White Roses

Lynette Rees

Dedication

To my lovely Mother. My biggest supporter and friend.
With Lots of Love.

Thank You!

Acknowledgments

To all at 'Merthyr Writes' for your encouragement and support. Namely, Thea Hartley, Betty Osment, Claire Jones and Val Williams. Thank you, ladies!

To SallyAnn Cole for your proofreading skills. Many thanks.

Chapter One

Abercanaid, November 1867

Lily Jenkin stared at the grey stone walls of Chapel House. Was it only a few short months since she'd departed from her home and life as she knew it? Home as in Abercanaid and not this particular house either, for she had been living apart from her husband Evan for some time before leaving for America, the New World. It hadn't been easy she had to admit, but now his memory had almost returned to normal and he'd shown his love for her once more by seeking her out in Utah, they were back together again as man and wife and both stood hesitating outside the large black panelled door of 'Chapel House'.

Thankfully, it was very early morning and no one had seen the husband and wife with their daughter Mollie, trundling from the railway station to their home with their heavy luggage, through the village streets.

It was far too early for the gossips like Maggie Shanklin to have awoken as yet. Day was barely breaking, and it was much colder here than Great Salt Lake, causing Lily to stamp her feet and blow on her gloveless hands. The skies were greyer, the mountains more enclosed and a feeling of suffocation bore down on her. That was one thing she would miss, the large open space of Utah. It was almost as though there you could stretch your hand out and touch the sky, connecting to God in his heaven.

Trembling, Evan inserted the wrought iron key in the lock and turned it, glancing at his young daughter, he said, "Now you wait there Mollie for a moment, there's something I need to do..."

Mollie stood there, her large brown eyes blinking with surprise.

"Evan what's going on?" Lily asked.

"Something I should have done a long time ago, my sweet... now put that bag down."

Lily did as instructed and the next thing she knew she was swept up into Evan's strong arms as he carried her into the house and set her down again on the other side of the threshold.

"Welcome home Mrs Davies..." He said proudly, with a huge grin on his face.

Lily laughed. "Well, there's silly you are Mr. Davies..."

"I know..." he said, as he stared into her eyes. "I haven't been much of a husband to you have I Lily? Well not of recent months anyhow."

She stood close to her husband and through lowered lashes, said breathlessly, "Do not trouble yourself Evan, it was not your fault that you had a blow to the head up in 'China' and lost your memory. I feel partly responsible for sending you to look for my brother in the first place." She sighed heavily. "All is to change soon enough and now you have extra responsibility..." she patted her swollen stomach indicating the new life dwelling within.

Evan fell to his knees and hugged her from her waist and began to sob quietly. "Oh Lily, how can you ever forgive me? I almost lost you and Mollie, both. It's my own fault that you are with child from another man. Even though that is Cooper Haines' child you are bearing, I shall love he or she as if it is my own."

Lily looked down on her husband and ruffled her hands through his hair. "Ssshhh,"she soothed. "Please do not mention that man's name in this house again."

He nodded and rose to his feet.

It was a hard thing having to break the news to Cooper in Great Salt Lake she was breaking off her engagement to him and returning to Wales with her husband and child. The guilt had been overwhelming. She had broken a man's heart.

But she realised it had been the right thing to do. There were no winners in this at all. Only survivors.

Remembering Mollie, Lily called the child who appeared beside them, thankfully she hadn't witnessed her father's tears. On the arduous journey from Utah, Mollie and Evan had become reacquainted once more, and the child had stopped mentioning the name of Cooper Haines all together.

They were all home at last and back where they belonged.

***

Lily was awoken by a heavy banging on the door...she sat up in bed and looked at the mantel clock over the fireplace. It was a quarter past three in the afternoon. Had they really been asleep so long? Exhaustion seeped through every pore of her being as she dragged herself out of bed, checking on Mollie, who was in the bed beside them. She was still asleep, her rosy cheeks made her look like a porcelain china doll, the rise and fall of her chest reassuring Lily, all was fine.

The banging continued. She struggled to find her dressing gown as they hadn't properly unpacked as yet. Locating it from the back of the chair, she put it on and slipped into her carpet slippers. At this rate whoever it was, would wake the whole house up.

As she secured the tie on her dressing gown she peeped through the glass-panelled window of the door and spied a familiar looking figure. She drew open the door. "Mrs Morgan..." she gasped and fell into the elderly lady's arms.

"Oh Lily, there's good to see you at last. I couldn't wait to visit you."

Lily beckoned the lady inside and offered her a seat at the kitchen table.

"I've brought you some Welsh cakes, milk and bread..." Mrs Morgan drew them from her wicker basket and placed the items on the table.

"But how did you know we were home?" Lily asked incredulously.

"After I received your letter, I was on pins for weeks, then William was out with the pony and trap early this morning and said he noticed a light on in the window."

Lily nodded. "Yes, we got back very early."

Elsa Morgan frowned. "I'm sorry Lily, I disturbed your rest?"

"No. I should get up anyhow to get back into a routine, now how about a cup of tea, Mrs Morgan? We've got lots to catch up on."

"Well you get dressed, *cariad*, and I'll make the tea."

It was good to see a familiar face at last.

By the time Lily had returned, Mrs Morgan had kindled the fire and the tea was already brewed. Lily sat gratefully at the table across from the elderly lady. "It's been some time..." she said, as her eyes filled with tears.

"I know." Mrs Morgan's kindly blue eyes mirrored Lily's own. "So, are you going to tell me more about what went on in Great Salt Lake?" She lifted the steaming earthen ware tea pot and poured the tea into two floral china cups, then added the milk, passing one to Lily. "Sugar?"

Lily shook her head. "No thanks. I stopped taking sugar in my tea when I lived in Utah, and these days I prefer it that way. The Saints promote healthy living there. Many have stopped drinking tea and coffee altogether!"

Mrs Morgan shook her head. "So, did you pick up good or bad habits whilst away then?" She cajoled.

Lily raised her eyes to meet with Elsa's. "Oh Mrs Morgan you will hate me when I tell you something, but you must promise to keep this to yourself. Tell no one, not even Mr. Morgan for time being."

"Whatever is the matter, Lily?" Mrs Morgan's eyes were full of concern.

"Remember I told you in my letter that I was betrothed to Cooper Haines?"

"That middle-aged shop keeper? Yes, but you thought Evan didn't want you any more, didn't you?"

Lily nodded, and then bit her lip as if it would somehow assuage the guilt now wracking through her body. "Yes, but that's not the worst part. I'm carrying his child." She almost choked on the words. Verbalising them seemed to make the situation more real.

Mrs Morgan swallowed hard. "Oh Lily, I don't know what to say. Who am I to judge? You must have loved him at the time?"

"No I did not. I liked him a lot and I thought I would never see Evan again. So, I thought it was in Mollie's best interests for her to have a father in her life, a man who would care for the both of us. I feel so bad, as I know he really loved me. I broke his heart."

Elsa Morgan tutted. "Now, now...take this handkerchief, it's clean..." She passed it across the table to Lily, who took the lace cloth and dabbed at her swollen eyes. "It seems to me that you did the right thing. It was God's will that Evan came looking for you.... 'let no man put asunder' and all that..."

A few words from Mrs Morgan could make a dark cloud disappear, and this time, Lily cried, but her tears were healing. Mrs Morgan was correct. Evan was still her husband and the intended marriage was not to be. She was well aware she had made two grown men cry, but both for entirely different reasons.

***

Being back in the old school room at the Chapel Hall, reminded Lily of the school she'd taught at in Great Salt Lake. Her mind drifted back to those days of not so long ago. She missed the Mormon children there, but those were well fed and dressed, here the children were desperate for a good hot meal and warm clothing. She'd managed to provide both, along with a good education. There was much poverty and ignorance in the village. A memory of how poor little Betty had been mute when she first joined the school came to mind. The child had been abandoned by her parents in the squalor of their home. Yes, Mrs Morgan had done a good job bringing up Betty. Now the little girl was clean, well-fed and well-dressed. She'd become an active participant in the classroom and talkative too. Something Lily thought she'd never see. The child had also grown a couple of inches since Lily last saw her.

Hannah and Mrs Morgan had kept the Dame Style School running like clockwork during her absence. They'd even got someone in to give the room a fresh lick of paint, and this year, a couple of new children had joined the school.

The children of Abercanaid were doing well following the pit explosion of almost two years ago, where many men and young boys were killed, though it wasn't eradicated from people's minds, in fact, could it ever be? But there was now some blue sky appearing on the horizon.

Smiling proudly, Lily turned to Mrs Morgan. "Thank you so much Elsa. You and Hannah have carried out some sterling work here. You deserve to rest now I'm back though."

Mrs Morgan's forehead creased into a frown. "I suppose I should go back to working full-time at the shop. William has managed well, but his back isn't what it was. Mind you, I would still like to help out at the school when able."

Lily smiled. "How about you keep your hand in by giving the children reading lessons a couple of times a week, Elsa?"

The elderly woman nodded. "Right you are then, that's settled." She kissed Betty softly on the top of the head and left to go back to the shop to relieve her husband of his duties, leaving her young charge in Lily's capable hands.

Lily let out a long breath after Elsa's departure. Now she was back in command, captain of the ship.

**

On the approach to Christmas, there was the hustle and bustle of activity around the village. The Chapel was preparing to put on a Nativity Play and Carol Concert, just before the big day itself. Life had to go on, even though it included the anniversary of the pit disaster. Some of the men had been lucky to continue to work with their injuries, though some, who had to have amputations and severe burns, would never work again. That was if they were lucky enough not to have been killed in the first place.

Lily visited Doctor Owen, who confirmed her pregnancy and told her he expected she would give birth around April or May time. If he was curious about the date of conception, then he didn't say so. As far as the villagers were concerned, Evan Davies had set out to Salt Lake to bring back his wife and child, any pregnancy occurred at their reunion.

Only Mrs Morgan knew the truth. Lily trusted her with her life.

Up until now, Lily had dodged the evil tongues of Maggie Shanklin and her cronies. She had just smiled sweetly at the group when they attended chapel, but now Lily's garments were getting tighter by the day, and soon enough, people would see she was pregnant.

"Why don't we just come out with it, I'll make an announcement at next Sunday's sermon," Evan declared.

A rush of blood suffused Lily's cheeks. She shook her head. "I...I really don't know if it's the right thing to do, Evan."

Evan immediately came to her side where she was seated in their living room. "Let me tell you my sweet, it's the absolute right thing to do, it will show we are united as a couple. There were many who chastised me for leaving you go in the first place. Do it for me, please?"

She looked up from the armchair into her husband's smiling eyes and saw both the love and compassion dwelling within.

"Yes, we will do that Evan. But what if anyone should ask any awkward questions?"

He shrugged. "If they do, they do. Don't forget no one in this village knows about Cooper Haines."

Lily experienced a sharp pang of guilt, she chewed on her bottom lip and standing, took a deep breath and said, "I'm afraid they do, Evan. I confided in Mrs Morgan."

The colour drained from Evan's face. "Why on earth would you do that?" His nostrils flared with anger.

"I'm sorry," she squared up to her husband, "but I had to tell someone and Elsa Morgan is the most trustworthy person I know, she hasn't even told her own husband about the situation."

Placing both hands on Lily's shoulders, Evan stared into his wife's eyes, his voice trembling as he said, "But don't you see what you have done, Lily? It's wrong, now you have Elsa carrying the burden of your secret and keeping things from her husband. You should not have done it, it was totally wrong."

He turned on his heel and left the room, she had rarely seen her husband look so angry and it frightened her. Tears filled her eyes. What had she done?

She seated herself down and wept uncontrollably for a few moments, unaware that someone was watching her.

She opened her eyes to see Mollie stood before her blinking, wide-eyed with confusion.

"Oh Mollie, come here, *cariad*..." She swept the small child into her arms and onto her lap. "It's nothing for you to be concerned about, understand? It's just grown up things. I am all

right. I just got myself all upset over something and nothing."
She soothed.

The child gazed up at her mother, smiled and cuddled into her, giving Lily a feeling of peace, which was to last all of two minutes.

Hearing the front door slam, Lily put Mollie down beside her on the chair and stood in time to see Evan striding down the road sharply, as if in a hurry. Where was he going? What if he didn't come back? What if he never trusted her again? It would be more than she could ever bear.

Chapter Two

Lily stood staring out of the window, straining to see in which direction Evan was headed, but it was of no use, he had disappeared completely from view. The ticking of the mantel clock seemed to get louder with every beat of her heart. A sickening pain wrenched her gut, twisting and tearing her up inside. Evan had travelled half way around the world to find her and bring her home and had now abandoned her again.

But where was he going?

She took Mollie by the hand and walked to the hallway where she pulled a small, woollen shawl from the oak wood coat stand, wrapping it around the child's shoulders. Then she got her own shawl from the peg and threw it around herself. The weather was definitely getting colder. They were in the midst of Autumn, bordering on winter.

It was too late to follow after Evan to see where he'd gone. She sighed deeply, deciding she couldn't wait in the house any longer; she was going to warn Mrs Morgan that her husband might show up there at any time. The shop was empty of customers thankfully, when they arrived the short distance from across the street. Mrs Morgan was seated on a wooden stool across the counter, scribbling something in a big black ledger, her specs half on her nose. She peered over them when she heard Lily and Mollie enter the shop.

"Well, hello you two!" she greeted. "Come to pay me a visit have you?"

Lily wrung her hands. "Not exactly. I need to speak with you Elsa, if you have a moment, please?"

Sensing the urgency in Lily's voice, Mrs Morgan glanced at Mollie. "Betty's in the backroom, *bach*. Go and join her Mollie. There are some nice Welsh cakes I baked as well on the kitchen table. Run along now..."

The child happily skipped into the backroom in search of her young friend, whom she'd recently become acquainted with. Since being in Abercanaid, she'd grown to follow Betty around like a puppy dog at the school and was now also familiar with Mrs Morgan and the shop.

Lily dropped her hands to her side and exhaled deeply. "Thanks. It's Evan I've told him..."

Elsa raised her thin silver brows. "I'm not quite with you, *cariad*. Told him what exactly?"

"That you know about the baby, that it's not his."

Mrs Morgan frowned and shook her head. "Oh. *Diolch yn fawr*, Lily!"

"I'm sorry Elsa. I just felt bad keeping it from him. I thought he'd understand."

Mrs Morgan shook her head. "Well, maybe you shouldn't have told me in the first place. So he's angry I'm guessing?"

Lily nodded. "He's most irked about the fact I might have caused trouble now between you and your husband by asking you to keep my secret."

Mrs Morgan softened. "That's only natural, Lily. I'll have a word with Evan for you if you like?"

Lily smiled and relaxed. "Yes, please."

"Look I was about to lock up anyhow, let's go in the back room and have a nice cup of tea."

Before leaving, Mrs Morgan selected some lovely homemade fudge for Mollie, which she scooped into a paper bag and tied with a little pink ribbon. She was kind hearted towards the children in the village, even occasionally giving away her confectionary to the less fortunate in Abercanaid. Lily surmised her benevolence must have cost her a pretty penny, but the woman didn't seem to mind, in fact, Lily suspected it gave her a lot of pleasure to do so.

Feeling a little better when they left Mrs Morgan's place, Lily hugged Mollie. "Now there's a good girl you've been today. How would you like to have some of those sweeties Mrs Morgan gave you, after we've eaten our supper?" Mollie nodded eagerly. By the time they got back to Chapel House the place was in darkness, making it evident that Evan had not returned.

All thoughts of him going missing last year came back to Lily at full force, like a magic lantern show. What if he did something silly like getting himself inebriated at the Llwyn-Yr-Eos pub? Or even worse? She'd once heard a tale of a man from Abercanaid who had a blazing row with his wife. He consumed so many pints of beer at the pub that he came out disorientated and fell in the canal and drowned, leaving his wife and children distraught and penniless.

Men didn't seem to cope with problems in the same way as women who chatted about them over a cup of tea. Men would call that gossip. She called it facing up to life.

***

After feeding Mollie her supper and getting the child washed and ready for bed, she sat down exhausted in the armchair, patting her swollen stomach.

"Oh little one, what has life in store for you?" she said, gazing at the bump.

She jumped when she heard the front door slam and her husband stood staring at her from the entrance to their living room.

"Where have you been all this time, Evan?"

He entered the room and sat down facing her. Removing his cap and muffler, he said, "I'm sorry Lily. I just had to get out. I couldn't contain my anger at the situation and didn't want to raise my voice in front of you and Mollie..."

She let out a long sigh of relief.

"For a moment there, I thought maybe you'd gone for good."

"Don't be silly. I'd never abandon you again," he said softening. "I went for a long walk and when it got dark, I called in to see some of our parishioners. I figured it was better to think of others' problems and not my own."

"Oh I see. And did that make you feel any better?"

"A little. Maybe. But this is what I think..."

"Yes go on..." She wanted to hear what was on his mind. Needed to almost.

He drew in a breath and let it out again. "I'm not comfortable that Elsa Morgan has to keep your secret to herself."

Lily raised her brows in surprise. "You mean you think we should tell the whole village the baby is not yours?"

15

"No, no, of course not." He shook his head. "I mean that she should tell her husband too. That way there is no burden of her holding the secret to herself. How would you feel about that?"

Relieved, she said, "Yes, you are right Evan. I shall tell her to pass on the information to her husband and tell him it's to remain confidential." She trusted Mr. Morgan as much as she did his wife.

"Good then, we are agreed." Evan rose and kissed Lily softly on the head. "Now what's for supper? I'm starving."

"I've got a pan of *cawl* on the go. I'll warm it up for you and cut some crusty bread that Mrs Morgan gave me. It was left over from today, so we need to use it up before it becomes stale."

"Ah good." Lily stood to leave the room to prepare the simple meal for her husband and as she departed, he said softly, "Lily..."

She turned with her hand still on the door knob. "Yes?"

"You know I love you and always will..."

Nodding, she smiled and left the room.

***

Lily's stomach lurched. With trembling fingers, she opened the brown envelope. It was a telegram addressed to her. The first thought that came to mind were Dafydd and Delwyn, her twin brothers, who were still in Great Salt Lake. She had heard no word on the long journey home as there was no means of communication as she travelled back to Wales. She'd expected a hand written letter from both at some point, but a telegram, no.

How she wished Evan were here right now, not visiting a family in Troedyrhiw where the mother of the house was dying. He had gone along that morning to provide comfort and solace for those who would soon be bereaved. Evan himself had said it would be a miracle if the woman survived.

Lily tore open the envelope to read the words:

Home soon. Have news. Dafydd.

What did that mean? It could mean anything. Good news or bad news? And why was he coming home so soon? She comforted herself with the fact that at least he was all right though, no ill had befallen him.

The message both baffled and intrigued her at the same time. Yet something deep down told her this wasn't bad news. It warmed her heart at the thought of seeing him once again. They'd been parted for a long time. Even when they were reunited in Utah, the time was short before she left again for Wales with Evan and Mollie.

Later, when she told Mrs Morgan about the telegram, as they were both in the kitchen seated at the table at Chapel House, the elderly lady raised her brows. "Let me see the telegram, please, Lily."

Lily extracted it from her apron pocket and passed it across the table. Elsa placed her half specs on her nose and peered. "Hmmm..." she sniffed. "He's not a man of many words your brother, is he? Granted. But he was probably being wise and saving his hard earned coppers. Looks as if you are going to have to air out the house at Chapel Square for him then, *cariad*. Unless of course you are going to move him in here?"

Lily hadn't really thought about that. She ran her hand over her brow. "We don't really have the room here for him, Elsa. We would put him up of course if needs be, but I think you are right, we will have to sort the house out for him. He and Evan departed in such a rush to look for me at Salt Lake, that he left the house in quite a tip I can tell you. I was going to tidy it up when I returned, but Evan said not to in my condition and there didn't appear to be any particular rush at the time. But now this could mean he'll be back for Christmas..."

"Let's hope so," Elsa said, as she sipped her tea and stared thoughtfully at Lily.

***

Several weeks later, there was still no sign of Dafydd. Evan had hosted prayers for his safe return at the chapel. Most people in the community were supportive of the prayers except for one woman and her band of sour-faced friends, Maggie Shanklin. Rumour had it that she was putting the poison into people's minds by claiming that Dafydd Jenkin was a blaggard and drunk and that he should remain in Great Salt Lake with the 'Saints of Satan' as she called them.

It made Lily's blood boil that Maggie was implying that those of the Mormon faith like, Delwyn and Rose, were not Christians and were nothing but Heathens. In fact, in Lily's opinion, the Saints were far more committed to their faith than some Baptists were to their own, in the village of Abercanaid. Silently she cussed the old crone.

One Sunday she could bear it no longer and marched up to Maggie as she stood on the chapel steps gossiping away. Noticing Lily's approach, Maggie smirked openly in her face. "Mrs Davies..." she greeted and then turned to carry on chatting to one of her friends.

"Mrs Shanklin," Lily raised her voice an octave to get the woman's attention. "A word or two, please!"

Maggie turned to face Lily, the false smile on her face disappearing into a wrinkled jowl. "Yes?"

Lily let out a breath. "It has come to my attention that you are slandering the good name of my brother Dafydd around the village?"

Maggie stiffened. Obviously she hadn't thought for one moment that Lily would pay attention to her. "No, it isn't me that is slandering his name but I have heard rumours, yes."

"Well if it is not you, and you are usually the harbinger of most of the bad news and gossip in this village, then who is it?"

"I'm not at liberty to say..." she snorted with derision.

Lily trembled from top-to-toe as she replied, "I am going to get to the bottom of this Mrs Shanklin and if I discover it is you who is responsible for slandering my brother's good name, then there will be repercussions."

"What good name?" Maggie chided, glancing at her friend with a smirk.

Lily balled her hands at her side into fists. How she would love to knock the woman's block off, but she couldn't, she was the minister's wife and even if she could, it wouldn't be right in her pregnant position.

Turning on her heel, Lily returned inside the chapel to help her husband collect the discarded hymn books.

Her husband had already collected most of the books with the help of young Hannah Griffiths. "What's the matter, Lily?" he asked, turning towards his wife as she seated herself in the wooden pew beside him.

"It's that old crone, Mrs Shanklin. I fear Evan, she's spreading gossip again around the village, this time about my brother."

"Delwyn?"

"No Dafydd. It's got back to me that she's calling him a blaggard and a drunk. I don't like it one little bit. She will turn the villagers against him."

Evan sat at her side as Hannah tactfully stacked the hymn books well away from earshot. "Don't worry so. It's not good in your condition. No one pays that much attention to that old gossip. Everyone knows what she is, a sharp-tongued, old witch."

Lily giggled. She'd never heard her husband speak that way before. "Yes you're right Evan..." she snuggled into him.

"And furthermore, Dafydd was practically a hero when he left here after that mountain fight. It was just Maggie and her cronies who are against a man having a few pints, who make trouble. Dafydd went through a horrendous time when he was involved in the pit explosion. He suffered a lot of pain and then there was your Mam's death. He did have his reasons after all. In any case that is all in the past now..."

Lily heard the sense in her husband's words and sincerely hoped he was right.

Chapter Three

Lily busied herself for the festive season. Evan had bought a Christmas tree in Merthyr market. The family had spent the previous evening trimming it. Mollie had squealed with delight as her father lifted her up to place the silver angel on the top. It looked a treat with all the trimmings, and now, Lily was busy baking in the kitchen. The festive spirit was truly here as she took in the smells of citrus and cinnamon that were wafting all around the house. She'd finished icing a fruit cake and was just taking a batch of mince pies out of the oven when there was a knock at the door.

Thinking it was Mrs Morgan calling around for a visit with Betty, she laid the tray of mince pies to cool down on the table and wiped her floury hands on her pinafore.

Unlocking the heavy oak door, she pulled the handle towards her. "You're both earl—" she was about to exclaim when she saw two figures outside, one familiar though slightly gaunt from the man she remembered. The other was one of the most beautiful women she had ever seen in her life. The woman's long auburn hair cascaded onto her shoulders and her sparkling emerald eyes shone with a life force she'd never seen before.

"Aren't you going to invite us in Lily Jenkin?" her brother Dafydd asked, with a mischievous grin.

Lily felt exhilarated to see her brother again. They embraced and he swung her around on the doorstep so she felt giddy.

"Oh Dafydd, how I've longed for this day to arrive!" she said, when she'd finally got her breath back and had both feet on solid ground. "And who is this young lady, may I ask?"

"Well if you invite us both inside, I shall tell you..." he teased.

"Now, where are my manners, come in both of you, it's freezing out there."Lily said warmly, noting the absence of luggage with the couple. "Evan's taken Mollie out for a walk they should be back soon..."

"Well I've got something to tell you..." Dafydd said, when they had all seated themselves in the parlour. "Kathleen and I have got wed."

Lily blinked several times. "Married? How? When? I had no idea of this at all."

"No, of course not, and why on earth would you?" the young woman said in an Irish accent.

"What a beautiful voice you have, Kathleen," Lily enthused in awe.

"Aye, it's even better when she sings!" Dafydd announced proudly.

"Oh go on *you*." Kathleen blushed. "Anyhow, 'tis why we're here to tell you of our marriage. We were married a week ago in Cardiff. We've just dropped our luggage off at Chapel Square, and I love that little house already!"

"Cardiff?" Lily could hardly believe her own ears.

"Yes," Dafydd joined in. "Remember I said I met Kathleen on the crossing to New York, aboard ship? I knew her family were about to join the Saints at Salt Lake, so after you and Evan returned to Wales, I searched for her."

"Then why all the secrecy about the wedding?" Lily frowned.

"Because..." Dafydd continued, "Kathleen's father did not approve of our relationship. He wanted her to marry another Saint and I wouldn't convert to the faith. It's not for me. So secretly we left for Wales and I brought her here to be my bride."

Lily forced a smile. "I'm pleased for you both...I really am..."

"But?" Dafydd stared at his sister.

"I suppose I'm being selfish as I wanted to be there when you got wed."

"We're sorry Lily..." Kathleen faltered. "The reason we got wed so quickly and in Cardiff, is in case my father sent some of our family from Ireland to look for us here in Merthyr Tydfil, to prevent the wedding from taking place."

Lily bit her lip. "I suppose I can see your reasons. I tell you what, even though you are both already wed, we can have a special celebration later when Evan and Mollie return. I'll ask

Mr. and Mrs Morgan too, if that's okay with you both? There's plenty of food in the house."

Dafydd and Kathleen both nodded, beaming with happiness.

When Evan returned with Mollie she asked him to bring Mr. and Mrs Morgan over for a celebration. Evan was surprised as she was about the wedding, but made no comment about that, just shook Dafydd warmly by the hand and greeted his new bride. Evan and Dafydd had become close as brothers-in-law after their quest to find Lily in Utah.

While she was making a cup of tea for the couple in the kitchen, Lily's eyes fell upon the Christmas cake she had iced a couple of hours earlier. The icing wasn't fully set but it would do as a wedding cake and there was a silver set of bells on the Christmas tree. She took those down and placed them on the cake as decoration.

This would be the next best thing to a wedding celebration for the couple who would now make their new home at Chapel Square.

***

Tongues were wagging in the village now that Dafydd had brought his young bride to the village, none more so, than Maggie Shanklin's. In an effort to silence her, Mrs Morgan had told her at the shop that Kathleen was a nice Irish lady. This piqued Maggie's interest even more, being Irish herself, and she immediately went in search of her.

She knocked the door at Chapel Square and was invited in. Kathleen had not been forewarned of the woman's sharp tongue. Dafydd was out looking for work in Merthyr.

"So, you're settling down well to married life in Abercanaid, are you, Kathleen?" Maggie said, seating herself down in the small, sparse living room. She glanced around and sniffed loudly.

"Oh yes. My husband's family have been very warm and welcoming. Would you like a cup of tea, Mrs Shanklin?"

Maggie shook her head and cast a beady eye at a bottle on the shelf. "What's that?" she enquired.

Kathleen blushed. "It's a bottle of Irish whiskey Dafydd bought to celebrate our wedding in Cardiff, would you like some?"

Maggie shook her head vigorously. "No thank you, I never touch the stuff," she lied. "But maybe I will have that cup of tea..."

When Kathleen returned with the cups of tea, feeling she had met a fellow Irishwoman she could make a friend of, Maggie said, "And tell me, do you have anything from the old country?"

"Yes, I do, I have a beautiful Irish lace tray cloth my grandmother made. I'll go and get it for you now to show you, shall I?"

Maggie nodded and smiled. While Kathleen left the room to climb the small stone staircase, the woman uncorked the bottle of whiskey and tipped some into Kathleen's cup of tea. Then seated herself back down again.

Kathleen returned and handed the cloth over to her guest, who inspected it vigorously. "Hmmm nice stitch work, though not as intricate as my mother's handiwork, now she was a proper lace maker..." she tossed the cloth onto the seat beside her.

Kathleen tried not to show any upset and took a sip of tea then said, "This tea tastes a bit odd..."

Maggie nodded. "It's the Welsh water, dear. 'Tis different back in the old country, much nicer there."

Kathleen nodded and carried on sipping the tea, leaving Maggie with a huge smile on her face.

***

The following day, Dafydd turned up on Lily's doorstep, his face ashen grey. She beckoned him inside.

"Oh Lily..." He removed his cap and seated himself at the kitchen table.

"What's the matter?" She touched his hand, then seated herself opposite him.

"It's Kathleen, there's something wrong with her."

"How can that be, Dafydd?" Lily frowned.

"When I returned from Merthyr after hunting for a job yesterday, her speech sounded slurred and then she vomited several times. Today, she has spent the whole day in bed and refuses to tell me what the matter is."

It was evident, from his tone of voice, just how concerned her brother was. For a moment, Lily wondered if the young woman was pregnant, before she had a chance to utter a word, Dafydd continued. "I know what you're thinking and it's not that. We didn't start trying for a family until we got married a couple of weeks ago. This is something different."

"Could she be sickening for something then?"

He shrugged. "I don't know."

"Maybe we should get Doctor Owen to see her, Dafydd."

He scratched his chin. "Look, I know you're busy with Mollie and the school, but please could you pay her a visit when you get chance?"

Lily smiled and patted his hand. "Yes, of course I will. Evan is due home soon and there's no school today, we've finished for the Christmas holidays. He can take care of Mollie whilst I come with you back to Chapel Square. He'll be home within the hour. Do you think she'll be all right? Maybe you're best getting right back to her?"

He shook his head. "No, she's sleeping now. I'll wait and escort you as it's getting dark."

"As you wish. I'll make a cup of tea."

Evan turned up a little earlier than expected, so she quickly explained the situation, claimed her shawl and bonnet from the hallstand and made the short journey with Dafydd to Chapel House. When they arrived, the house was unlit, though there were still the embers of a fire in the grate.

"Has Kathleen eaten?" Lily asked.

Dafydd shook his head. "No, I tried her with some soup earlier, but she was still nauseous."

"I'll go up and see her now..." Lily said, removing her shawl and bonnet and leaving them on the kitchen table. When she got to the top of the stairs, she softly called out Kathleen's name.

The woman stirred and groaned. Lily knew the bedroom like the back of her hand as this was her old room when she was growing up. She made her way over to the bed where the last light of a flickering flame, illuminated Kathleen's petite frame. "Are you all right?"

Kathleen stirred and opened her eyes to focus on Lily. "I don't know what happened...I've been feeling nauseated all day."

Lily sat herself on the edge of the bed. "Think back to when the feeling started, did you eat something that may have disagreed with you?"

Kathleen pulled herself up into a sitting position in the bed, her long hair tousled and untidy, and the dark rings beneath her eyes, evidence of how sick she was. "No, I hadn't eaten much, I was all right when Mrs Shanklin called yesterday."

The blood in Lily's veins turned to ice. "That woman was here, yesterday? Why?"

"She called to pay me a visit and we had a cup of tea together."

A shiver of apprehension skittered down Lily's spine. "Did she say anything to you?"

"No, nothing out of the way, at least I don't think so. I showed her a lace tray cloth my grandmother had made back in Ireland. She didn't seem all that impressed with it in all honesty, and after we had tea together, it all went a bit of a blur. I can't even remember her leaving here."

"Lily!" Dafydd shouted up the stairs. "Please come here a moment!"

Sensing the urgency in her brother's voice, Lily left Kathleen a moment to join him in the kitchen.

"What's the matter, Dafydd?"

He held up a half empty whiskey bottle and whispered. "Lily, Kathleen must have drunk this...it was full when I left to go to Merthyr yesterday. She's turned to the bottle..."

Lily shook her head. "No, I think I have an idea what's happened. She told me Maggie Shanklin paid her a visit yesterday. Do you think Maggie might have poured some whiskey in Kathleen's cup of tea or given her some neat?"

Dafydd's nostrils flared with anger. "That bloody woman again!" He gritted his teeth. "She is always meddling in our business. I've a good mind to go down there and speak with her husband, she could do with a good slap!"

Lily touched his arm. "It won't do to hit a woman, Dafydd. There are better ways to deal with the likes of her sort. Believe me."

Lily took Kathleen a glass of water and told her to sip it slowly. "I have to ask you this, Kathleen," Lily began, "did you drink any of the whiskey from the bottle downstairs yesterday?"

Kathleen vigorously shook her head, her eyes widening with horror. "No, Lily."

"Half the bottle has gone!"

"I don't understand, it was full when Mrs Shanklin arrived here as she remarked on it. Oh my goodness. That tea I made yesterday tasted odd, but Maggie said it was the Welsh water." Kathleen trembled as realisation dawned.

"I think it's best you keep away from Maggie Shanklin, she's not to be trusted. I should have warned you as much. The woman has caused a lot of trouble for this family. Did she ask you any awkward questions?"

"Not that I can remember, but oh Lily...I can't remember much at all about yesterday." Kathleen burst into tears as Lily comforted her.

"There, do not worry yourself over what's happened. I shall be having sharp words with her, and she will not be welcome in chapel again. She was given a chance last year and she has abused both my own and Evan's trust. Now sip that water and if you still feel nauseous afterwards, I shall fetch Doctor Owen."

Fortunately the sickness subsided soon after, so no real harm had been done, but Lily's patience with Maggie was starting to grow thin and she wondered what her motivation for causing Kathleen's state of inebriation might be.

Chapter Four

Christmas was only a few days away, and Lily suggested to Dafydd that Kathleen should sing in the chapel concert, thinking it would not only increase the young woman's confidence, but endear her to the people of Abercanaid at the same time. It was often hard to settle in the village for newcomers were viewed as outsiders.

Dafydd scratched his chin. They were sitting in Lily's kitchen enjoying a cup of tea. "I don't know about that Lily, she doesn't seem to want to go out anywhere after that Maggie Shanklin incident, she feels she can't trust anyone in the village now, apart from you and Evan of course."

Lily swept a loose tendril behind her ear. "Well, that's exactly why she must sing in the concert. She will get to know a lot of the villagers and you say she has a beautiful voice?"

"Aye she does. It's the sweetest, most melodious voice I've ever heard in my life. It's quite heavenly to hear."

Lily smiled, it was obvious that her brother was totally besotted with his new bride, she'd yet to hear Kathleen sing, but if her speaking voice was anything to go by with its gentle intonations and Irish lilt, then it must truly be a magical experience.

"Well if you like, I'll give her a word of encouragement, Dafydd. I'll call around this evening?"

"As you wish, but don't go expecting miracles, mind you. I think she's missing her family and the home country to be honest with you."

"This is her home now, Dafydd," Lily said wisely. "And this is why we need to make her feel welcome and wanted here."

Her brother nodded and then carried on sipping his tea.

***

It had worked, Lily had persuaded Kathleen to sing, and now Lily waited with bated breath for Kathleen to stand on the podium at the front of the chapel to sing. The place was packed to the rafters. A group of young children had just performed 'The Nativity' and now Kathleen stood before them in her best, green velvet gown, her auburn hair elegantly swept up and pinned neatly. The young woman trembled slightly as she gazed around the chapel, no doubt wondering what people thought of her.

But when she opened her mouth to sing 'Silent Night', the place fell quiet as the incessant chatter faded into the ether of the old beams of the building.

Lily glanced around, people were mesmerised as Kathleen put her heart and soul into the song.

"Silent night, holy night
Son of God, love's pure light
Radiant beams from Thy holy face
With the dawn of redeeming grace
Jesus, Lord, at Thy birth
Jesus, Lord, at Thy birth "

The Spruce Christmas tree at the foot of the stage twinkled as the candle lights flickered with each note of her voice and the silver star atop, glittered magically. It felt as though Christmas was here at last.

Lily watched as everyone stood after the performance, including Evan, who had Mollie in his arms, in the pew beside her. Kathleen beamed; a slight blush appeared on both cheeks, making her look even more beautiful. When the applause faded, Dafydd took to the stage to help his wife down. Thankfully, there was no sign of Maggie and her friends.

Afterwards, when they all had tea and mince pies in the chapel hall at the back of the building, a smartly dressed man in a cravat, dress shirt and black silk suit, approached Evan.

"That young lady—" he began, his white whiskers twirled into a moustache, "the one with the voice of an angel, who is she?"

"She's my sister-in-law," Evan explained. "Would you like to meet her, Sir?"

The man smiled broadly. "I would indeed."

Evan led the man to where Kathleen stood, surrounded by church members, keen to find out where she was from and how long she'd been singing for.

"There's a gentleman here who would like to meet you Kathleen..." Evan began. Kathleen smiled shyly. Obviously not used to such attention. "Excuse me, Sir, I didn't catch your name?"

"I'm Walter Bartholomew. I'm a theatrical agent and I'd like to represent you, my dear."

Kathleen blinked several times. "Represent me, but how, Mr. Bartholomew?"

Dafydd shook his head. "Now look here, what are you proposing?" he said, squaring up to the man as if about to start a boxing match with the fellow.

The man chuckled. "Whatever you're thinking, it's not that. I take it you are Kathleen's husband?"

Dafydd's jaw jutted out. "I am indeed. Well, what are you proposing, Sir?"

"I'd like to become her agent. I think she is good enough to sing on stage at such places as the Temperance Hall Merthyr, and even maybe later, on stage in Cardiff and Swansea. With the right coaching she could go far."

Dafydd shook his head and raised his voice a notch. "I don't like the sound of that. It's one thing for my wife to appear on stage at the local chapel, but quite another for her to mix with the likes of those performers who get up to all sorts of shenanigans. She is not a common whore you know!"

Evan intervened. "Calm down, Dafydd." People were beginning to stare. Kathleen shifted about uncomfortably. Evan continued, "Mr. Bartholomew seems perfectly respectable to me. It would be a great opportunity for Kathleen. She should do it if she wants. What would you like to do, Kathleen?"

Kathleen lifted her head and through lowered lashes said, "I will not do something which would displease my husband."

Lily looked at the woman in front of her and then at her brother and back again. "Kathleen, this could be a big chance for you. What would *you* like to do?" Dafydd's nostrils flared, Lily was well aware that he was trying to keep his temper in check.

Kathleen looked at Dafydd for what seemed the longest time and then, Dafydd softened and smiled at his wife. "If it's what you want, then who am I to stand in your way?"

She smiled and threw her arms around him, then turned to Mr. Bartholomew and replied. "Yes, Sir. I would like to take you up on your very kind offer."

***

Christmas passed peacefully that year and by the time 1868 arrived, Lily was looking forward to the future with renewed hope and vigour. The new life inside her was growing rapidly and kicking like a Billy goat. The winter had been mild up until now, but by the time January arrived, temperatures plummeted and the hillsides and valley were under a heavy fall of fresh white snow, people worried how they would get enough food to eat.

The people of the village helped one another by eking out the little they had and Elsa Morgan kept her shop running as best as she could, but getting new supplies was difficult. Eventually the snow began to thaw and people were able to get about once more, much to their relief.

It was around this time that Kathleen took to the stage at the Temperance Hall for the first time. She wasn't star billing, she was right at the bottom of the list. The star of the show was Bella Montovani, an operatic singer who claimed to be an authentic Italian, who in reality was Welsh through and through. She came from Cardiff but her dark Celtic looks, gave the crowd the impression that she was an Italian Soprano, tickets sold well as a result.

Kathleen O'Hara, as she was billed, was just below a juggling act and expected to warm up the crowd who were baying for blood that Saturday night. Dafydd hadn't been keen on her not being allowed to keep the Jenkin name for her act, but her agent had been insistent that she keep her Irish surname.

She stood in the wings trembling from top-to-toe. "It will be all right, you'll see," Lily said, patting her sister-in-law on the shoulder, reassuringly.

"But what if I can't sing a note?" Kathleen asked.

Dafydd and Evan were already seated in the audience, Lily knew how much it would mean to her brother for people to see his wife through his eyes.

"You will be all right, you'll see, just close your eyes for a couple of seconds and take a deep breath, that works for me."

Kathleen smiled and was directed on stage by a man in a bowler hat. She stood behind the thick red, plush curtain, edged with gold fringing, waiting for it to open. She closed her eyes and took that deep breath Lily advised. The curtains opened and she was met with a sea of faces, the spotlights directed on her. Then the light in the hall dimmed and she began to sing, The Rose of Tralee. She heard one or two shouts about the Irish, then someone yelled, "Be quiet at the back..." and it was, a silence fell upon the auditorium and she felt as if the audience was with her, taken in and mesmerised by her performance.

> *The pale moon was rising above the green mountains,*
> *The sun was declining beneath the blue sea;*
> *When I strayed with my love to the pure crystal fountain,*
> *That stands in the beautiful Vale of Tralee...*

Receiving a rapturous applause that warmed her heart, she confidently bowed and stood for the second song, which was, *The Ashgrove.* Walter Bartholomew had suggested she sang this song as it was a Welsh aria. She sang the first verse in English and the second in Welsh, bringing down the house, finishing the third in English

> *The ash grove how graceful, how plainly 'tis speaking*
> *The harp through its playing has language for me.*
> *Whenever the light through its branches is breaking,*
> *A host of kind faces is gazing on me.*
> *The friends from my childhood again are before me*
> *Each step wakes a memory as freely I roam.*
> *With soft whispers laden the leaves rustle o'er me*
> *The ash grove, the ash grove alone is my home...*

She stood and took the applause then the compere ushered her into the wings. "The incomparable Miss Kathleen O' Hara!" he boomed. "This little lady will be back in the second half to stir up your senses!" People cheered loudly and she rushed off the stage. Kathleen's heart hammered beneath her red satin dress, her bosom swelling with pride.

When she returned to the dressing room expecting to see Lily, she was faced with Bella Montovani who stood in a breathtakingly beautiful shimmering, sea-blue gown. The folds of the dress rustling as she walked towards Kathleen, fan in hand, for her performance. "Leave before the second half..." she hissed with venom at Kathleen. Kathleen frowned, whatever could the woman mean, was this some kind of joke?

She was just about to reply when a dresser at the theatre sidled over to her and whispered in her ear, as Bella strode off in the direction of the stage carrying a white frilled parasol. "She's really annoyed as you stole the show, Miss. You were far better than she is. Don't pay no attention, it's sour grapes that's all." Then the woman began picking up Miss Montovani's discarded clothing, hanging them on pegs, tutting to herself as she went along.

On Bella's dressing table, Kathleen noticed a large basket of white roses, with a small card. She picked it up and read it, *"For the finest singer in Wales. Yours M. X"* For a moment she wondered who 'M' was. One day she decided she'd love a beautiful bouquet of white roses just like those, if she ever reached the top of the bill.

As if reading her mind, the dresser turned to her and said, "Those roses are from her suitor, Maurice. He makes out he's French but he's from Ferndale. He's no more French than I am."

Kathleen tittered, just as Lily entered the room. "You were wonderful out there," she beamed, hugging Kathleen.

"Aye maybe so, but I've gone and made an enemy of someone..."

"Who?" Lily blinked.

"Only the star of the show, but the dresser just told me she thinks she's jealous of me."

"And so she should be too," Lily muttered. "I heard her practising earlier and she's not a patch on you, Kathleen. One day you'll have star billing here, you mark my words..."

And as Lily helped Kathleen to change into her evening gown for the second performance, Kathleen smiled at the thought of taking centre stage out there.

Chapter Five

Word was despatched to Evan by letter from his father, that his mother, Olwen, was unwell. She had been experiencing strange turns, fainting fits and nausea, which the doctor had put down to her 'time of life'. Evan's worried frown told Lily of his genuine concern, he hadn't seen his mother since their falling out earlier the previous year. Now he was wracked with guilt, even though the woman had done some dreadful things to the family, and no more so than trying to turn him against his own wife.

"What are you going to do?" Lily asked, handing her husband a cup of tea as he was seated at the kitchen table.

"I don't know. She made me so angry Lily, she could have helped us out once upon a time, but chose not to, and of course, there was that incident where she drugged Mollie with the Syrup of Poppies..."

He took a sip of tea and put his head in his hands. Lily stood behind him and gently massaged his shoulders.

"What's past is past, Evan. We need to let it lie now. The thing with the medicine, I think she genuinely didn't realise how dangerous it was and thought it would quieten Mollie down as she was particularly fractious while I was at work. The woman has learned her lesson about that. Life is short, you need to see her."

He took his wife's hand and held it to his cheek. "Oh Lily, whatever did I do before I met you?"

She smiled inwardly. "I don't know Evan, but you had a few fiancées before you met me, from what your mother told me."

He laughed. "I think Mother has given you the impression that I had a harem of nubile young ladies at my disposal, there were only two and Mother drove those away. You are the one that remained standing."

Lily drew away and seated herself at the opposite side of the table.

"Third time lucky for me then, isn't it?" she said brightly. "Why don't you catch the next train to Pentyrch? Go and see how she is. I'm sure she'd appreciate a visit from you."

He nodded. "Yes, I think I might do that."

Evan finished his tea and went to get his coat and muffler from the hall stand. "Any message you'd like to pass on to my mother?" he asked.

"There is one I'd like to pass on to her but I'm too much of a lady to say so..."

Her husband laughed. "I'll send her your regards then, shall I? Now you get off to the school and don't keep those children waiting. It won't do for the teacher to be late, what kind of an example would that set?" He scolded her in a light-hearted manner.

"Mr. Davies, I would never let those children down!" She declared.

He smiled, locking eyes with hers. "I know that, Lily." He walked towards her and pecked her quickly on the cheek, then left the house for the journey to the railway station.

Today, she particularly didn't want to be late, as Kathleen was going to help at the school. She needed her around as now she was getting awfully tired. Young Hannah Griffiths and Elsa Morgan were a great help, but she needed someone who could control the children and Kathleen could do it easily. The children were mesmerised by Kathleen's soft Irish lilt. She was great at teaching them to sing new songs, she also played the piano too, and it was good to have someone so musically minded in the school room.

Her sister-in-law's performances at the Temperance Hall were only far and few between to begin with, but she'd been promised more work by her agent in the future, and hopefully, maybe one day would move up the bill.

"The problem I find about performing," Kathleen said, later that day as she handed Lily a pile of discarded books the children had left on the classroom floor, "is the sort of people the music hall attracts."

"You mean that opera star?" Lily enquired, "Bella what's-her-name from Cardiff?"

Kathleen shook her head, "No, not her. I mean there are certain sorts that go there for their fun and frolics..." She blushed, a deep shade of magenta from the neck up. Then lowered her voice, so that the children who were now putting on their coats for home time, could not hear what she was about to say.

Lily raised her eyebrows. "Sorry, I'm not sure I'm entirely with you?"

"Ladies of the Night!" Kathleen hissed.

Lily blinked profusely. "Oh, I had no idea..."

"Yes, they go there with some of the more affluent male members of the community."

"You mean those gentlemen attend performances without their wives?"

"Yes, and they get up to all sorts of shenanigans. Sometimes I notice the fumbling that goes on up in the balcony area. I try to avert my gaze, but it's shameless. I'm sure if Dafydd knew he'd stop me performing there. Those poor wives left at home while their husbands make mischief with those shameless whores of Babylon!"

Lily swallowed. "Kathleen, you mustn't upset yourself so. Those working girls probably come from the China area of Merthyr. Dafydd has told you about the district, I assume?"

Kathleen swallowed hard. "Yes, he has. He told me it was a hell hole and not safe even for the police to walk around alone."

"Yes, that's very true. Evan got attacked there once."

Memories of the time Evan got hit over the head and robbed, flooded back to Lily with a vengeance.

"Was he all right?" Kathleen looked deep into Lily's eyes with genuine concern.

"Not exactly. Physically, he wasn't too bad but mentally, not so good. He lost his memory and couldn't remember me for the longest time. That's how I ended up in Utah with the Saints."

Kathleen's emerald green eyes darkened. "Sorry, Lily, I'm not entirely following you?"

Lily exhaled loudly. "He forgot I was his wife. He remembered who I was around the time of the awful pit disaster that we had here, but couldn't remember marrying me or even that we had a child together."

Kathleen put her hand on Lily's shoulder as Lily fought to hold back the tears at the memory of such a traumatic event.

"That must have been terrible for you, Lily."

Lily nodded. "Yes, so when Delwyn and Rose set off for Utah, I followed not long afterwards. You met them when you were there, I'm assuming?"

Kathleen beamed. "Oh to be sure, what a lovely couple and their son Meirion is such a cherub."

Lily lowered her voice to barely a whisper. "Then I'm assuming Delwyn would have told you about Cooper Haines, the man I almost married?"

Kathleen turned away to watch the last of the children depart for home. "Yes..."

"Then I need tell you no more about what happened out there." She patted her swollen stomach. "That's why you must never breathe a word of this to anyone..."

"I understand. Delwyn confided in Dafydd before we left for home that he was extremely shocked at the situation. He thought Mr. Haines a very fine man and that you were making a mistake returning to Merthyr."

Lily trembled at the thought of how circumstance had almost made her marry someone she didn't love. She'd cared for Cooper, but she'd been thinking of Mollie and having a good man to help care and provide for her child. That had been her aim, and now she chastised herself for putting herself in that position.

Kathleen intruded into her thoughts. "Dafydd explained that you thought Evan no longer loved you, but when they both turned up at Salt Lake together in search of you, then you realised how much he really loved you to undertake such an arduous journey."

Lily smiled at the thought of seeing him again, so out of the blue, it had stirred up all her own buried feelings. She frowned momentarily. "The only thing is I felt bad breaking off my engagement to Cooper Haines. Did you ever meet him while you were in Great Salt Lake?"

"No, but I heard a lot about him and visited his store once. You could have been a very wealthy woman, Lily."

"Well I have all I need here and more..." Both women walked towards the main door and Lily took the key from her dress pocket and locked the school room for the day behind them. Some things were best left under lock and key.

***

The following day while Kathleen was helping at the school, Lily sent her to Mrs Morgan's shop to purchase some flour, butter, sugar, eggs and currants as she intended making some Welsh cakes with the children.

"It will do them good to have a cookery lesson," Lily had said, "we will show them how to make them and they can eat their efforts afterwards. I have a bakestone here, we can use it on the stove."

Kathleen had loved the idea. When she arrived at the entrance of the shop with her wicker basket hooked over her arm, she was surprised to see a small crowd of women gathered inside and Mrs Morgan trying to usher them through the front door.

"If I hear any more talk like that then you'll all be barred from this shop!" Mrs Morgan said brusquely. She picked up a broom and proceeded to brush the gossip mongers out of the shop, who were tutting and shaking their heads in disbelief.

Kathleen stood awkwardly gazing at the scene before her. "What's going on, Mrs Morgan?" she asked, when the women had departed and the elderly woman had allowed her inside.

Elsa leaned her broom against the wall and dusted her hands together, quite pleased with herself by the look of it.

"Some evil-tongued woman, whose name I hate to mention, has once again been spreading rumours about Lily in this village."

Kathleen swallowed. "Oh, no!" Her hands flew to her face in horror as the blood in her veins turned to ice. "What kind of things is she saying?"

"Awful things, which I wouldn't repeat, but you will hear them soon enough I have no doubt. They are making allegations that the child Lily is carrying is not Evan's. Had you heard anything of the sort yourself, Kathleen?"

Kathleen's mouth was parched with panic as she vehemently shook her head. "Please, tell me who is the person spreading the gossip in the village, Mrs Morgan?"

Elsa rolled up the sleeves of her brown dress, dusted down her white cotton pinafore and snorted derisively. "Maggie Shanklin. Her, from Nightingale Street. She has nothing better to do."

"Please Mrs Morgan, might I sit down for a while?"

"What's the matter Kathleen? You've gone quite pale, cariad?" Mrs Morgan dragged a stool over to the young woman. "Please sit, dear."

She took a seat and caught her breath. "I...I..."

"What's wrong? Please take your time..."

"Oh, Mrs Morgan," Kathleen's head slumped and she stared at the floor. "Mrs Shanklin came to visit me when I first moved into the village..." she continued, then looked up at Elsa through lowered lashes.

Elsa's gaze narrowed. "You didn't tell her anything did you, about Lily?"

Kathleen shook her head. "Not intentionally, no."

"What do you mean?"

"'Tis not as it sounds, Mrs Morgan. I became ill after her visit and we discovered that half a bottle of Dafydd's whiskey went missing. Both my husband and Lily think Maggie slipped it into my tea."

Elsa raised a brow. "So, you think that she had a motive maybe?"

"I'm not too sure, but it could be. I have little memory of her visit that day."

"Well if I know Maggie, she was trying to get the guts out of you, and might have already succeeded by the way those old crones were wittering away in here earlier." Elsa raised her voice an octave. "How else could they have known?"

Kathleen began to sob. "Take no notice of me, dear. It's them I'm angry with and not you. Maggie in particular, she has already tried to blacken Lily's name once. So I take it you knew about the baby?"

Kathleen wiped away a tear with the back of her hand. "Yes. But I should hate it if my loose tongue has caused trouble for Lily and Evan, especially now that they've become reacquainted with one another."

Elsa straightened her pose and with jutted chin, said, "Let me tell you, there is only one loose tongue in this village that I know of that causes trouble, and it isn't yours. Now what is it you came in for?"

Kathleen smiled and passed her shopping list to Elsa. "It's for the children to bake with Lily at the school this afternoon."

Mrs Morgan unfolded the list and peered at it over her half rim specs. "Yes we have all you need here. I'll pack it up for you and then I'm closing up the shop for ten minutes so we can have a cup of tea, then you can compose yourself before you get back to the school. I don't want Lily knowing any of this. We need to find a way to quell the gossip, are you with me on this?"

Kathleen smiled and nodded. It was good to find another ally in the village.

***

Evan and Lily were having supper together in the kitchen at Chapel House. "You didn't tell me yesterday how it went other than you visited Pentyrch, were things there all right, Evan?"

He chewed on a tough piece of meat and set down his knife and fork, then looking at his wife said, "To be honest with you Lily, Mother didn't seem herself. Physically she looked well, but sounded a little vague to me."

"However do you mean, Evan?"

He let out a long sigh. "There was just something odd about the whole experience. She didn't once ask how Mollie, her own grandchild was, and you know how keen she used to be about her, even once ripping her from your arms and running off with her..."

Lily remembered that experience all too well, how the woman had turned up on the pretence of a visit and ran off with her down the road, only to be stopped dead in her tracks by Dafydd, who had finally shown up after weeks of having gone missing.

"So, you suspect something is wrong?" She studied her husband's face. He looked tired and worn.

"Maybe." He scratched his chin thoughtfully. "Father didn't seem too worried about her mental condition, seeming more concerned about the fact she wasn't eating properly. And to be honest with you, although she looked fine, she did look a little thinner than usual. He seemed to think it was 'the change of life'."

"That's entirely possible though, Evan. Maybe next time Mollie and I will accompany you to the house, we need to make things up after all that's happened."

Evan smiled. "I really would appreciate that Lily. It's so good of you, after all my mother has done in the past. Many would never forgive her..." He reached across the table and squeezed his wife's hand. At least they were both back on track, even if everything else in life seemed to be off it. That thought comforted her. She decided it was time to bury the hatchet with her mother-in-law, guessing that her mental state might very well be a form of depression caused by her advancing years, and the fact she hadn't seen her only grandchild in a long while.

Chapter Six

Lily had become increasingly concerned about two young children at the school named, Emily and Luke Howells. Their father, an ironworker at Cyfarthfa, had taken to drink and absconded from the area with a young woman from the notorious China area of the town.

The children's mother, Lucy, had taken on a job of washerwoman to make ends meet, but had fallen in with a bad crowd. Frequently, the children were left to their own devices according to local gossip, as their mother mixed with a bawdy, drunken crowd, who worked together at the wash house.

Lily made her way around to the woman's home in Canal Row, with a slab of *bara brith* fruit cake for the children in her basket. She had baked it the night before, with them in mind.

As she approached the house, which was embedded into the bank of the canal, she looked around tentatively to watch for any sign of life inside. The living room appeared to be in darkness and quite bare except for an old rickety table and a couple of chairs. There was no fire in the grate and it concerned Lily greatly.

She knocked on a neighbour's door to be met with a stern-faced, middle-aged woman, with a large chin. "What do you want?" the woman asked rudely.

Lily straightened, took a deep breath and said, "I am concerned about the whereabouts of two children from my school, they live in this house next door to you, Emily and Luke Howells. They haven't shown up for a couple of days now. Do you know what's happened?"

The woman stared at Lily. "So, you're the one they're all talking about, are you? The school teacher, married to the minister?"

Lily's face grew hot. "Talking about? I don't understand and who do you mean by 'They'?"

"I mean the villagers of course!" The woman cast a beady eye over Lily as if she were something disgusting she had just trodden in.

"And what might I ask are they saying?"

"That the baby you're carrying is not the minister's!"

Hardly believing her own ears, Lily fought to keep a modicum of composure. Remembering why she was here in the first place and her concern for the two children, she replied, "I don't know what people are saying but none of this is anyone's business. Please, if you see the children, then send them to me at Chapel House!" She turned on her heel to depart.

The woman shouted after her, "So, you're not denying it then?"

Lily's neck shrank back into the collar of her dress. Although it was a cold afternoon, heat rose in her body and her heart beat quickened. She must not show this woman how upset she really was. As she rounded the corner, she trembled and broke down sobbing, grateful the side street was deserted.

How on earth had word got out?

It shocked and saddened her that people could be so vicious.

When she got back home, Evan was waiting for her by the door with Mollie in his arms. "Lily, where did you go?"

She struggled to find the words. "Evan I am so upset...I..."

"Come in and warm yourself by the fire, *cariad*." They both entered the living room and sat with Mollie between them on the couch. Lily hugged the young child.

"Go on, Lily. What has upset you so much?"

Lily stared into the flickering flames on the hearth. Taking a deep breath and letting it out again, she said, "I went to see about the welfare of two children from the school who both live in Canal Row. They are brother and sister. When I asked a neighbour about them, she told me she knew all about the fact this baby I'm carrying isn't yours, Evan. It upset me greatly."

Evan draped an arm around his wife and hugged both her and Mollie. "But I don't understand how she would know such a thing. I know the Morgans would never say anything. Does anyone else know?"

"Yes, Dafydd and Kathleen. Delwyn told them before they left for Merthyr."

Evan muttered something under his breath in Welsh that sounded like a swear word. "That man has caused some trouble for you, Lily. I know he's your brother, but if it wasn't for him you would never have met Cooper Haines in the first place!"

"Don't be too hard on him, Evan. He did what he thought best, he wanted myself and Mollie to have a good life. After all, he did think you'd abandoned us."

Evan sighed deeply. "I suppose so. But look at how these secrets have a way of getting out even though it all occurred thousands of miles away!"

That was true, she supposed. If she had remained in Salt Lake, this wouldn't be happening and she would be living a wealthy life-style with a man she didn't love. Maybe she might have grown to love him in time. Who knew?

What she did know for certain, was that the man she really did love, the only man she had ever loved, was with her right now.

***

"Why didn't you tell me you knew about this gossip, Mrs Morgan?" Lily said in hushed tones the next day when Elsa was at the school helping the children to read. The class was taking a break, eating homemade biscuits and supping ginger beer the elderly lady had made herself.

"I'm sorry Lily, but Kathleen and I agreed to keep it from you..."

"You mean to tell me, my own sister-in-law knew too, and didn't say anything to me?"

Elsa nodded. "You can blame me. I told her to keep quiet as I didn't want you finding out and getting hurt. I was going to have a word with Maggie Shanklin the next time I saw her to put things straight."

Lily exhaled deeply. "What's the point? What's out there, is out there now. Evan said he will make an announcement in chapel on the weekend. Being a man of God he can't lie to the villagers, and now this is out, neither would I want him to. It would go against the grain."

"But what about your good name, Lily? It will be tarnished if Evan confirms that you had relations with someone who was not your husband?"

"Evan shall explain that I almost converted to Mormonism, as I followed after my brother and Rose when he abandoned both Mollie and myself, when he lost his memory. He will tell them that both Cooper Haines and I were engaged and due to marry shortly afterwards as in the Mormon faith our marriage would be permissible."

Elsa shook her head vigorously. "Oh *cariad*, please think what you are both doing, it would be better for your good name if you lied about this."

"But where has lying ever got anyone, Elsa? Ask yourself that?"

***

News had got back to Lily that the Howells children were being cared for by their grandmother in Pentrebach, a small village close to Abercanaid, much to Lily's relief. Their mother, Lucy, had not been seen for days and the grandmother, Gladys Morris, was greatly concerned.

"Don't worry Mrs Morris, the children will be well cared for at the school, I shall do all I can to help at this difficult time," Lily said, when the middle-aged lady escorted them to school that morning.

"The poor little things walked all the way over to see me in Pentrebach. They were barefoot and starving half to death. They said their Mam had been missing for a couple of days. Emily said her mother, when she last saw her, smelled strongly of alcohol and kept trembling. I blame that father of theirs, John Howells!" She spat out his name in disgust. "He took to drinking up in China and then ran off with a floosie. Now their Mam is going the same way. I brought her up to be a good girl, but since he left her with those young 'uns to care for, she has not been the same since. She had to get a job at the wash house and has been mixing with a rum lot..." she lowered her voice an octave. "Now there's talk that she might be working as a 'lady of the night'... if you get my meaning?"

Lily nodded, shocked that poor Lucy Howells had resorted to selling her body for beer money, while her children were left to fend for themselves. "Mr. Davies and I will do all we can to help," Lily comforted.

"A few prayers for her poor lost soul would not go amiss." Gladys sniffed and dabbed her eyes with a handkerchief.

"Yes, of course. She shall be remembered in our prayers." Lily laid a sympathetic hand on the woman's arm.

"Thank you Mrs Davies, you are a good kind person, there aren't many like you around, and don't let anyone tell you otherwise."

Lily smiled. "Before you leave Mrs Morris, do you have any idea where your daughter might be at this moment in time?"

The woman nodded. "It's got back to me from one of the men in the village that she's been staying in China and working for a man called, Twm Sion Watkin. He's known locally as Sioni. The man from my village says he pays women and girls their wages so they can drink in the pubs in the area. Some of them are in a bad way; they'd do anything to get their hands on a drink at those evil beer taverns frequented by all sorts of undesirables, some don't even speak the Welsh language!"

Lily straightened. "And how does your neighbour know about this?"

Gwladys put an arm around Lily and drew her near the door, as several children approached with their slates ready to make a start for the day. "Well, he admitted to me, see, he goes there himself. His wife died of the cholera when we had that outbreak a while back and a man has certain needs. I think it took him a lot to tell me about our Lucy being there. He promises that he has not touched her mind, and I believe him. For heavens' sake they were brought up at Sunday School together, as young children. It does not bear thinking about that he could defile my daughter."

"Don't concern yourself, Mrs Morris. I will help you all I can. You and I shall go and look for Lucy together. Tomorrow, I shall be leaving the school in safe hands."

Gwladys Morris broke down and wept, wiping her tears away with the fringes of her shawl. "Oh Mrs Davies, I have never encountered so much kindness in all my born days."

Elsa Morgan stood near the kitchen door of the school room. Lily beckoned her over. "Mrs Morgan, I'm just about to start class for the day, can you take Mrs Morris into the kitchen and make her a nice cup of tea as she's a little upset, please?"

Elsa nodded and ushered Mrs Morris out of the room. Sometimes Lily felt she was more than a school teacher and minister's wife, she seemed to get involved in people's problems, but she couldn't walk away from them either. Mrs Morris's heart was broken with grief for her daughter, who was a lost soul, she didn't want to see her distress go on any longer.

Lily carefully sat herself down at her desk, her ever growing bump making it difficult to move easily these days. "*Bore Da*, class!" She greeted, as the children sat themselves down.

"*Bore Da!* Mrs Davies," The class chanted in unison.

***

"Lily, I forbid you to go to China with Mrs Morris," Evan said angrily that evening, when she told him of her plan. "Have you not forgotten what happened when I went there? I could have died when I was attacked."

"But Evan, I can't allow Mrs Morris to look for her daughter on her own. Her husband is ill."

Evan's face softened. "I know you mean well, my sweet. But you have to think of our...I...I mean the baby."

Ice-cold water washed over Lily. "You stuttered there for a moment, Evan, when you mentioned the baby. This is *our* baby. Please say so. I don't care what anyone in this village thinks, and you shall tell them on Sunday to set the record straight. But please, I implore you, we have to help this woman find her daughter before it is too late!"

"All right then, but I think you need to take Dafydd with you. He can handle himself and he's still at hand as he hasn't found work yet."

Lily nodded. "Thank you, Evan. Yes, I worry about Dafydd, his savings have dwindled since returning from Utah."

"He could always go back to bare knuckle fighting, just to tide him over," Evan implied.

"Oh Evan, you're a man of God. How could you say such a thing?"

He placed both hands on her shoulders and gazed directly into her eyes. "Don't forget Lily what Dafydd did for me and you, he took on and boxed the hardest man around these valleys, so you and I could have the money to be reunited. Even though I finally got the money from my parents in the end, he was quite prepared to sacrifice even his life for us both."

Lily swallowed. "Evan, you're right. I suppose as long as God knows the motive behind the fight, then maybe He will understand."

***

The following day, Dafydd and Lily set out for China. Evan went to see Mrs Morris to pray with her, thinking it would be in the woman's best interests if she remained at home. After all, no one knew what would happen if Lucy were found, Mrs Morris was not in good health.

By the time Lily and Dafydd arrived in China, she was breathless after walking from Abercanaid.

"Are you all right, our Lily?" Dafydd's voice was full of concern for his sister.

She nodded, leaning against the wall. "Yes, I'm fine, just need to get my breath back that's all, Dafydd." She rested a while, and then composed herself. "Right come on then, we need to find Lucy Howells for the sake of her Mam and those poor young children." The thought helped spur her on.

At the approach to one of the arches of China, were a couple of young urchins, their feet bare and clothes ragged. The poor mites looked as though they had not eaten for days. The stench of the area permeated Lily's nostrils making her want to retch, it was not easy for a pregnant woman, but thankfully, Dafydd was at her side.

In the distance, smoke arose from one area, thick, acrid and putrid, the ground awash with muck and waste. It really was as some described, 'a hell on earth'. Her mind wandered back to the time she had looked for Dafydd herself when he'd taken to drink.

A gang of children ran past, almost knocking her over. "Hey, steady on there!" Dafydd shouted, but they had already gone, disappearing somewhere along a narrow alleyway, their voices echoing in the distance. The area was rife with pick pockets and Lily felt for her own drawstring purse, which thankfully remained untouched. She slipped it into her pocket, out of sight.

"Even the police fear coming here," she sighed. "And when they have done, the locals all stick together, surrounding them, some spitting and hitting them onto the ground," Lily said sadly.

Dafydd nodded. "Yes, I know. They're very suspicious of outsiders in these parts, that's why we need to be careful what we say to them, Lily."

"I agree. We need to be mindful we don't turn them against us."

"This is no place for you in your condition, Lily!" Dafydd scolded.

She let out a laboured breath. "Yes, but it might evoke their sympathy if they see a pregnant woman."

Dafydd shook his head. Lily realised that her brother knew she was a force to be reckoned with when she got an idea into her mind.

"What did you say the name of that man was who runs the girls?" Dafydd asked.

"Twm Sion Watkin. Otherwise known as, Sioni..."

Dafydd's eyes widened. "I know of the name!" He shuddered. "Where from?"

"When Evan and I visited here to find out what happened to him after the blow to his head, we encountered a prostitute. She was accosted by a thick-set man with a dog whilst we were speaking to her. He tried to strike her with his cane..." he gazed at the ground beneath his feet.

"What is it you're not telling me, Dafydd?"

He looked up. "I fear we may have made things worse for the woman. She told us as she'd been seen speaking to us, she would get a worse beating from the man than she already had received. I fronted up to the man, see, and warned him off."

"It was a brave thing to do, Dafydd."

"Brave or foolish, maybe. Who knows if that poor woman is still alive?"

"Hopefully, she is," Lily tried to reassure her brother. "And maybe that was down to you by preventing her having a beating."

Dafydd shook his head. "You don't understand, Lily. The woman told us that the man was the one who beat Evan and caused him to lose his memory."

Lily gasped. If it hadn't been for that brute, Lily might not have lost Evan in the first place. Anger seeped through her veins, making her more determined than ever to save Lucy from a fate worse than death.

Chapter Seven

It was getting dark and Lily and Dafydd had spent hours asking around and knocking on doors in China to find the whereabouts of either Lucy Howells or Sioni, the man in charge of her. But to no avail. Doors where closed in their faces, some people didn't even speak the same language, answering them in some strange tongue they couldn't understand. Others, Lily could tell, were in fear.

Whoever Twm Sion Watkin was, he made people tremble.

Dafydd turned to Lily and said, "I think we need to get you home now, Lily. It's been a long day."

She finally had to admit defeat. They had lost their bearings and passed a house that seemed a little larger than the others, the bedroom window was open. Hearing sounds of a female's protestations from inside, they hesitated.

"Get yourself back in here you bloody wench!" a man cried out. "He's paid a good day's wage to have you for a couple of hours!"

The downstairs door was ajar. Lily noticed people swigging from pewter tankards and smoking pipes, the sound of raucous laughter drifted outside. There was a strange odour in the air which she couldn't identify; it was neither snuff, nor tobacco. She pushed the door open further but, Dafydd, took hold of her arm and put her behind him. "Sssh leave this to me," he advised, as he entered first.

As he stood in the room with Lily behind him, trembling, the laughter abruptly ceased. In the far corner were a couple of men and half-dressed women in corsets and pantaloons, reclining on what appeared to be an old horse air mattress and sharing something from a long pipe that sent large puffs of white smoke into the air; their faces sleepy and dreamlike. The group seemed even unaware of the strangers' appearance on the premises.

Lily wrinkled her nose in disgust, whatever that substance was it seemed the work of the Devil to her.

"Those whores wink at evil for the source of profit..." Dafydd whispered in Lily's ear.

"What do you want?" asked a large-faced man, who had the reddest hair she'd ever seen to match his bushy sideburns. He clasped two foaming tankards and had a towel draped over his shoulder.

Dafydd cleared his throat. "I've come to look for a lady called Lucy Howells from Abercanaid."

A couple of the men laughed.

"Well, do you know her?" Lily asked, stepping out from behind her brother and noticing for the first time, that some of the clay pipe smokers seated around a long wooden table, were young lads not much older than those she taught at school.

"Once you've had one whore, you've had them all!" A beefy, dishevelled, drunken man in the corner shouted, making the pack crease with laughter.

Dafydd straightened. "And what makes you think she is a whore?" He narrowed his eyes with suspicion.

The laughter died away as Lily heard one man hiss to the drunk, "Shut up for goodness sake!"

The landlord's penetrative gaze, unnerved Lily. "There's no one of that name here, Miss."

"And what about Twm Sion Watkin, Sioni?"Dafydd asked, his chin jutting out in defiance.

There was a deathly hush about the room. People began muttering and shook their heads.

"Come on Lily," Dafydd said, taking his sister's hand. "This is no place for the likes of us."

Lily stood her ground and pushed her brother's hand away. "Look," she explained, trying to appeal to the men's better natures, "I know this lady and she's fallen upon hard times, her children need her." She turned to the side so they could see without doubt that she was with child and put both hands behind her back as if in some discomfort.

No one answered, but one old man looked at Lily, his eyes drawn upwards to the ceiling as if to say, "She's upstairs."

Not wishing to get him in trouble with his friends, she ignored his gesture and followed Dafydd out of the place.

"That was a bloody waste of time!" Dafydd said, stomping off down the road, forgetting how exhausted his sister was from her confinement.

"Hang on one moment, Dafydd," Lily pleaded for she could hardly keep up with his huge strides.

He stopped, and softening for a moment, smiled. "Sorry."

She caught up with him. "No, that wasn't a waste of time. I know for certain that Lucy is in that house. I have a feeling it belongs to Sioni. An old man there indicated to me with his eyes she is upstairs."

"Then let's go back there immediately and fetch her!" Dafydd's eyes gleamed with excitement.

"No," Lily advised. "We need to bide our time to get her safely away from the snare of that Watkin man."

"But how will we do that?"

"Kathleen!" Lily exclaimed.

"No, Lily, I think I know what you're going to say."

"Look, she has the right sort of look, she can pretend she's asking for work there and get the girl out."

"I'm not sure about that Lily, she could get hurt."

"I'd do it myself, but as you can see, I'm in no condition to!"

He frowned. "But I can't place my own wife in danger."

"No, and you shall not have to. What you could do is pretend to be someone who wants to pass her on to Sioni for a small fee."

"But I'd be recognised in there. Evan would have to do it. It might work I suppose as long as I am close at hand."

"Well Dafydd, if things got out of hand you know how to handle yourself. You should have been a policeman."

Now that was something he hadn't considered before. A policeman. It was worth a thought.

***

Evan was most displeased when Lily got home. He stood to square it up with Dafydd. "What hour do you think this is bringing my wife back home and in her condition too?"

Dafydd let out a long sigh. "Sorry, Evan, it took us the best part of the day to get the information we needed."

Lily looked at her husband. "Evan, it's my fault you know how strong-minded I am and not even a herd of horses could have dragged me away from that cess pit while I was on a mission."

Evan nodded. "Yes, I do know what you're like."

"Shall I tell him or shall you?"Dafydd looked at Lily.

Evan frowned. "Tell me what?"

Lily nodded. "Yes go on..."

Turning to Evan, Dafydd said good-naturedly, as he slapped his brother-in-law on the back. "Get your glad rags on. Mr. Davies, the Minister of Abercanaid, is to become a whore master for one day!"

Evan stood there opened-mouthed as Dafydd left them standing in the hallway of Chapel House.

Lily smiled to herself and removing her cloak, hung it on a hook on the wall behind her.

***

A couple of days later, when his ministerial duties allowed, Evan set out for China accompanied by Kathleen, whom Lily realised would be willing to help regarding the poor unfortunate's position. Trailing behind them at a good distance was Dafydd, for protection.

Lily had advised Kathleen to dress in more garish clothing than usual, so she borrowed a stage costume from the Temperance Hall. Lily heavily rouged Kathleen's cheeks and applied some to her lips also. So well perfumed and made-up, Kathleen entered China.

She gazed around in utter dismay at the hovels before her. "'Tis worse than I first thought, Evan. Back in the old country, I never once saw a sight such as this!"

He nodded. He was not used to wearing a top hat and had also been loaned a gold tipped cane and cravat, by Kathleen's agent, Walter Bartholomew.

"If this were not for such a good cause, I would turn around right now and depart from this very hell hole..." he muttered.

"Yes, but we need to do this for that poor woman and those children. 'Twas bad enough she was left to fend for herself and

53

those wee kiddies, but now to come to this." She noticed two men looking her up and down, a sliver of unease, coursed through her veins. She quickly brushed down her skirts, as if sweeping them off her person, like foul pieces of flesh. Kathleen walked on briskly.

Evan sniffed. "Lily described the place we're to go to as looking a little larger than the other houses. She said it was noisy and there was a broken window pane upstairs." His eyes searched the narrow lanes for anything that bore that description, most of the two roomed houses looked quite similar, one up, one down, stone-walled and thick with grime.

Kathleen gagged at the stench when they rounded the corner, holding her shawl to her nose.

"Are you okay?" Evan asked.

She nodded. "I'll be all right, thank you. How people can live in this state I don't know. Great Salt Lake was a world away from this place."

"Do you regret coming here, Kathleen?"

She hesitated for a moment, "Sometimes, if I am being honest with you. I do. I miss my family and I don't just miss Utah, but I miss Ireland too." Her eyes welled up with tears, forcing them back, she swallowed down her grief. "But my love for Dafydd is the greatest thing of all and worth missing home for."

Evan smiled. "Now, let's ask someone if they know where that house is."

***

Lily felt as though she were sitting on pins. "I'm sorry Elsa..." she said as they were taking a break at the school room. "I'm not myself today with Evan and Kathleen going to China. If something goes wrong it will be all my fault."

Elsa touched Lily's shoulder. "Don't be so hard on yourself, *bach*. It's a great kindness that you're all doing for Lucy Howells and those children." She glanced over at Emily and Luke who were hungrily biting into a hunk of bread and cheese. "Look how happy they'll be to get their mother back home where she belongs."

Lily sighed. Deep in her heart she knew that Mrs Morgan was right.

***

"Twm Sion Watkin, you say?" The old man shook his head. "No one of that name in this place." Then he turned his back, leaving Evan and Kathleen flummoxed.

"'Tis a great shame but it looks as if people are not speaking to us, Evan," Kathleen shrugged.

"Yes, I agree. No doubt, they are afraid of the consequences of speaking to strangers. I've heard that they all gang up on any outsiders here."

Kathleen shivered. "We don't want to go upsetting them then, we need to tread carefully."

Evan nodded. They decided to enquire only about Lucy Howells instead of the bully boy Watkin, but no one claimed to know her.

Kathleen took Evan's arm, causing him to pause for a moment. "It could be that she has changed her name...I knew a woman back in my hometown in Ireland who become one of the unfortunates. She changed her name to something that sounded more exotic."

Evan made a sound that sounded something akin to "Harrumph..."

"Yes, the name seemed to be in keeping with her new image. It suited her I thought."

"I can't see Lucy Howells changing her name to be honest. She's quite a plain, homely sort in normal circumstance."

"Maybe not."

"I think the reason these people aren't telling us anything about either person, is that the bully has threatened some of them."

Kathleen exhaled loudly, and it was then, she noticed a house that stood out from the others befitting with the description that Dafydd and Lily had given them: the larger house, the broken window, and the loud voices from inside. "I think we've arrived at our destination."

"Time to put on a performance of a life time," Evan said, "and if anyone knows how to perform, it's you, Kathleen Jenkin."

Kathleen shivered. "On stage, singing maybe, but I've never acted before."

"What about the time you sang as a woman who was left waiting at the altar? That was a fine act!"

She let out a breath. "That was a song though."

"Same thing...it's all a performance." He pushed open the heavy door, which was ajar.

Kathleen had never seen such a dive before. There were men of all shapes and sizes sitting on benches around a long table, supping from tankards and smoking their pipes. Some looked as young as her brothers. In one corner was a woman, who appeared to have seen better days, her face heavily made-up, sprawled over a gentleman who appeared quite out of place in the establishment. She wondered if he was one of the bosses at the Iron Works or Pit maybe? She'd heard they frequented the hovels of China. He turned his head when he saw them both as if trying to conceal his identity.

"You can wager he's a married man..." she whispered behind her hand to Evan.

A man sitting in the middle of the table, with a bald head and a scar deeply engraved in his left cheek, stood.

"What business do you both have here?" He stood his ground in a threatening manner, his broken nose making him appear highly menacing.

Evan cleared his throat. "My name is Tegwyn Thompson, Sir. I would like to speak to Twm Sion Watkin about some business I might be able to put in his direction."

The man relaxed his stance, momentarily. "Well, he's busy at the moment and doesn't want to be disturbed; he's testing out some goods upstairs." He glanced upwards and the men and boys at the table, laughed.

Kathleen guessed they were referring to his antics with one or possibly more of the women. *Nymphs of the Pave* they called them in Merthyr. It chilled her to the bone to think how contemptuously the men behaved towards the women folk, but she reasoned, if the young lads were brought up to think that way about a certain sort of woman from a young age, it was a no wonder they turned out to be beastly old men.

"Then we shall wait a while, if we are permitted to do so," Evan said firmly. "Until Twm Watkin has finished his business whatever that might be!"

A couple of the men sniggered.

"Right you are," said the scar-faced man.

Evan led Kathleen to an empty table. Then the landlord appeared and asked them what they wanted to drink.

"You'd better drink something," Kathleen whispered. She knew Evan did not touch a drop of alcohol as a rule unless it was for a special occasion.

Evan shrugged. "I'll have a pint of ale and anything the lady would like."

"Call her a lady, do you?" One of the young men from the opposite table shouted.

Kathleen's cheeks grew hot, but she was satisfied that her flamboyant appearance had the right effect.

"I'd like a gin, please," she said, and winked at one of the men, surprising herself with her own impudence. Causing lots of cat calls and whistles.

"Gin and a pint of ale, it is then," said the landlord, smiling.

It was a full hour and half before Twm Sion Watkin made an appearance. He stumbled down the stairs, his hair and clothing dishevelled. His large frame lumbering into the room. "Send some drinks upstairs, Emlyn!" he shouted.

The landlord turned to him, "There are a couple of people waiting to see you first..."

Sioni scanned the room and catching sight of Evan and Kathleen, strode towards them. Kathleen could see Evan's hands trembling slightly and he swallowed hard.

"Well, what is it you want?" he asked, looking directly into Evan's eyes.

"Tegwyn Thompson at your disposal, Sir. I was wondering if you might like to talk business with me? I shall pay for your drinks of course."

Sioni smiled broadly and sat down beside them, then clicked his fingers, "Landlord, drinks are on this fellow here!"

A foaming tankard was placed in front of the man and he took a long sip and placed it down on the table.

Visibly relaxing somewhat, Evan said, "I was wondering if you might like to employ the services of some of my ladies...."

Sioni narrowed his gaze. "And why would you ask me such a thing?"

Evan cleared his throat. "I want out of the business, see. I'm now a married man and I am headed North for a new job as a colliery manager. It wouldn't be fitting for me to mix with those, how shall I put it, less fortunate than myself."

Sioni's eyes widened. "I understand your position." His eyes swept over Kathleen, causing a shiver to skitter down her spine as he devoured her with his gaze. "And some of these ladies are quite tasty would you say, if they are all like this one..." He kept his eyes fixated on Kathleen.

"Thank ye kindly, Sir." She fluttered her lashes.

Quickly, the bully turned to face Evan. "You didn't tell me she was an Irish whore?"

"Well, what of it?"

"Some of the men they'd rather stick to their own kind. Communities keep within communities around here. The Welsh and Irish often fight one another; there was a big fight last weekend near Quarry Row. The police had a hard time of it I can tell you, there were stones flying everywhere! Some of those lads from Tipperary and Cork are real fighters! But we got the better of the bastards in the end!" He announced with an air of pride. "Don't know whether I want one of their whores in this lodging house."

Evan rubbed his chin as if mulling things over. "How about another drink?"

Sioni drained his tankard and wiped the beery foam from his whiskers. "Aye, all right then."

Evan had made a point to make his pint last as long as possible having neither the taste nor inclination for it. He summoned the landlord over and ordered another drink for Sioni.

"Think about it..." he said, looking the man squarely in the eyes. "An Irish girl might be a bonus, some of the men like something a bit different. They might like the idea of having carnal knowledge of one of those Irish bastards' women!"

Sioni's eyes gleamed. *"Di iawn.* Yes! I hadn't thought of that..."

Chapter Eight

It was arranged that Kathleen would start working for Twm Sion Watkin the following day. Dafydd assured her that he would not be far away as he would partake of a pint of ale in the bar of the house in the room below, thereby posing as a potential customer.

She arrived alone at the premises, where Sioni was waiting for her. "Upstairs!" he growled. Petrified, she did as told, climbing the rickety stairs, until she approached the landing area. Her heart pounded heavily with anxiety, her hands cold and clammy. This house was bigger than the others in the area, the upstairs divided into three small rooms, for the girls to entertain men, she assumed.

Sioni pushed her roughly into one of the rooms. "Now, what did you say your name was?"

Nervously, she steadied herself and glanced around. The room was bare, save a straw mattress spread upon the floor. An odour of damp and stale sweat permeated her nostrils. Her mouth was parched with fear. She took a few seconds to respond. "Colleen McNamara, Sir."

He ran his wooden cane over her body, softly skimming the curves of her breast, and taking the tip, placed it just beneath her chin, tilting it backwards. She swallowed hard.

"Now my dear, I need to try out the goods..."

He dropped his cane and began unbuckling his belt. "Get your clothes off...it's the only way for me to tell..."

She stood, tall and proud. "I'm sorry Mr. Watkin, but that's not possible right now."

The whites of his eyes were beginning to show as his nostrils flared. "You'll do as I tell you woman, you belong to me now!"

"I mean I can't...I am having my monthly. I will finish soon though..."

He stepped back and sighed heavily. "All right, but as soon as you are off, I'm on top of you lady. I always make a point of fornicating with my girls before anyone else has been there. Do you understand?"

She nodded. "Maybe there are other things I can do meanwhile?" She batted her lashes in expectation.

"Aye, maybe. Anyhow meantime, there's washing to be done at the wash house next door, you can help some of the girls there and tonight, there's a fellow coming here. Married. I promised him something a bit different and you are certainly that all right. I have a little something that I want you to slip into his drink...and then..."

"And then what, Sir?" she asked innocently.

"And then rob him of course! He'll have plenty of money on him, I'm sure of that, maybe a nice silk cravat, an expensive waistcoat. You slip it into his drink and get him upstairs here. You understand?" He handed her a small brown bottle of liquid with a corked top.

She nodded. "Yes." She took the bottle from his grasp, wondering what it was.

"How long have you been working the streets, you seem a bit naive to me, but maybe that's a good thing..."

"I'm new, Sir, I only started working for Mr. Thompson last month."

"Good," he smiled. "And have you been broken in yet?"

"Not properly, Sir. I mean a few men have messed around with me..."

"So they touched you, did they? Got their big mucky paws into your drawers?"

She nodded and lowered her head.

He began laughing. "Well fuck me, if we don't have a virgin here. I am definitely going to have a fine time breaking down your maidenhead. You can be my special girl..." He drew her to him and squeezed her buttocks. "Maybe we could have a bit of fun before then." He began to unbuckle his belt. "On your knees, sweet Colleen..."

Fear compounded her as her heart beat like a drum.

A gruff male voice resounded up the stairs. "Sioni, you're wanted downstairs!"

He shook his head. "You'll keep," he said, pushing her roughly to one side, "now get in the wash house next door and

61

tell them who you are, you can work for your keep that way meantime!"

She brushed her skirts down and headed next door, that had been a fortunate escape for her. Once outside, she caught her breath and noticed Dafydd speaking to a middle-aged, suited-man, in the street, as she approached, the man scurried off into the shadows.

"Who was that?" she whispered.

"Pay no mind to him," Dafydd assured.

"Please tell me?"

Dafydd let out a long breath. "Well if you must know he was offering me one of the girls from the wash house next door. It seems to me, there is a link with that lodging house and tavern belonging to Twm Sion Watkin and that wash house..."

"Yes, you are correct with your assumption. He has just sent me next door..."

For the first time Dafydd appeared to come to his senses. "He didn't touch you, did he?"

She shook her head. "He was about to though. He said he always took the new girls first."

A look of relief came over her husband. "Sorry, I didn't think he would try it on so soon. You are going to have to be careful. I will take a drink in there this afternoon so that if anything happens, you'll have me around."

She nodded. "I need to get in the wash house. We mustn't let anyone see us together. I'm going to ask the women there if they know where Lucy Howells is."

"Good. But do be careful, Kathleen. I shan't be far away, all you have to do is scream as loudly as you can and I'll be there in a flash. Are you sure you want to do this, I can take you back home now if you wish?"

"No," she said firmly. "I feel I owe this to Lily. I need to redeem myself for being loose lipped with Mrs Shanklin about Lily's pregnancy."

Dafydd sighed and taking her by the shoulders said, "But that was no fault of your own...but if by doing this, it will help salve your conscience, then I am by your side."

She smiled. "There's just one other thing I feel I must mention, he intends that I should rob a gentleman this evening. I feel that I cannot do such a thing. 'Tis not right in my eyes."

Dafydd gazed softly at her. "Oh Kathleen, whatever you decide to do will be for the good, look on it that way. You need to play the game..."

It was a game though that she was afraid she might not have the winning hand for.

***

As she entered the wash house, clouds of steam greeted her.

She heard women's voices and battled her way between make-shift clothes lines drying men's combinations, ladies' pantaloons, petticoats, towels and bed linen.

A large woman in a long black dress, white frilled apron and mop cap, peered at her over half specs. "What do you want doing, Miss?"

"Er sorry. I am not here in that capacity. I have been taken on to work here by Mr. Watkin."

There was a deathly hush as the women stopped chattering to stare at her.

The woman approached Kathleen, looking her up and down.

"You'll do, I suppose. You look strong and well fed enough to me." She sniffed. "You know you have to work upstairs, next door, as well?"

Kathleen nodded. "Yes."

"And you know you have to service the men?"

"Yes."

"And you might have to service them here also?"

This Kathleen hadn't been told. "No? That I did not know."

The woman shook her head. "Although this is a wash house, we have a little room just here, where there's a bath for the men. The gents like a little something else, some of them do. They work hard and need to relax. They don't get the full works here, mind you. Just a hand to send them on their way, if you understand my meaning." She lowered her voice to barely a whisper. "It's something we do to get a bit of extra money for ourselves. Mr. Watkin doesn't know, so keep it to yourself, all right?"

Kathleen nodded, open-mouthed. "Yes, I shan't breathe a word."

"I don't know how they'll take to you being Irish, but some of those men would let an old woman see to their pleasure, so I am guessing they'll not mind." The woman studied her for a moment. "What's your name?"

"Colleen McNamara." She could not give her real name, it was fraught with danger.

"Well, Colleen...remove your shawl and roll up your sleeves, I've a tub-full of washing for you!" She pointed towards a corner of the room. "There's plenty of soap, a wash board, and a pinafore hanging behind the door. Your hands will get red raw before the day's out. Mr. Watkin works us hard, mind!"

One of the girls standing behind her tittered and she wondered if one of those was Lucy Howells.

***

Kathleen gazed around the room and gulped, the Wash House looked like such hard work. One of the young women smiled at her and she smiled back. "Don't worry, you'll get used to it, Colleen," she reassured. The girl had her curly black hair secured under a mop cap, her face smattered with freckles. The woman's smile lit up her face. "I'm Jess." She introduced.

Kathleen returned her smile. "Well, you already know my name, but it's nice to meet you."

"Don't worry about Mrs Harris, she's not so bad to work for. She ensures we have plenty of rest and we've always got the kettle on the go for a cup of tea. She's good to us in many ways, and if you don't mind doing the odd bit of extra work in the bathroom with the men, there's a bit more money you can earn for yourself."

"Thanks. 'Tis reassuring to know that, Jess..." Kathleen reached for the pinafore from the hook on the door, slipped it over her head, and Jess tied it tightly for her.

The morning went quite quickly. There was much hilarity in the Wash House as the girls chatted and sang as they went about their arduous tasks—they were all enthralled by Coleen's voice.

"'ere you should be on the stage!" a girl who introduced herself as Meg, announced.

Kathleen swallowed. *They mustn't find out,* she thought. "Oh, I don't think I'm that good, honestly."

At midday they all stopped for a brew of tea, seated at a wooden table with two benches either side. Kathleen really enjoyed working with the women and for a moment, almost forgot why she was there. "I was wondering..." she began, as Jess poured her a cup of tea into a tin mug. "If any of you know a Lucy Howells..."

A cup of tea began to spill over the table as Jess lost concentration. "Sorry." She glanced around the room as if to ensure Mrs Harris was not around. "She left here last week. Why do you want to know, are you a friend of hers?"

"No...not really." Now how would she explain herself? "I...er...just know her mother, she told me she worked at this Wash House. She's very concerned about her daughter's welfare."

"Oh I see." Relaxing somewhat, Jess carried on filling the cups. "Between me and you, she has a drink problem, she's probably in the pub right now. She could have done well for herself working here and upstairs next door, but she got in with a bad crowd."

Seeing Mrs Harris enter the room, Jess averted her eyes.

"Have you finished those sheets, Jess?" the woman called.

"Yes, Ma'am."

"Good, then take your time all of you with your tea, you'll need your energy for this afternoon."

Kathleen hoped she was referring to work in the wash room and not the bathroom, or even upstairs in the house next door. She wondered how Dafydd was doing there.

***

"Haven't I seen you in here before?" the landlord asked Dafydd in the house next door.

It was no use lying if he didn't wish to arouse suspicion. "Yes, I was here with my sister the other day, looking for someone."

"What brings you back here?"

"I've been looking for work. I just remembered this place and thought I'd call in for pint."

"Well, there's not much going in these parts. You could ask Sioni, the owner of this establishment for a job, I suppose. He's always looking for big, strong men like yourself to recover unpaid debts. That doesn't go without its pitfalls mind you. Some of his men have ended up in court charged with assault. Other than that, you could go to the Vulcan Inn and ask to see one of the managers from the Iron Works. A lot of the workers from Cyfarthfa drink their wages away in there. You might be lucky to catch one of them there who will know the whereabouts of the manager."

"Thank you, I might call into the Vulcan later. Meanwhile, I wouldn't mind resting here awhile, I've been walking since early light. Could I order a pint of house ale, please?"

"Certainly, Sir."

The landlord returned with a tankard of foaming ale and set it down in front of Dafydd. He was going to have to be careful he didn't drink too much. He'd caused enough of a problem for his family last year when he took to drinking after the death of his mother. He was going to have to make this last, especially as Kathleen might need his help.

***

Kathleen and Jess were busy folding sheets together. "Do you know which pubs Lucy frequents?" Kathleen asked.

Jess stopped mid fold. "There are several she drinks at, but she'll be back to stay next door without a doubt. She needs the money for the drink, exchanging a few hours on her back for a few hours drinking time."

Kathleen considered it would be better to spend time at the house next door rather than go traipsing around the various pubs to find the girl.

"Have you known her for long?" Kathleen enquired.

"Only for a couple of months. When she first came here it was to earn money as that no good husband of hers left her and the children in the lurch. But as time has gone on, she seems to have got in a bad state. She no longer takes care of her appearance. She's fond of the gin see and we all know what a mother's ruin that is. If she doesn't clean her act up, I can see Sioni throwing her out onto the street. He likes his girls to stay pretty. I'm sure you'll end up being one of his favourites with your lovely auburn hair, Coleen."

Kathleen nodded her head and smiled as her cheeks burned red hot at the thought of being one of Sioni's favourites. She considered the time Maggie Shanklin had laced her tea with alcohol, that had been bad enough, but to live in that state of stupor every day like Lucy Howells, didn't bear thinking about. "Please Jess," she implored, "if you catch sight of Lucy, please let me know as a matter of urgency."

"Yes of course, I will..." she lowered her voice as Mrs Harris entered the room. "I will let you know right away."

***

Being in the house next door to the Wash House was reminding Dafydd of the time he'd spent in a China lodging house, which had forced Lily and Evan to go in search of him last year. It was beginning to make him feel uncomfortable and could be a particular lifestyle, if he were not now married, that he could easily slip back into, especially now as he had no work to go to. He had left the pit for Utah and now he was back, jobless. It might well be worth his while going to the Vulcan later to see if he could speak to a manager from the ironworks as suggested.

He watched the men around him, some were playing cards and others were sitting there in a state of despair staring into their tankards. Maybe they were lonely and this was the life they chose for themselves.

Even the young boys of no more than 12 and 13 years of age, were like young men, they worked hard and acted like grown-ups, drinking ale and smoking pipes, even frequenting with the likes of the prostitutes upstairs. What kind of life was that? It wasn't what he'd want for one of his sons.

A couple of women in gawdy dresses, made their way down the stairs. One wore a dress with a low laced bodice, so that her breasts were spilling over the top, he could almost see her nipples. Her dark hair was pinned up tightly onto her head, with a red flower secured to the side. If she'd had a normal life, she'd probably be a good looking girl with natural beauty, but this woman was weary worn and overly-used, he'd no doubt she'd lost her last flame of youth.

She sauntered over to his table and bent over, allowing him a long look at her bosom, which made him feel guilty with Kathleen in the room next door, but he knew he needed to play the game. "Buy a girl a drink, Sir?" she beckoned.

He nodded. "Yes, come and sit beside me, darling." He patted the bench. Vigorously clicking his fingers for the landlord and ordering another pint of ale and a gin.

The woman smiled. Her pan-sticked face and heavily painted lips gave her face a theatrical look. "Thank you kindly, Sir." She sidled up next to him, smelling heavily of lavender. It made him shudder to think that not so long ago, he was exactly like one of the men in here himself and that thought didn't bode well at all.

Chapter Nine

Dafydd fought to keep his composure as the woman beside him writhed around, lifting the underskirts of her dress and showing her legs. He had encountered this previously the time he had stayed in China, but he was single then. He swallowed, he was just a man and a man with certain temptations at that.

"Come upstairs?" she beckoned, as she fluttered her lashes.

One or two of the men across the room winked and egged him on as they made baying noises. In another circumstance, he might well have taken the lady up on such a generous offer, but he needed to keep his wits about him should the need arise.

"Sorry, some other time, maybe. I'm busy today, got a bit of business to attend to, see."

She dropped her petticoats, and looking him boldly in the eye, said, "You're not one of those queer gentlemen that I see around from time to time are you? Those that take part in unnatural practices?"

Dafydd knew full well what she was referring to, men that lay with other men. "No, of course not," he said stiffly. If he wasn't careful, he might alienate some of the people or make them suspicious.

"Then what is it?"

He firmly took hold of her wrist. "Say nothing, I'll take you upstairs and pay you handsomely."

She smiled a knowing smile that told him she realised he only wanted to go for appearances sake and just talk.

He finished his ale, slamming his tankard down loudly on the table to catch the men's attention, then followed the woman upstairs, realising he had to make this look real.

***

The working day in the Wash House had been quite a rewarding one for Kathleen, as well as discovering a little more about Lucy, she felt she had made a friend in Jess. As they went about their tasks, they nattered amicably and laughed at the same things. In another world, she dreamed of having a good friend.

Sometimes the isolation in this old, grey town was all too much for her to bear. She helped at the school occasionally which was rewarding too and then there was the odd bit of theatre work, but she longed to have a friend to call her own. The theatre performers acted as though they were above themselves sometimes and she wondered if certain folk treated her in a particular manner due to her Irish accent and upbringing.

The door to the laundry room swung open and Mrs Harris stood there peering over her spectacles. "There's a gentleman just turned up to use the bathroom. Would you take care of him please, Coleen?"

Kathleen stood there for a moment, open-mouthed. By 'take care' surely Mrs Harris didn't mean having to provide an extra service for the man? She gulped. "What would I need to do, Mrs Harris?"

The woman sniffed loudly. "Just add some jugs of boiling water that are on the stove to the bath tub and fill the remainder with cold. Test it with your elbow before he gets in. One silly girl here recently didn't do that and the gentleman almost got a good scalding, luckily he only placed his foot in the water, but we lost custom over that."

"That's all I need to do?" Kathleen visibly relaxed.

"Just give him the soap and flannel off the shelf and there are some clean towels next to those."

Kathleen let out a breath. "Right you are, Mrs Harris."

She was just about to leave for the bathroom when Mrs Harris added. "Oh and if he asks for anything else, I am assuming you know what you need to do, else you wouldn't have been employed by Mr. Watkin?"

Kathleen's heart slumped to her feet as Mrs Harris stood there arching an enquiring eyebrow. "No, actually." She glanced across to Jess as if in support.

"So, he's not broken you in yet? Mr. Watkin?" Jess asked.

Kathleen shook her head and Mrs Harris rolled her eyes and muttered under her breath, something in Welsh which she didn't understand.

"I'll go with Coleen and show her what to do..." Jess offered.

Mrs Harris stood there blinking for a moment. "Yes, all right you are then, Jess. Then next time Coleen, you shall know what to do for a customer, should the need arise."

A sliver of guilt coursed through Kathleen knowing that now she was making Jess do what she should be doing herself, but reassured herself that the girl had probably done this many times before.

Both girls went off to the bathroom as Jess whispered. "Don't worry, you'll get used to it here and you'll also come to know the preferences of certain men folk. Some don't even ask for anything at all."

The gentleman was waiting as they entered the room. He was smartly dressed in a black dress coat, white shirt and cravat.

"Good afternoon, ladies," he greeted and tipped his hat. Which Jess took and placed on the shelf, alongside his cane.

"Good afternoon, Mr. Pomfrey." Jess curtsied slightly and Kathleen followed suit. "He's one of the managers from the Ironworks," she muttered under her breath.

The girls busied themselves carrying enamel jugs and basins of hot water back and forth from the stove, being careful not to scold themselves and eventually topping up with cold water. Jess bent over the bath and tested it with her elbow.

Unbeknown to Kathleen, the gentleman had already undressed behind a curtain and she swallowed when she saw him standing there, pot-bellied and his pubic region on show. She had not even seen her husband like that, as they often made love in the dark, so it was an absolute shock to see the stranger that way. In her eyes a man's private parts should remain just that—private.

He lowered himself into the bath and lay back closing his eyes. "Full works for me today, Jess..." he said.

Kathleen watched as Jess went about scrubbing the man's back and front, then appeared to lose the soap and flannel as her hand reached out between his legs. She showed no look of disgust about her face, just a look of determination that Kathleen had seen when she scrubbed the collars of shirts on a washboard in the room next door.

The man's eyes remained closed, but a small smile appeared on his face as Kathleen experienced a wave of utter amazement as Jess appeared to jerk her hand up and down in the water as the gentleman's private part grew bigger and harder.

He began to make some strange groaning noises which didn't seem to affect Jess at all, then it was over as quickly as it began as the man sprayed his pearlescent fluid into the water and lay back with a look of contentment on his face. Kathleen cleaned him off with a flannel and went off to wash her hand.

"Fetch Mr. Pomfrey a clean towel, please," Jess ordered and Kathleen averted her gaze as she handed it over to him.

He took it and vigorously rubbed himself down. "Maybe next time you can do the honours, young lady?" He suggested, looking at Kathleen.

She nodded, hoping that she'd never have to witness anything like that ever again. It was both seedy and sordid in her eyes.

When the man had dressed himself, he slipped Jess an extra shilling for her time. She beamed at him. "Thank you, Sir" and dropped the coin into her pocket.

After the man's departure, both women set about cleaning up, then put new pans of water to boil on the stove. "You'll get used to it, don't worry," she assured Kathleen. "We only do a little here, the full business goes on next door, that's why I prefer it here."

Kathleen nodded. "That gentleman was married?"

"Yes," Jess said. "His wife is with child. So you can understand why he uses our services. To be fair to him he doesn't even go next door. Just comes here like that once a week. He's one of the nicer ones."

Kathleen frowned. "What's the worst thing you have to do?"

"Some of the girls will fellate a fellow, well they get paid extra for that particular service and understandably so."

"Fellate?" Kathleen was mystified; she had never heard that word before.

"They will take the man's organ in their mouth and both lick it and suck it until he reaches a happy ending as it were..."

Kathleen retched, she would never even do that to her own husband, never mind a stranger.

"Have you ever done that, Jess?"

Jess's face flushed bright pink. "Only on a couple of occasions, if I can avoid it I will, but there's a few who would as the payment is understandably much higher."

Kathleen shuddered at the thought of it. "I don't know if I could ever, in all honesty."

"Believe me, Coleen, if there's mouths that want feeding back home, you do it, close your eyes and try to think of something pleasant!"

Kathleen blinked in horror. "You mean you have young children, Jess?"

"Yes. Why do you think I work here in the first place? My husband was a good man, but he died of dysentery last year...I could easily have fallen apart, and I did for the longest time, but realised I needed to keep going for the children." She leaned over the bath tub and scooped up some of the used bath water into a large enamel basin.

A strong admiration for the woman and what she had to endure, swept over Kathleen. "Here, I'll help you with that, Jess," she said, taking the basin from the woman. "Where do I tip it?"

"Down the trench outside...it leads to the river. A lot of the waste goes down that way, that's why it smells so bad around here."

Kathleen watched as the woman wiped the sweat from her brow and leaned over the bathtub to remove the flannel and the soap. Life was hard in Merthyr Tydfil and for some, even harder than most.

***

Dafydd sat himself on a wooden chair in a curtained, partitioned off, part of the bedroom over the bar. The whore stood with hands on hips, breathing so heavily that her bosom almost toppled out of her low cut dress. "So, you're just one of those gents who would like to talk? You love your wife, but she misunderstands you?"

He shook his head. "No. I want to ask you a couple of questions and I shall pay you quite handsomely for any relevant information you might offer."

"Very well," she shrugged and sat herself down on the straw pallet near the window, with her knees tucked underneath her.

"What do you know about Lucy Howells?"

Her eyes widened, the whites now on show, and she shrank back into the corner. "N...N...Nothing. I know nothing at all."

"Look, I will not harm you," he spoke softly. "I'm here to find Lucy and take her back home to her children where she belongs."

"It's not that I won't tell you, I can't..."

He saw the genuine look of fear in her eyes, she was afraid of something or someone. "Is it Sioni that you're scared of?" He asked.

She nodded. "Us girls we'll get a beating, see. We've got to do as we're told or else..."

"Or else what?"

"Or else he might even kill us...one poor girl got beaten black and blue for speaking to the police last year. She never recovered properly, and even now, walks with a slight limp. There has been talk that one girl who didn't do as she was told, ended up with her head caved in, floating down the river."

Dafydd nodded. "I understand your concern. Look, if you were to talk to me I could even get you out of here, find you refuge with the chapel. My sister is married to a minister in Abercanaid, they would take care of you."

The girl began to cry. "No, it's just not safe. This is all I know anyhow. Look, all I can tell you is that Lucy was spending a lot of time at the Vulcan Inn just over the way. But it ain't good, she was being passed around like a piece of meat between the iron workers last time I saw her."

He nodded. "I see. That sounds an awful way for a mother of two young children to spend her time." He stood and went to offer her a shilling from his pocket, but she raised her vertical palm and shook her head.

"I don't want anything to do with this. Now listen, you need to stay up here a little longer or they'll be suspicious downstairs and word might get back to Sioni."

"Well, if that's the case then I have to pay you for your time or it will create even more suspicion."

She nodded. "I suppose so."

He knelt on the floor beside her and softly traced the contour of her cheek, as a lone tear coursed its way down her face. In another circumstance he might well have taken her like he did those whores last year when he went missing in the area, now he could see what victims they all were, at the mercy of bullies like Twm Sion Watkin and the hearts of lustful men.

"Thank you, Sir," she said, gratefully.

A few moments later, Dafydd heard footsteps approaching up the stairs. "We better make this look good...take off your dress...." he ordered.

She did as told, leaving herself robed only in petticoat and pantaloons. He quickly undid his belt and lowered his trousers.

"Get on your knees," he shouted loudly so as to be overheard.

A man's voice laughed outside the curtained area and Dafydd knew that it was Twm Sion Watkin returning to check on things.

"Now in your mouth, woman!" he commanded, surprising himself at the veracity of his own voice.

For effect, he let out a long moan. Then they heard the footsteps retreating down the stairs.

"Sorry about that," Dafydd touched her face, "go and get dressed."

He lifted his trousers and buckled himself up.

She stood and did as instructed, taking her dress from the straw bed and placing it over her head and pulling it into place and lacing up the bodice. When she was decent again, she said, "I wish they were all gentlemen like you, Sir."

A pang of guilt surfaced as he remembered how un-gentlemanly he was last year when he had taken to the drink and gone off around China with the whores, blaggards and drunks.

He slipped her the shilling earlier offered and an extra sixpence for good measure. "I meant what I said you know, if you need any help at all, call to 'Chapel House' in Abercanaid, the home of the Minister Evan Davies and his wife, Lily."

She nodded and taking the money, slipped it into a pocket of her dress.

Deciding it was too dangerous to hang around much longer, he made his way down the stairs, through the bar and over to the house next door.

***

Kathleen's muscles were aching and her back felt broken in two. It was hard manual labour this constant washboard scrubbing and pegging the clothes out to dry, and then there was the ironing she was expected to do, too. Her poor hands were almost torn to shreds, where once they had been a light pink, they were now red raw and beginning to crack from too much soap and water.

The laundry room door swung open and there, stood Mrs Harris with Dafydd at her side. Astonished, Kathleen blinked profusely.

"This gentleman needs a young lady to take care of him in the bathroom," Mrs Harris began. "Any particular preference, Sir?" She asked, looking at Dafydd, who was stood, cap in hand.

"I'd like that one to attend to my needs," he said, pointing to Kathleen. "The one with the red hair."

Kathleen found herself blushing, she looked at her husband in disbelief.

"Very well," Mrs Harris agreed. "But this one will cost you mind, she hasn't had her maidenhead broken in as yet. It's her first time. You'll have to pay twice the going rate."

A small smile appeared on Dafydd's face as he nodded in agreement, causing Kathleen's blush to spread to her neck and bosom area. It was already hot enough in the wash room as it was.

"Run along then Coleen," Mrs Harris advised. "You know now what needs to be done?"

"Yes, Ma'am," Kathleen nodded, then followed her husband into the bathroom.

Once inside, Dafydd collapsed into fits of laughter. "Hasn't had her maidenhead broken in! Oh 'Coleen', you do make me laugh so much!"

She began to giggle, then said, "Sssh or the others might hear you and then we'll be in trouble. Why have you come anyhow?"

"I came to warn you, I don't think it's safe here. I spoke to one of the 'ladies' next door and it sounds as if some of the women could be in danger from Sioni, which raises my concerns for Lucy Howells. Look, I will take that bath and any extras offered to me..." he flashed her a huge grin, "then we need to get out of here and over to the Vulcan Inn to look for Lucy."

She nodded. "There's a door at the back here, we could go now. I'd prefer to get out of here myself as before too long Mr. Watkin might well demand his rights in the bedroom."

He let out a breath. "You're right, it's just a risk we cannot afford to take. We've got some information and need to find Lucy before he does. Her life might depend on it."

Chapter Ten

"I feel so guilty..." Kathleen said, addressing Dafydd, "leaving the other girls in the lurch like that, especially Jess." The truth was she'd grown quite fond of the girl and sensed she was a kindred spirit of sorts.

They were stood in the alley way beside the Vulcan Inn. Dafydd lifted his wife's chin with his thumb and forefinger, and met her gaze with his. "Now look here Miss Coleen, Kathleen or Mrs Jenkin, whatever you happen to be calling yourself these days. I wouldn't want a wife of mine working in that wash house or the whore house next door, come to that. I know it appears you did exceptionally well on your first day, but it's a hard life." He lifted one of her hands and placed a kiss upon it. "Just look at your poor hands. I shall have to ask Lily if she has some soothing balm you can put on those."

Kathleen nodded, feeling torn in two at her hasty departure from her new found friend. It felt akin to leaving a little lamb in amongst a pack of rabid wolves.

Dafydd pushed open a side door to the Vulcan Inn, which was packed out with workers of all descriptions, grimy and coal dust black, or weathered and weary from the iron works, supping tankards of ale and putting the world to rights as they did so. Dotted around the place was the odd 'nymph of the pave' as people referred to the prostitutes of the town. They stood out with their garish dress and flamboyant style, the type of attire that many of the wives and girlfriends of these men, would never dare to wear. Those 'angels of the house' would not dream of setting foot in a tavern in the first place. There were rich pickings to be had in this boom town if you knew where to look, and the prostitutes certainly had a keen eye for those.

Kathleen scoured the room, but there was no sign of Lucy Howells, she knew what she looked like as she had come to collect her children from the school on the odd occasion. Her heart sank.

She turned to Dafydd. "No sign of her here."

"Well we'll hang on a while, we're here now," he said firmly. "It's the best place to look for her."

Once her husband had something in his mind, there was no stopping him, he was rather like his sister in that respect.

***

Lily and Mrs Morgan were tidying up the school room at the end of another arduous day. "I hope all is going well up in China," Lily said, picking up a couple of slates the children had left on the floor.

"Here, allow me to do that for Lily. You shouldn't be bending in your condition." Elsa bent over to retrieve the discarded slates, puffing loudly.

Lily stood for a moment and rubbed her lower back. "I'm not finding it any easier, grant you, but at least I haven't had any scares this time like I did when I was pregnant with Mollie."

"Yes, I remember that well. It shows this is going to be a healthy pregnancy. You're a strong woman, Lily. In more ways than one. What are you so concerned about anyhow? Kathleen has Dafydd by her side and no man would touch her with him around."

"I just worry something could go wrong. I suppose I am looking on the black side after what happened to Evan there with the bump on the head that particular time."

Mrs Morgan exhaled loudly. "Yes, but forgive me for saying this to you Lily, but the man was foolhardy going there alone. He's not a fighter your husband, well not in the way Dafydd is."

Lily supposed Mrs Morgan was right. Evan was a peace loving man and that's what she loved about him, he fought with his faith not his fists.

"I just hope we can get Lucy Howells back home for the sake of the children." Lily wiped her brow.

"Otherwise the consequences just don't seem worth thinking about," Elsa said sadly, shaking her head.

***

A dishevelled drunk approached Kathleen inside the Vulcan Inn, while Dafydd was busy speaking to a group of ironworkers, asking them if they knew the whereabouts of Lucy Howells.

"Come on outside by the alley way Miss...I'll give you sixpence for a nice fumble around in your drawers..." the drunk leered.

Kathleen turned her back towards him and then felt a hard slap on her bottom. Swiftly, she spun around. "Keep your hands off me, Sir!" She ordered.

"Come on now, dear. You're a working girl and you could do with the money, I'll be bound. Give a poor hewer a bit of pleasure for a few minutes to make his life worthwhile..."

Was this what it had came to? Men who worked hard underground and in the iron works, spending their hard earned money on whores and the evils of alcohol, while their families suffered in silence at home? She shuddered at the mere thought of it. Yet, she knew she needed to keep up the pretence.

"I've been bought for the afternoon by that fellow there," she said, pointing at Dafydd.

The man's eyes grew wide, he muttered something and shrank back into the corner, obviously afraid to challenge her husband. It made her feel proud that Dafydd was feared by most men.

She was just about to turn to stand nearer to Dafydd as protection, when there was a loud commotion as a man and woman entered the room supporting a woman between them. Their arms linked with hers. The woman's head bowed so low that her garish bonnet had almost fallen off. It was then, Kathleen gasped as she noticed blood dripping onto the flagstone floor as the woman's feet dragged heavily. A hush fell upon the bar room and the crowd moved back so the trio was stood in the midst of them.

"What's happened?" a collier shouted.

The man and woman did not reply but left the lifeless, battered body of the woman fall onto the floor, as it became immediately evident that the woman was dead.

Kathleen looked at Dafydd. "Lucy Howells?" she murmured as a wave of nausea surfaced inside.

But it was not Lucy Howells. The woman was named by someone as, Bronwyn Pritchard, and she was said to originally have lived in the Penydarren area of the town, so how she ended up in China was anyone's guess. But the talk in the Vulcan was that she had hit hard times and worked for one of the bullies, though this was not one of Sioni's girls.

Kathleen's stomach lurched at the grotesque sight before her. The woman's open eyes appeared to be taunting them all as she stared catatonic-like at the ceiling, a trickle of blood running from her mouth. Her ragged garb was hoisted above knee level, her limbs splayed as her body almost looked ready for business. A grotesque scene to behold. Kathleen turned her head away in disbelief.

Dafydd hugged Kathleen to his chest and softly patted her back, then lay a kiss upon her head. "Don't look, *cariad*. Best not to..."

The landlord beat his way through the crowd. "What on earth is going on here?"

"A man and woman just dropped her off here, do you know her, Sir?" Dafydd replied. "Some of the men are saying she's Bronwyn Pritchard from Penydarren."

"Aye, she does look a little familiar. But why leave her here when she's already dead?"

A man in a bowler hat, who was better dressed than the other men, walked toward the landlord. "To make an example of her, that's why!"

The men around him muttered sounds of, "Yes", "Aye" and "That sounds right."

"Who's that?" Kathleen whispered to Dafydd.

"Looks like one of the bosses to me, maybe at the pit or ironworks," he replied.

"No doubt," the man continued, "she had crossed the man she works for. It's a warning for the other women who work this way."

Kathleen looked around the bar and noticed the other prostitutes slowly leaving the premises, one or two looking fearful. It was imperative, Lucy Howells be found now at all costs, before it was too late.

***

Kathleen and Dafydd watched as a couple of men were employed to remove the body into another room at the inn, whilst a doctor was contacted to officially pronounce the woman dead.

Kathleen shivered as Dafydd draped his arm around her, and then he escorted his wife safely out of the pub.

"Hang on a moment!" the landlord shouted at them. "I've never seen you two in here before, how do I know you're not involved in this murder?"

"I can assure you we are not, Sir!" he said angrily. "In fact we were here to find out the whereabouts of Lucy Howells from Abercanaid."

The landlord's forehead creased into a frown as he narrowed his eyes with suspicion. "And why would you be wanting her, run some girls yourself do you?" He looked Kathleen up and down as if appraising her, which made her feel somewhat cheap and degraded.

"No, most definitely not!"Dafydd's chin jutted out with annoyance. "We would just like to return her home safely to her young children who need her. She's taken a wrong path since the death of her husband."

The landlord let out a breath and lowered his voice. "Very well. I know where she is, but come with me quietly as I don't want the others to hear."

Kathleen felt puzzled, but said nothing as the landlord led them behind the bar and up a stone flight of stairs, along a corridor and into a bedroom. He pushed open a door. There, lay a young woman fast asleep on the bed. Her long hair covering the pillows as her chest rose and fell with each breath. She looked comfortable and cared for.

"Lucy? I d...d...don't understand..." Dafydd stammered.

The landlord went over to the bed and lifted the blanket over Lucy to tuck her in, where she had pushed it off in what appeared to have been, a fitful sleep. She looked rested now though.

"No, why should you?" he said softly. "I've been secretly taking care of her here this past week or so, since she got away from the bully Sioni. I know she's been abandoned by her husband, and has young children, that's why I've tried to take care of her, sober her up, like. The trouble is a pub like this isn't the best place to keep someone like her."

Dafydd nodded. "Well if you wish, when she wakens, we'll take her back to Abercanaid with us."

"She's in a weakened state mind you, might not be able to walk the distance. But I have a friend with a pony and trap, he'll take you and the er...lady?" He shot Kathleen a look.

Dafydd smiled. "I know what you're thinking, that this lady is a whore, but she's not, she's my wife. We came here today to try to find Lucy, that's why she looks this way. Kathleen went to work in the wash house to try to gather some information, and I went to Sioni's home and got some facts from a prostitute there. That's what led us to this pub."

"I see," said the landlord and then glancing at Kathleen said, "I'm sorry Ma'am about the confusion."

Kathleen smiled warmly. "There was no reason why on God's green earth you should know who or what I really am."

"Anyhow," the landlord said, "I want to make sure Lucy's fed and watered before she leaves tonight, so we'll all eat together."

"Sounds as if you care greatly about her," Dafydd said.

"Aye, maybe I do. She fell on hard times, that's how she's ended up in this state, it happens to the best of us."

"Yes, I know." Dafydd become thoughtful, then turned to the landlord and said, "You don't know if there are any jobs going around these parts do you?"

The landlord scratched his stubbled chin. "Who's after a job then?"

"Me!" Dafydd said brightly.

After a swift appraisal, and the landlord taking in Dafydd's well-built physique, he replied, "Well, actually I could do with someone here to collect the tankards and throw any trouble makers off the premises. I couldn't afford to pay you much though."

"That sounds fine by me..." Daffydd said, holding out his hand to shake the landlord's, sealing the deal.

Kathleen wasn't so sure though that her husband being surrounded by ale and the temptations it brought, was such a good idea.

***

Later that evening, Kathleen and Dafydd took Lucy to Lily's home so she could be cleaned up and borrow a new dress before going back to her children. Lily thought it best for the woman to stop a few days with her until she was absolutely sure she was well enough to go back home.

As they were tucked up in bed later at Chapel Square, Kathleen laid her head on Dafydd's chest as he ran his fingers through her hair. A candle flickered on the cabinet beside them, sending a warm glow around the room.

"I'm glad we found Lucy today, Dafydd. I never want to see that place again, it's vile and disgusting. Life seems to be cheap there. It's right what they say about it being a hell on earth."

"I know... but one good thing about us looking for Lucy is that I've now got some employment at last before my savings run out."

Kathleen sat up in bed suddenly. "But it concerns me though, you working in that pub."

"You're afraid in case I get into any fist fights are you, Kathleen Jenkin?"

"No, I know you can handle yourself and it would be a foolish man to take you on, but I worry about something else."

He looked at her thoughtfully. "That I'll take to drinking alcohol again, you mean?"

"Yes, your sister told me all about what happened to you that time you went missing in China."

"Well, I'm not proud of myself. It was silly, I just couldn't cope with my leg after the pit accident and then Mam dying."

"Delwyn coped though?"

"Yes, I know, but he's stronger minded than myself. His religion has kept him on the straight and narrow."

"Promise me one thing?"

"Just name it, *cariad*?"

"You'll not touch a drop of that evil stuff whilst you are working?"

"I promise."

She hoped that his vow to keep his promise should not be breached.

***

Lucy had settled in very well with Lily and Evan. After a few days of keeping herself clean and away from alcohol, she was now being well fed with meat stews, apple pies and all sorts of heart warming foods, and so was beginning to return to her former self.

"Oh Lily, I don't know what I would have done if you hadn't all helped me," she said, when she was helping Lily to peg the washing on the line early one morning. It was getting harder for Lily to bend every day. To be truthful, Lily wondered the very same thing herself.

"The most important thing of all is now you're back in Abercanaid and Evan thinks it would be a good time to reunite with your children at the weekend. It will be arranged for your mother to bring them here. I will tell her at school tomorrow when she brings them first thing."

Lucy smiled a thin watery smile as if somehow dubious of the outcome. "I...I..."

"What is it?" Lily touched the woman's pallid hand.

"I just don't know if they will ever forgive me for abandoning them like that."

"Of course they will, they will be only too pleased to see you. They've known for the past few days you are here, but I've told them you need rest and prayers until you feel well enough again."

"Where did they think I was?"

"We didn't want to lie to them, so I told them an abbreviated version of the truth, just that you got involved with some bad people at your work at the wash house in China and became unwell."

Lucy frowned. "I expect the tongues have been wagging about me."

Lily nodded. "Ah well, it's only to be expected, but as far as the villagers know it's just that you hit the bottle, following your husband's departure, they don't know about the other side of things," she said, referring to the prostitution. "And that's the way it shall remain as far as I'm concerned."

Lucy pegged the final item on the line. "I hope so, I really hope so."

"Come on," Lily took her arm. "Let's have a nice cup of tea and give thanks to God that you're home at last."

Chapter Eleven

Dafydd began working for the landlord at the Vulcan Inn and
Kathleen still made her occasional performances at the
Temperance Hall. Even after being there for a few months, she
found she was still an outsider to the likes of opera singer, Bella
Montovani. The woman paid her hardly any heed except if she
wanted something. It was "Katy, fetch my gown!", or "Could
you pick that up from the floor..." "Put my flowers in fresh
water, dear..." If they passed in the corridor between
performances, Bella, sniffed loudly, holding her nose in the air.

One day... Kathleen thought to herself, *One day I will be the
big star here and you will be a 'has been', you diva!*

One Saturday night, Kathleen had finished a performance and
was waiting for Dafydd to walk her home after his shift at the
pub. He had kept his word about not drinking alcohol, though
she guessed it must be difficult, in amongst the temptation.

As she waited for him, she felt a tug on her sleeve, turning,
she was amazed to see Jess stood there. "Well if it isn't *Miss
Coleen*!" She spat angrily at her. "The big star herself on that
stage!"

Kathleen shivered. "I'm sorry Jess, please let me explain to
you what I was doing that day in the wash house..."

"I can't believe a word that comes out of your mouth, lady!"
By now Jess was trembling with anger and had her fists balled up
at her side. She looked better dressed than she had that day at the
laundry. Now she wore what looked like might have been her
best dress, woollen shawl and bonnet.

"You were there inside?" Kathleen asked. "You saw my
performance!"

"Yes, and it was even better than your performance as a poor
washer woman! I trusted you. I told you things and later
discovered you lied to me!"

Kathleen shook her head. "No, I didn't lie to you Jess. Only
about my name. I came that day to try to find Lucy. That was
all."

"Why couldn't you have told me you were pretending to be one of Sioni's girls?"

Kathleen relaxed. "I could hardly do that could I? If one of the other girls had happened to overhear, who knows what might have happened if it had got back to the ears of Mr. Watkin!"

Jess nodded. "I suppose you're right." She reluctantly admitted.

"Anyhow, we found Lucy and she's back with her family."

"We?"

"Me and Dafydd, my husband. The man I took into the bathroom before I scarpered."

Jess giggled. "I wondered what had happened to you. Mrs Harris was not best pleased, let me tell you. She informed Sioni and he was livid. You should have seen his face, all bulging eyes and that vein on his neck almost popped out!"

Kathleen laughed along with the woman, helping to ease the tension between them. "I'd love to have seen that."

Jess blinked several times. "So, your real name is Kathleen O' Hara. Like it says on the billboard on the wall?"

"Yes. Well that was my maiden name. I'm Kathleen Jenkin these days. Are you still working at the wash house?"

Jess removed her gloves and held up her hands which were sore looking and cracked. "Yes. I think these give my profession away, don't you?"

"I could ask if there's any work going at the theatre, if you like?"

Jess's eyes shone, her eyes brimming with tears. "Yes, please. I would love to work with you again. I'm sorry I was so off with you earlier, but now you've explained..."

"That's all right, Jess. Look, where can I find you if I can secure you a position here?"

"Send someone over to the Wash House to ask for me. Better not be you, mind. Otherwise, Mrs Harris might duck your head in that water tub and scrub your cheeks on an old wash board!"

She waved goodbye to Jess, who set off in the opposite direction, just as Dafydd came the other way along John Street. Kathleen ran to greet him.

The following day, Kathleen was helping Lily at the school, who was finding it more and more difficult to move around. "I think the time has come for you to stay at home until your confinement," Kathleen advised.

"Maybe, you're right," Lily said, slowly easing herself into a chair. "Do you think you can cope here?"

"Yes, Mrs Morgan will provide extra help, she said as much, and Hannah Griffiths is a good girl. How did it go with Lucy and the children? I notice they're not in today."

"Oh Kathleen," there were tears in Lily's eyes. "It was a wonderful thing to see, a mother reunited with her children; how they all laughed and cried too. I've given them the day off school so they can spend some precious time together."

"How do you think Lucy Howells will cope with the gossips around the village?"

Lily let out a long breath. "Well if I have anything to do with it...I'll get a big scissors and cut out their evil tongues."

Kathleen laughed at the very thought of it. "Yes and I'll collect them all in a little bag and throw them in the River Taff!"

"I've told Lucy to come along to the Sunday service at the chapel with the children and hold her head up high."

"'Tis quite right and proper too. Who knows what we might do ourselves if faced with those circumstances."

Lily tasted bitter bile in her mouth as she remembered being abandoned herself not so very long ago, but she'd been lucky to have the support of her family and Mrs Morgan at the time.

"Can you assemble the children please for morning register, Kathleen?"

Kathleen did as requested, ensuring the children sat quietly.

After register was taken, Lily explained she would stop working at the school for a short while and that Kathleen would be taking her place. The children seemed happy with that arrangement, they loved Kathleen with her sing-song voice and musical ability, and she brightened up the room.

***

Lily and Kathleen headed over to Mrs Morgan's place later that day to explain the situation. The elderly woman was just closing the shop for the day and called both women into the backroom. Once Lily had told Mrs Morgan about the school situation, the elderly lady's face took on a serious look.

"Now sit you down Lily, and you too, Kathleen. The tongues are wagging again. All sorts of things are flying around about Lucy Howells and her involvement in China. It's none of my business I know, but when these things keep getting repeated in my shop, then it is my business. I don't know what to do about it to be honest with you."

Lily stood. "Nor do I. Wasn't it enough that Maggie Shanklin and her cronies besmirched my name and that dreadful old witch got Kathleen intoxicated, but now she's causing trouble for Lucy and her family. Hasn't that poor woman been through enough?"

"Please sit, Lily," Mrs Morgan soothed. "It's no good you getting aerated in your condition. We'll have to come up with a plan, but first, let's all have a nice cup of tea."

Lily finally seated herself and this time Kathleen stood. "'Tis not time for tea Mrs Morgan, 'tis time for action!" She strode purposefully out of the shop, shouting, "I know where that wicked woman lives!"

***

Kathleen hammered hard on the wooden front door in Nightingale Street. Finally, it was pulled open and Maggie stood staring at Kathleen in the street, one arm leaning against the door jamb.

"I've heard you read the tea leaves, Mrs Shanklin?" Kathleen asked sweetly.

Maggie nodded. "Yes I do, but I always choose the right time, I usually arrange a gathering, why you want to come, do you?"

"Yes, but I wondered if you could do it for me over at Mrs Morgan's house. She is about to make a pot of tea. I'm sure I could give you a sixpence and Mrs Morgan too, maybe she'll even give you some Welsh cakes to be going home with."

Maggie smiled, a glint in her eyes. "All right you are then, I'll just go and get my shawl and follow you over there."

Kathleen ran back to the shop where Mrs Morgan had already put the kettle on to boil. "Change of plan Mrs Morgan, there's an extra one for tea."

Elsa furrowed her already wrinkled brow. "But I don't understand?" she said.

"I've been to Maggie's and invited her here to give us a reading of the tea leaves."

"*Fy Duw.* My goodness, Kathleen, why did you invite that woman into my home?"

"Because," said Kathleen, "I want to hit her where it hurts!"

***

Mrs Shanklin showed up at the shop ten minutes later. She'd obviously made an effort as she'd put on a different dress and shawl. The woman was about to put on a performance and revelling in the attention.

"Sit yourself down, Mrs Shanklin," Elsa offered, trying to be on her best behaviour.

"Lily..." Maggie said, "I wasn't expected you to be here..."

"Likewise," Mrs Shanklin. Lily turned her head away.

"Right, I'll brew up the tea and you can read the leaves then, Mrs Shanklin," Elsa said with a big smile on her face, and behind the women's backs winked at Lily and Kathleen.

The women made idle chit chat for a few minutes as they sipped their teas and nibbled their Welsh cakes. Although they spoke there was an odd atmosphere in the room, as the incident with Kathleen and the whiskey in her tea was not mentioned, almost as though it had never happened in the first place. Mrs Morgan got up to poke the fire in the grate, then sat herself down again.

"Now then, are we all ready to commence the reading?" Maggie asked, studying their faces. All the women nodded. "Very well, then let's begin."

Firstly, Maggie took Elsa's cup, turned it upside down on her saucer and turned the cup three times. Then she peered in, her large hooked nose almost poking inside the cup. "They're not bad leaves Mrs Morgan. They show pretty good health for your age and the possibility of a small windfall, sometime soon."

Elsa beamed, and then as if remembering why they were then, stopped smiling. "Well that's good news at least."

Kathleen handed her cup over and Maggie did the same thing, she peered in. "There's some good and there's some bad..." she said, "Do you want to hear both?"

"Aye, better had. Give me the bad first." Kathleen sat waiting anxiously.

Maggie straightened in her chair. "There's some misfortune in the family soon involving the perils of drink."

Kathleen bit her lip, remembering how Maggie had spiked her drink and nodded. "And the good news?"

"There's a lot of success coming your way young lady and it's to do with you singing. I see you on the stage..."

"Yes, but I already do that..." Kathleen protested.

"But I see you taking centre stage in a big city somewhere, maybe even London." Kathleen gasped. Could she really believe what the old crone said? It was probably all stuff and nonsense to be taken with a pinch of salt.

"Now on to Lily..." Elsa said.

Maggie could not make proper eye contact with Lily and kept lowering her head. Then she read the leaves. "They are not bad leaves at all. I see a reunion of sorts and a long journey."

"You mean I am going to see someone overseas?"

Maggie shook her head. "No, they are coming to see you that is all I can say for now...from a place on distant shores..."

Kathleen inwardly shook her head, the woman was talking utter nonsense and had distracted her from the real reason she wanted her there with them.

Sitting forward in her chair, she said, "Mrs Shanklin, do you remember that time when I first moved to Abercanaid and you thought it fit to visit me?"

The woman nodded, the whites of her eyes now on show.

"And do you remember we had a cup of tea together?"

"Y...yes of course..."

"And do you remember me saying how strange it tasted and you said it was something to do with the water."

"Yes, I do..." Mrs Shanklin sniffed.

"Well it was nothing to do with the water at all, was it?"

There was a long silence that could be sliced in two in Mrs Morgan's back room, all that could be heard was the sizzling of the coals on the hearth.

Quite suddenly, and with great force, Kathleen banged her hand on the table, causing the rest of them to jump. "Was it, Mrs Shanklin?"

Elsa and Lily looked at one another in surprise.

"I really don't know what you're referring to, dear..." Mrs Shanklin made to turn her head away, but spying the poker Elsa had left in the fire, Kathleen stood as the others watched and returned to the table with the red hot instrument.

Maggie shrank back in her chair. "What are you doing with that thing?"

"I'm doing what many in this village would like to do Mrs Shanklin. You've put around such malicious rumours about my lovely sister-in-law, Lily, myself and now, poor Lucy Howells. Where I come from we sometimes use a Scold's Bridle to silence the gossip mongerers or even a hot poker...."

There was a hard scraping sound as Maggie Shanklin moved herself back on her chair with fear. "Well, what's it to be then? Do I burn your evil tongue or do you keep your mouth shut from now on?"

Kathleen glanced at Lily and Mrs Morgan who were doing their best to stifle their giggles. If they were initially shocked by Kathleen's behaviour, now they found it hilarious. Maggie Shanklin being silenced by a red hot poker held by sweet little Kathleen.

Maggie reached into her purse and slammed some coins down on the table. "Please keep your money all of you. I shall not say another word, you have my promise."

"Not even about Lucy Howells?" Lily asked.

"No, I will tell everyone I was mistaken about her involvement with men up in China. And you Lily, I am so sorry." She hung her head in shame.

"Well, get out of here then!" Kathleen shouted at the woman, causing Lily's mouth to drop open with surprise.

Maggie stood. "There's just one thing you should know before I go..." she had that evil glint in her eye again. "When you, Kathleen, were loose-lipped from drink, you told me about Cooper Haines and the baby. I got the name of his store from you and I wrote to him. He thanked me for the very kind information and said he was going to make his way over here in time for the birth!"

Maggie hastily made her retreat, leaving Kathleen with the red hot poker in her hand and Lily feeling faint with Mrs Morgan in attendance. It really was the last straw.

***

When Kathleen got home to Chapel Square, she hastily put on a pan of Irish stew to boil for her husband when he returned from work and wondered what he'd have to say about the fact that Cooper Haines might well show up at any given moment and would he blame her.

She looked at the mantel clock on the hearth, he should have been home by now, but there was no sign. She could always reheat the stew later thankfully, but where on earth was he? He didn't arrive home until two and a half hours later, and by then she felt ready for her bed.

He looked so tired, there were big dark circles beneath his eyes.

"Oh Dafydd, where have you been?" She ran towards him as he opened the front door.

"Nothing to concern you, *cariad...*" he mumbled.

"No, you must tell me."

He removed his cap, jacket and muffler and sat down at the kitchen table. "I heard some bad news tonight and hung around to speak to the police."

"Go on, what is it?" she said, seating herself at the table and holding his hand.

His eyes began to well up with tears and for a moment, she feared the big strong man she knew, would break down and cry like a baby. He sniffed and swallowed hard to stop himself.

"Remember I told you about the prostitute I got the information from?"

"The one at Sioni's house?"

"Yes, well she was found in an alleyway, dead in China. It appears that she was strangled by someone."

Kathleen's hands flew to her mouth in horror. "But who would do such a thing?"

"Well, it's not that difficult to work out is it? Twm Sion Watkin my money's on!" Dafydd clenched his fists, the whites of his eyes now showing, nostrils flared.

"Surely not, he wouldn't do that to someone who worked for him?"

"Don't be naïve, Kathleen!" He stood and began pacing around the room.

"Sit yourself back down," she said softly.

He did as told. "Anyhow," he said more quietly now, "I've told the police what I know and about what we did to get Lucy Howells back home."

"What did they say?"

"That they could do with someone like me to join them!" He laughed scornfully.

"But don't you see, Dafydd, this could be your big chance? Didn't you say anything to them about looking for a job?"

"No, it didn't seem appropriate. Maybe I should though."

"Yes, I think it wouldn't do any harm."

"But I've already got a job, haven't I?"

"I wouldn't call collecting tankards and throwing people out of the Vulcan Inn, a profession of sorts."

He smiled. "You're right. I will go to see the Inspector tomorrow. You know, I got a sense of satisfaction when we were trying to find Lucy and bring her back home, it made me feel good."

"Me too." Then remembering what news she had, she straightened in her chair. "Dafydd, I have something to tell you…"

His eyes clouded over. "It's not Lily is it? Has she gone into labour?"

"No, no. But it does concern her and the baby."

He frowned. "What is it?"

"Maggie Shanklin informed us this afternoon that the day she spiked my tea, she got Cooper Haines's name out of me and the name of the store he owns in Salt Lake. She wrote to him back then telling him about Lily's pregnancy and she claims he's on his way here to Abercanaid."

Dafydd narrowed his eyes. "That old witch must be lying!"

"No, I don't think so, Dafydd. She sounded as if she meant what she said. I only got the information from her as I threatened her at Mrs Morgan's home. Otherwise, we'd have known nothing whatsoever."

"Does Lily know any of this?"

"Yes."

"It will not do the remainder of her pregnancy any good that's for sure, but at least forewarned is forearmed. Evan will need to know. We all need to be on our guard now."

***

There was no sign of Cooper Haines over the following month and things settled down into a slightly uncomfortable dis-ease. Thoughts of him were pushed into the background, and Mrs Morgan said that maybe he had thought not to come after all. A telegram had been sent to Delwyn in Salt Lake to see if he knew anything of this, but there was no reply. Lily took this as a sign that Mr Haines would be coming, but others were doubtful, claiming it was unlikely he would make such a gruelling journey.

Dafydd had been to see the Police Inspector at Merthyr Police Station, who told him he would give him a job and he could begin work next month when there would be a uniform ready for him to wear. The Inspector warned him how short staffed they were and his beat would involve a wide area of Merthyr Tydfil. He specifically warned him not to enter China alone in his uniform. He would have been safer as himself before he became a policeman than he was now.

Kathleen was really proud of her husband and began to tell people so, beginning with Jess, whom she'd managed to secure a job for, cleaning at the Temperance Hall. It was a start, not the best job in the world, but better than being wash house prey for the bosses from the iron works and coal mines.

On her first morning at the theatre, Jess beamed as she faced Kathleen. She wore a cloth mop cap, long white pinafore and had her striped dress tucked into her bloomers to begin cleaning the place. The auditorium could get in a right mess the next day following a lively performance. If the crowd didn't like a particular act, they pelted them with rotten fruit and vegetables. Fortunately, that hadn't happened to Kathleen, but she guessed there was always a first time.

"How will you feel now you are going to be the wife of a police constable, Kathleen?" Jess asked, tucking in a strand of hair that had dislodged from her cap.

"Proud, really proud." Kathleen beamed. "He really needs this job, Jess. Did the police speak to you about the prostitute who was murdered from Sioni's place?"

"Yes. Her name was Amelia Morris. We called her Amy. I didn't know her that well but she was a lovely girl. I'm so glad you got me out of that place. I shudder to think what could have happened otherwise. Since Amy's death and the involvement with the police, Sioni has disappeared, so it was easy for me to get away."

Kathleen realised that probably her husband's assumption that Sioni had killed Amy, was correct then. She shuddered at the thought of it. Trying to banish the vision, she smiled and then spontaneously hugged her friend. "I have to rehearse for tonight now, Jess, but if you stay in here cleaning up a while longer, you can listen for free!"

Jess beamed. "That's one of the great perks of working here, listening to the beautiful voice of an angel."

Kathleen stiffened as Bella Montovani made a grand entrance on the stage, in preparation for that night's performance. "I'll be on after that Prima Donna," she whispered.

Jess giggled. "She does like herself, doesn't she? I prefer your voice myself, Kathleen. It's much sweeter and pure."

On that note, Kathleen left to dress for her rehearsal leaving Jess to pick up the discarded items from the previous evening's performance.

***

At the end of Kathleen's rehearsal, she was surprised to find Jess waiting for her in the dressing room, Bella had already left the building and now, here was Jess waiting. "I've brought you a nice cup of tea. I reckon you could use one after singing your heart out like that."

"Thank you, Jess. Could you help me out of this dress, please?"

Jess stood in awe as she helped her friend and hung it up on a hanger for her and placed it on a large hook on the wall. "That's the most beautiful blue satin dress I've ever seen. Drink your tea quickly as there's a man sitting in the auditorium who's asking to see you."

Kathleen slipped her day dress back on and covered herself with a shawl as it was quite chilly in the dressing room. "Me? Did he say what he wants?"

For one moment, she feared it might be Cooper Haines and her veins filled with dread.

"Don't worry so. Drink your tea, I told him to give you a few minutes. He has a London accent I think. Looks quite well dressed to me, like one of those bosses at the Iron Works."

Puzzled, Kathleen sipped her tepid tea and went in search of the man with Jess trailing behind her. She found him seated towards the back of the theatre in the semi-darkness. "Ah, Miss O'Hara…" he said, standing to greet her. He was well-dressed in a grey wool suit, white shirt, and black cravat, and held a black bowler hat in his hand.

"You wished to see me, Sir?"

He nodded. "Please sit beside me." He patted the seat next to him. Tentatively, she did as ordered. "My name is Clement Johnson. I'm a London agent. I came here looking for talent and have found it in you, my dear." He took her hand and laid a kiss upon it.

"Me?" But why would he need to see her when the true star, Bella Montovani, had been on stage too?

"Yes, I believe I could get you work on the London stage."

She gasped. Her heart began to thud loudly and she feared he would hear. "B..b…but I already have an agent."

"And has he got you any work at any of the famous London theatres?" His sky-blue eyes shimmered, mischievously.

"No, but he said he might eventually get me work on stage in Swansea or Cardiff."

Clement threw his head back and chuckled. "I admire your loyalty Madam, but I can help you hit the big time, if you'll only allow me to do so. You have such a beautiful singing voice, so clear and pure, the voice of an angel."

Wasn't that what Jess had said earlier too?

He handed her a small card. "Here are my details, and I've written the name of the hotel where I'll be staying over the next couple of days. I hope to hear from you. I will also be at this evening's performance should you need to speak with me."

"That's very kind of you Sir, but I need to talk this over with my husband."

"Very well, as you wish. But this could be a golden opportunity for you, my dear."

He stood to depart, leaving her with the embossed card in the palm of her hand. This was something she could have only previously dreamed of. What would Dafydd think? And most of all, what about Bella Montovani? It didn't sound as if her current agent was going to take her to London.

Jess came scurrying over, lifting the hem of her dress in either hand, to saving her from tripping up. "What's happened?"

Kathleen looked up at her. "I've just been made an offer by that man over there. He's an agent, Jess, and he wants to put me on the London stage!"

"Cripes Kathleen, it's all happening, ain't it!"

Chapter Twelve

Breathless with excitement, Kathleen left the Temperance Hall in search of Dafydd, who was still working at the Vulcan Inn. She pushed her way in past the hordes of men who'd gone there to waste their wages away on alcohol after work. Beery fumes wafted her way and the odd odour of stale sweat and toil hung in the air.

A few men looked her up and down, making her feel slightly embarrassed as though she was some sort of wild prey and they were the hunters. She found her husband speaking to a crowd of men in the corner, who were seated on benches around a large wooden table. He was handing over some foaming tankards from a tray. She watched a while as he cracked some sort of joke to them as the men began to chuckle heartily. He had a way with people, that much was evident, and she thought he'd make a fine police constable when he began work at the Merthyr police station.

She tugged on his sleeve and he turned about face. "Kathleen, what are you doing here, *cariad*?"

"Is there somewhere we could talk?" She glanced past him, at the men who were eyeing her up with keen interest.

"Yes, come out the back room with me, I'll tell the landlord I'll be five minutes."

He shouted something across the bar to the man she'd recently met when they came in search of Lucy Howells, and Dafydd led her into a small room full of wooden beer kegs. It was drafty and cold, but at least they were away from prying eyes.

"What's the matter? Is it our Lily?" He looked into her eyes with concern.

"No, 'tis not Lily. It's me. When I was rehearsing for tonight's performance, Jess told me there was a man waiting to see me. I wondered who on earth this man could be. When I went to meet him, I discovered he was an agent who can get me more work."

Dafydd frowned. "But you've already got an agent, Mr. Bartholomew?"

"Yes, but so far, he has only secured me work locally, this gentleman says he can get me on the London stage!" She quivered with excitement.

Dafydd bit his lip. "Don't be fool hardy, Kathleen. We don't know this man. He could be anyone. If he takes you to London, who knows what he has lined up for you? You could end up walking the streets like the whores of China."

Disappointment surged through her. "He gave me this..." she handed him the card.

He fingered the business card and pondered over it, then handed it back to her. "That doesn't prove anything. He might have paid to have it printed to lure gullible females like yourself."

"Come along tonight," she said desperately. "He will be in the audience for the performance. You can meet him then and speak with him."

He vehemently shook his head. "No, certainly not, Kathleen. Be happy with what you're doing already, it's enough for a married woman as it is. You've already got on the stage and the people of Merthyr love you. You can't go upping sticks and moving to the big city, when I am about to embark on a career with the Glamorgan Constabulary!"

Tasting the overwhelming bitterness of bile in her mouth, she took a deep breath and let it out again. "This could be my big chance, Dafydd."

"We'll hear no more of it, Kathleen. Those London theatres are filled with good-time girls, and men with more money than sense." He held her by both shoulders at arms' length, then pecked her on the cheek. "I'll walk you home from work tonight." He turned his back on her and walked away, leaving her standing there feeling desolate and alone.

Tears filled her eyes and threatened to spill down her cheeks. By the time she got back to the theatre, Jess was busy mopping the passage way leading to the dressing rooms. "What's the matter, Kathleen?"

"I've just been to see Dafydd at the inn and he is against me going to London. He won't even consider it."

Jess rested her body on the handle of her mop and smiled sympathetically. "Don't be fretting so. I'll make us a cup of tea and you'll feel better, you'll see that you will."

Even the tea did little to fill the dull ache in Kathleen's heart. She knew singing was what she was born to do, and lately had such extravagant dreams of being on stage somewhere quite posh, with the landed gentry gazing on in awe. They'd peer at her through those exquisite little opera glasses, the women in fancy satin dresses and long white gloves, with hair styles twirled and piled high upon their heads. The men in evening suits, crisp white shirts and bow ties, it was all so fanciful; such gentile folk there to see her perform.

People would pull up outside the theatre in their horse-drawn carriages. There would be a big poster outside bearing her name, Kathleen O'Hara, Voice of an Angel. People would queue to get in for one of her performances. Bouquets of flowers of all descriptions, white roses mainly, her favourite bloom, would arrive after a standing ovation, filling her dressing room with a soft fragrance. There'd hardly be room for her to change out of her dress. The biggest bouquet would be from her own husband, that proud of her he'd be, seated enamoured in the front row. The people would adore her. There'd be numerous standing ovations as she took curtain call after curtain call. The newspapers would print the most wonderful reviews. Famous at last. She let out a long sigh as the dream slipped away from her and she came back to reality.

Jess stood behind her, as Kathleen was seated looking at herself in an old smudged, cracked mirror in the dressing room. How many people had watched themselves before a performance in this mirror? She wondered.

"I tell you what I think, Kathleen, is that if it is meant to be, it will be," Jess said, breaking into her thoughts.

Kathleen forced a smile. *But if it's not what your husband wants, then it won't be possible at all.* She thought to herself.

Her performance on stage that evening at the Temperance Hall, was the best it had ever been, despite the hurt, maybe even because of it, the emotion was there, as she sang from the heart, her voice reverberating from the rafters. People stood to applaud afterwards, but she did not go in search of the agent, instead, she quietly left the theatre from a side door and went to meet Dafydd outside the pub. She was a few minutes early as she hadn't even bothered to remove her stage makeup, wanting to slip away before Clement Johnson could find her again.

What was the use? In fact what was the use of it all? Maybe it would be better if she gave it all up and just went back to being an ordinary wife and started a family with her husband.

She'd speak to Jess about it in the morning; she seemed to be the only person who understood. Lily would have made a fine confidante, but she was heavily in confinement, and it would not be fitting to speak about her brother that way. Mrs Morgan would probably have old fashioned ideas, so thank goodness for Jess, her best friend these days.

***

No more was spoken about the theatre at home and Kathleen swallowed the lump in her throat as she carried on being a good wife to Dafydd, he would have enough on his plate soon starting his new job at the police station. Had he been single, he would have been expected to sleep there too, as the Inspector and his wife lived on the premises as she helped look after the single constables, ensuring they had a hot meal and kept their uniforms neatly pressed and their shirts well laundered.

If Kathleen's family knew she was married to a policeman, she'd wondered how they'd react. But in fairness, the whole family had changed from any wrong doing since taking up the Mormon faith and now she was in Wales, she wondered about her old faith at the Catholic Church. At one time it had brought her a lot of comfort. The chapel in Abercanaid was nice enough, but seemed sparse and bare in its simplicity compared to the beautiful ornate church with its stained glass windows and statues of the saints back in the old country.

She missed her family dearly and wished she hadn't run away from Salt Lake like that, but realised her father would have forbade her wedding to Dafydd, as he wanted her to marry someone he had lined up out there. Someone from another wholesome Mormon family.

Now she felt lonelier than ever.

Dafydd knelt to stoke the fire in their small house, saying nothing. She stared at his broad back and shoulders, he was a handsome man whom she loved so much, but her dream now crushed, she wondered how their relationship would survive.

***

The following day, Kathleen spoke to Jess in the dressing room. "Mr. Johnson is only in Merthyr for a couple of days. I've got the name of his hotel on this card!" She handed it to her friend.

Jess studied it wide-eyed, blinking several times in the process. "That's only on the lower High Street, a stone's throw away. Why don't you call to see him, maybe he'd have a word with your husband for you?"

"I've half a mind to, truth be told, but don't tell anyone of this for now, I would not want Bella Montovani blowing up. She could make things difficult here for me if she learned I was ear-marked for the West End of London."

Jess shook her head. "Me and her, we don't have those sort of conversations. I find her abrupt and abrasive. Go and have a word with Mr. Johnson later, Kathleen," Jess urged.

With renewed optimism, Kathleen said, "I believe I will. I'd like to see him anyhow as last night I left here without thanking him for his generous offer; it was most rude of me."

Later that afternoon, after rehearsal, Kathleen called at the hotel, only to be told that Mr. Johnson had cut his visit short and taken the train back to London that morning. Her hope of stardom now dashed.

She walked home to Abercanaid in a daze and downhearted, thankfully, there was no performance that night at the theatre, and Dafydd wouldn't be back until late. So she let herself in the house and made a cup of tea, pulling a couple of photographs of

104

her family out of an old tin she kept in the cupboard. "I wonder what you'd have said, Da?" she said, studying the dog-eared, black and white photograph of her mother and father. Her father stood tall and proud in his best Sunday suit and beside him, seated in a chair, was her mother, wearing a high-necked dress and her favourite locket; the one that carried a photograph, one side of her husband and the other of her four children.

Kathleen sighed deeply. She was about to get up and begin the evening meal when her hand slipped into her dress pocket and she felt the business card there. On one side the agent had scribbled the name of the Merthyr hotel, but the other side read:

Mr. Clement Johnson
Theatrical Agent
17 Chester Square
Belgravia
Westminster
London

She had some savings put by that she kept in an old jam jar, she was going to write to Mr. Johnson to see if she could still go to London.

That evening, before Dafydd came in from work, she sat down at the table and drafted a letter to the agent. By the time her husband returned home it was late, and they sat almost in silence eating their meal, with only the odd spit and crackle from the coals on the hearth. She toyed with the idea of mentioning the letter but thought better of it, hiding it in her pinafore pocket with the intention of showing it to Jess the following day.

Dafydd looked up from his bowl of stew, broke off a hunk of bread and gazed at Kathleen. "You've not been getting any more ideas about any of that London stage stuff, have you?"

She shook her head, hardly daring to meet with his eyes for fear that he should tell she was lying.

"Good, as you'll be busy enough looking after me when I begin work at the police station next month..." he dunked his bread in his stew and took a bite, followed by a large spoonful of the hearty stew. He chewed and swallowed, then said, "Why don't you find yourself something else to do instead of the theatre? Ask Mrs Morgan if she'll take you on at the shop to fill up your time when I'll be at work."

Although her husband was making what he probably thought was a helpful suggestion, for her, it really had become the final straw. He was telling her he didn't rate her much anyhow. She was nothing more than a stupid shop girl, whose aspirations were best kept to serving customers over a counter rather than being centre stage in life. The grease paint and the footlights were not for the likes of her.

She pushed her bowl of stew into the middle of the table.

"Don't go wasting that, Kathleen, I'll have it…" he drew the bowl towards him, then looking into her eyes said, "you're not hungry anymore?"

"No, I've lost my appetite." It was true, she had been ravenously hungry before he came in, now she had a bellyful of disappointment.

"I know another way to fill your time…" he said with a big grin on his face. "Why don't we get started on trying for a family tonight? Now that would give you something else to think of, having a young baby in your arms. You won't be bothered about the theatre then!"

She stood, looking down on him, her knuckles white as her fists were closed so tightly on the table, "Maybe you're right. But not tonight, I have a headache…" She clenched her teeth and then left the kitchen and climbed the winding stone staircase, to bed.

***

Next day, she took the letter out of her pocket to show, Jess, at the theatre. "What do you think?"

"You've worded it beautifully, Kathleen, but won't your husband be upset about this?"

She shrugged her shoulders. "I don't much care what he thinks anymore. If he had his way, I'd either end up working in a small shop or having his babies, or maybe both. He doesn't understand that this is my dream. T'will be a long time till I get a chance like this again."

Jess blinked. "So, what will you do?"

"If Mr. Johnson still wants me to go to London, then I will. I have some money saved from my theatre performances. And I have a small favour to ask of you, Jess?"

Jess's eyes widened. "Just name it?"

"I'd like it if you came with me. I'll try to get you work in the theatre…"

"But I can't leave the children…"

"If you could leave them for a few weeks with someone you trust, you would earn far more there than you do here. Think of all the nice things you could treat them to when you return, maybe you could bring the whole family to London to live eventually."

"I think you've been reading too many stories about how the streets of London are paved with gold, Kathleen!" Jess laughed.

"Aye maybe, but if we don't try it, how will we ever know? We don't have to go forever. Promise me you'll think about it at least?"

Jess nodded. "I will give it some thought, yes."

"I'm just going out for a while to post that letter, then we'll have a cup of tea before I rehearse."

"Right you are. I'll have these floors mopped before you get back and the kettle on the boil."

***

It was almost a month before Kathleen received a letter from the agent. It arrived one morning in a sturdy white envelope addressed to her in the most elegant copperplate hand writing she had ever seen in her life. Thankfully, Dafydd had gone to visit his sister. Kathleen's hands trembled with anticipation as she slit open the envelope and extracted its contents. She unfolded it and read:

Dear Miss O'Hara,

It was with great pleasure that I received your recent correspondence. The offer still stands, and in fact, I can guarantee if you come to visit me next week at the above address, two o'clock sharp on Wednesday, then I think I can get you a slot performing at the Royal Standard Music Hall in Victoria Street, Westminster, within a couple of weeks.

I shall reimburse you both the return train fare and your first week's accommodation. Should you choose to come, I can arrange lodgings for you.

I sincerely look forward to hearing from you, if you can send me a telegram confirming your decision to meet me on that day, I would be most grateful.

Yours Faithfully,

Mr. Clement Johnson ESQ.

Theatrical Agent

Kathleen shook from top-to-toe with excitement and couldn't wait to tell Jess. But what was she going to tell Dafydd? Maybe it would be best to just go, but somehow she realised, it wasn't just a note she'd leave behind, but her heart too.

Chapter Thirteen

Over the following couple of days Kathleen made plans with Jess to leave Merthyr. Jess had apologised and said she couldn't go, but would help her. The plan was for Kathleen to attend her afternoon rehearsal and slip out the side door of the Temperance Hall and down to the station to take a train to Cardiff. She'd find a hotel there for the night, and leave next day for a train bound for London.

Her heart beat so loudly, she feared someone might hear, but apart from Jess who knew of her excitement, no one else seemed to notice, and if her own husband did, then he wasn't saying so.

She managed to bundle some of her clothes into a bed sheet and took them to the theatre with her the following day. No one would question this as it would appear that she was going to one of the wash houses in the town. She'd borrow an old trunk that had been used as a prop at the theatre.

The guilt that washed through her was not enough to counterbalance the excitement she felt at the thought of performing on a London stage.

That evening after a riveting performance, she bade the other performers 'good night', hid the trunk of clothes under the stage, and went home with her husband after his shift at the inn. "You're quiet tonight, *cariad*," he said, as he wrapped his arm around her as they walked down Merthyr High Street past the many shops, hotels and taverns on their way.

"No. Just a little weary 'tis all, after tonight's performance."

He let out a long breath. "That's all it is. Well then you can put your feet up when you get home tonight, no cooking for you my girl, there's enough stew left from last night to be going on with."

She sighed, heavily assuaged with guilt knowing it would be their last night together.

When they arrived home, the fire in the grate had all but gone out, so the room was quite chilly. Darkness was beginning to fall, so she lit a couple of oil lamps. Dafydd knelt down and set about kindling the fire, while she put on the remainder of the stew to boil and cut some hunks of bread.

She laid the table with lace cloth and cutlery and went back to warming the stew. She was about to dish up, when she felt Dafydd's strong arms wrapping around her waist and he was kissing the back of her neck making her tingle all over. She knew what he wanted that night and couldn't make another excuse to get out of it. She owed him that at least, as soon he would come home to an empty bed of an evening.

She forced a smile. "Your stew is ready, please be seated, Dafydd!" Reluctantly, he pulled away and sat himself down in expectation. He still had his shirt sleeves rolled up to his elbows from working at the inn, and looked so handsome in his waistcoat, her heart flipped over. The fire was now nicely alight, crackling and spitting on the hearth, and this was all that she should have needed. Many young women would give their eye teeth for a moment such as this with the man they loved.

Having little appetite, she forced every mouthful down to find Dafydd staring at her, just like he had the other evening. "This is getting to be a habit, Kathleen. You not eating properly, you don't eat enough to keep a bird alive these days." He shook his head.

It was true, anxiety was preventing her from eating or sleeping much these days as there was a battle going on between her heart and mind. "I'm fine," she mumbled. "Just a little worked up that's all as I've been asked to learn a new routine at the theatre. I'm finding it difficult as it's a Welsh song."

He stretched his hand out across the table and took hold of hers and placed a kiss upon it. "I am proud of you, you know. I don't always show it, but I'd be lost without you."

Those words pierced her heart and she blinked away the tears beginning to form. Before he should notice, she stood. "I'm just going to make us a nice cup of tea." It was a way to change the subject, so he shouldn't see her crying. So he'd never realise the cause for her concern.

That night, she tried to banish all thoughts of tomorrow and gave herself wholeheartedly to her husband in their bed. She would miss their love making, but the London stage and footlights were strongly beckoning her away from Wales.

***

The following morning, she was alarmed to find she had woken up later than planned after last night's fitful sleep and love making. She stretched out and touched the empty spot in bed beside her. Dafydd had already left for Merthyr as he had said he would be calling into the police station to be measured up for a new uniform, before his shift at the Inn.

She was now running about half an hour behind time, so got herself quickly washed and dressed, forgoing breakfast. She would take some bread and cheese with her to sustain herself and eat it later with a cup of tea at the theatre.

It was with a heavy sense of foreboding, that she left a note on the table for Dafydd, telling him of what she had planned, her reason for going to follow what was in her heart. He would not get to read it until that evening, and by then, she would be in Cardiff, staying at a hotel for the night.

By the time she arrived at the theatre, breathless, but excited, Jess was waiting for her in the dressing room.

The young woman blinked. "I thought you'd changed your mind, you're normally here by now, or else had decided to leave the theatre all together?"

"No, Jess. I overslept that was all. I had difficulty sleeping last night, but I'm fine now." She laid a hand on her friend's shoulder, then they both hugged warmly.

"I'm really going to miss you, you know…" Jess whispered in her ear.

"I'll miss you too," Kathleen sobbed. "But I have to go. Do you think I'm being selfish, Jess?"

Jess pulled away and looked into her friend's eyes. "No, not at all. It's different for me. I have young children who depend on me and I couldn't bear to leave them behind even for a few weeks. It's that pig-headed husband of yours who is causing this. If he supported you, you wouldn't be running away in the first place!"

Jess's words hit home for the first time. The woman was absolutely right. There was no reason on earth why she shouldn't follow her dream. The train was due to leave Merthyr station half hour after rehearsal finished, so there would be plenty of time for goodbyes.

"Would you like a cup of tea?" Jess asked kindly. "Looks to me as if you could do with one, Bella Montovani's running late, so we've got time."

Kathleen nodded, grateful to have someone like Jess in her corner.

***

Rehearsals seemed to take an age and now she worried she might miss the train and have to catch a later one as she kept one eye on the clock. She cussed Bella under her breath and then heaved a sigh of relief when she realised she had ten minutes to get to the station. She quickly kissed Jess and handed her a small daisy brooch, she'd been given as a child. "This is for you, Jess, a reminder of me if we never see one another again."

"Please don't say that, Miss."

Kathleen blinked several times. "Jess, that's the first time you've addressed me as 'Miss'."

"I know, but now you're going to be a someone, a somebody, a star…"

She smiled and kissed her friend on the cheek. "Now, I really have to go as I'll be late."

"I had one of the stage hands to deliver your trunk to the station," Jess said.

Kathleen smiled. "Thank you so much!" She hugged her friend warmly. "Now I really do have to go—" She turned abruptly and stumbled as someone blocked her path.

"Kathleen!" It was Dafydd standing there, his forehead creased into a frown. "Where are you going?"

Her heart thudded so hard she could hear it in her ears, the blood drained from her body and she feared she might pass out.

"I..I'm going to—" she glanced at Jess's face which had gone a deathly shade of ivory.

"Anyhow, stop what you're doing, we need to get home, Evan sent Mr. Morgan on his trap to get us. Lily's gone into labour. Elsa's sitting with her right now. Come on, you're needed. There's no sign of Doctor Owen, you might have to help with the birth…"

Breathless, he stood there in anticipation, a concerned look in his eyes. He was very close to his sister, especially now that Delwyn was living so far away in Utah. All resolve about Kathleen's departure from Merthyr Tydfil, left her body and dissolved into thin air. How could she leave at a time like this? She quickly glanced at Jess.

"Please explain to the stage manager, I have to leave and probably won't make tonight's performance, they'll have to use the understudy, then turning to face her husband, she forced a smile. "I'm all yours, Dafydd," she said, swallowing down her severe disappointment and heartache. She liked her sister-in-law a lot and couldn't let her down in her moment of need.

As Dafydd helped her on to the pony and trap awaiting outside the theatre, with William Morgan in the driving seat, she suddenly felt a wave of fear wash over her entire being.

The note! She had forgotten all about it.

Chapter Fourteen

When they arrived at 'Chapel House', Evan was already outside the door with Mollie in his arms. His face stubbled and unshaven, shirt collar open, hair tousled. Not the smart, well-groomed minister, Kathleen normally saw most days. The dark rings beneath his eyes, testament to his lack of sleep.

"We're both here now, Evan," Dafydd announced, patting him on the shoulder.

Evan managed a concerned smile. He nodded gratefully. "Mrs Morgan is sitting with Lily upstairs, but there's still no sign of Doctor Owen, I sent word out a couple of hours ago." He bit his lip. "Kathleen, would you go upstairs, just in case you're needed?"

"Yes, of course."

"No fear," Dafydd said. "I'll ask around to see if I can find the doctor for you."

"Thanks. I didn't want to leave Lily for too long." Evan pointed up towards the upstairs window.

Dafydd set off in the direction of the canal bank and Kathleen guessed he might be headed for the Llwyn-yr-Eos pub. It wasn't that Doctor Owen was a big drinker, but it was common knowledge he sometimes popped in there on his rounds for a pint or a cup of tea. In any case, even if he wasn't there, there was always the possibility that someone might know his whereabouts.

"Let me make you a cup of tea, Evan," Kathleen said kindly.

"Would you please go and see my wife first, see if there's anything she needs or you can do?"

Kathleen nodded and climbed the stairs, where she found Lily in the bedroom, door ajar, propped up on pillows. Mrs Morgan was sitting one side holding her hand. Lily's eyes were closed tight, lips pursed as if wincing in pain.

Elsa Morgan looked up and smiled at her entrance. "Thank goodness you're here, Kathleen, you might have to help with the birth, we can't find the doctor."

"Aye, I know," Kathleen said. "How is she?"

"The contractions are coming every ten minutes now…"

Kathleen removed her bonnet and shawl and threw them over an armchair. "I think we need to light a fire to keep this room warm," she said firmly. "We need to boil a few kettles too. Can you go downstairs and do that for me, Mrs Morgan?"

Elsa nodded. She glanced at the grate. "Looks as if there's coal in the scuttle by there, I'll start that fire first."

"How are you feeling, Lily?" Kathleen asked, taking her sister-in-law's limp and pallid hand.

Lily's eyes flicked open. "Something's going to happen soon…" she held her breath and let it out again and winced.

"Yes, I think it is. Now don't worry, if the doctor doesn't get here, I have helped at a birth before. I had to help a few times when my cousin went into labour in Ireland. She was always having children, nearly every year…" She laughed to make light of the situation.

Lily nodded gratefully and Kathleen hoped she sounded more confident than she felt.

Within a few minutes Elsa had a nice fire going in the grate and then went to boil some kettles. "I'll make some tea for us all, shall I?"

"Yes, but better just bring a glass of water for Lily in case it upsets her stomach."

Elsa nodded.

She returned later with the tea. "We're going to need some sheets and towels too," Kathleen said.

"In the cupboard, there…" Elsa pointed. "I know as I helped out before Mollie was born. Lily had a bit of a scare just before and had to go on bed rest…" she whispered.

"I understand. Don't worry, I think she'll be fine this time." Kathleen decided to act as confident as was possible not to spread any fear or panic.

Kathleen propped Lily up and took the glass of water to her lips which looked parched. She took a few sips, then laid her head back down on the pillow.

"We're going to need something to put the baby in when he or she arrives," Elsa pointed out.

"We can always use one of the drawers from the cupboard there..." Kathleen glanced at the wooden chestnut cabinet in the corner.

"Good idea." Elsa smiled.

Lily opened her eyes. "No need," she mumbled.

Kathleen drew up close to hear what was being said. "Pardon, Lily?"

"Evan has made a small cot; it's in Mollie's room…"

Kathleen walked across the landing and pushed open the child's room, gasping to see a small white painted, wooden cot on a rocker. It was lined with a beautiful patchwork quilt that Lily must have made herself, she guessed.

"Oh it's so beautiful," Kathleen exclaimed, loud enough for the women to hear. She returned to the room next door to see Lily smiling proudly.

"Yes, Evan worked hard on that. Every spare moment he had, he hammered away at it. Can you bring it in here so we can keep it warm in front of the fire, please?"

Kathleen brought the cot in, still staring in awe at the creation by both parents and soon there would be another new creation by them, for all the world to see.

***

Doctor Owen finally turned up with Dafydd in tow. "Sorry you couldn't find me, my workload is huge today, but I finally managed to get away," he said, entering the bedroom. Elsa took his hat and coat and he rolled up his shirt sleeves.

He glanced at Kathleen. "How is she doing?"

"The contractions seem to be coming every couple of minutes, Doctor, and she's feeling the need to push."

He nodded. "If you would stay, my dear, while I examine her and everyone else leave the room."

When they were on their own, he took Kathleen one side and whispered, "I suppose you heard what happened with her last pregnancy?"

Kathleen nodded. "Elsa Morgan, did make reference to it, yes."

"Well we mustn't alarm her, but I feel there might be a weakness in the womb, she was bleeding quite heavily and had to go on bed rest for a while before the last birth. Any sign of any bleeding so far?"

Kathleen shook her head. "None as far as I can see."

"That's good then." Turning to Lily with a smile on his face, he said, "Well let's deliver this baby…"

An hour and a half later, Joshua Thomas Davies, entered the world kicking and screaming. "Well, he's got a healthy pair of lungs on him, I'll say that," Doctor Owen said, handing the baby to his mother.

Kathleen beamed with pride, she had been at the doctor's side throughout and very proud to assist. "You did a fine job both of you." Doctor Owen smiled at the two women.

Lily was cradling the infant to her bosom, ready to feed him.

"You can wash your hands there, Doctor," Kathleen pointed to a jug and bowl in the corner. She tipped some water in and watched while he soaped his hands and arms in the warm water. Then she handed him a towel to dry off. He adjusted the sleeves on his shirt, put his jacket on and lifted his black leather bag and hat. "Just let me know if there are any problems, and you, Lily, will need to get some rest." He winked at Kathleen. "Just ensure Mrs Davies eats some nourishing food as soon as possible, her body has been through a huge trauma."

Kathleen showed the doctor down the stairs and out of the house, then went into the living room where Evan stood beside Dafydd. Mrs Morgan was sat on the settee with Mollie. All eyes turned in Kathleen's direction. "It's a boy!" she said proudly. "A bouncing baby boy!"

Evan beamed and kissed her on the cheek, then went upstairs to see his wife and new child.

"Now," said Mrs Morgan, "we could all do with feeding up, especially Lily. I've managed to make some mutton stew. Let's eat and celebrate!"

They all smiled and then Kathleen remembered the note. "I need to get home and change out of these clothes," she said, excusing herself.

117

Dafydd shot her a glance. "That can wait, eat first, Kathleen!"

"No, I'd much rather change first out of these clothes, they got a bit messed up after the birth. I won't be long."

Before he had chance to protest, she was out of the house and running along the canal bank home. She hadn't even gone back to the bedroom for her bonnet and shawl.

Breathlessly, she let herself into the house and went to the kitchen table in search of the note to destroy it, but her heart sank. It was no longer there. The table was empty, only overlaid with a dark red chenille cloth and vase of flowers, but there was no note propped up against the vase as she'd left it.

She broke down and cried. It was all too much, one moment she was almost on that train to live out her dream, the next she was called away to attend a birth, now the note was missing. Dafydd must have got to it first and read it, and now what would he say?

She heard the front door open and footsteps on the flagstone floor, and looking up through a haze of tears, she saw her husband stood there with the note in his hand. Then he was on his knees weeping along with his wife. "Oh Kathleen," he said as she softly cradled his head. "Were you really about to leave me?"

***

"Yes, I was about to leave you, Dafydd," Kathleen sniffed, her body stiffened.

He stood to face her. "I found the note when I went to look for Doctor Owen. I called to the house to change my boots and was astonished to see what you'd written. But am I really so awful that you wish to leave me behind?" Her husband gazed intently into her eyes.

She shook her head. "No, of course not. I love you dearly, but you wouldn't allow me to follow my dream. Since I was a young girl I've dreamt of standing on stage singing…"

He shook his head. "But you are already doing that very thing."

"Yes, but that's in front of the baying horde. Some of those people, though not all, are already inebriated when they come to the performances at the Temperance Hall. They're looking for an excuse to pelt performers with tomatoes and rotten fruit. It's a sport of sorts for them, I suppose. That's not how I want things to be."

"Please tell me they've never done that to you?" He frowned.

She smiled, relaxing her stance. "Thankfully, no, but I've seen them do it to others if they don't meet with expectations. But don't you see, it would be more up market on the London stage for me?"

He harrumphed loudly. "What makes you say such a thing? I very much doubt it!"

"I'm not saying there wouldn't be people like that there, but the gentry would attend. People with good breeding. More refined members of the audience."

He shrugged. "Perhaps. I just don't understand your desire to follow this dream all the way to London, isn't Merthyr enough for you?"

She shook her head and began to gaze out of the window, the first buds of spring were starting to show, it was a time of new beginnings. Then she looked around the small room and realised how much she wanted to better herself. She took in a deep breath and slowly, let it out again. "Quite frankly, no, Dafydd."

"Then tell me, just what it is you want?"

She turned to face him. "You, are what I want, Dafydd…"

"Me? I don't understand, you already have me. Body and soul."

"No, I don't." Her chin jutted out in defiance. "I want you to be happy for me."

"But I already am, *cariad*," he said, softly now. He walked towards her.

"I want more…"

He stared into her eyes and she saw the pain there as he fought to come to terms with what it was she really wanted. Recognition dawned as he looked at her and said, "You would like me to come with you?"

"Yes."

"But I don't know if I can do that, I'm needed at the tavern and soon have to begin work at the police station."

"Well, I have decided, I'm going tomorrow. You're either coming with me or you're not. It doesn't have to be a permanent thing, Dafydd. Just for a week or two for me to settle in to see if it's what I want. I won't know until I try. You could easily explain your situation to the landlord."

He rubbed his chin. "I'm not really sure about that…"

She turned her back on him and climbed the stairs to take a nap. It had been an exhausting day and his ambivalence was beginning to grate on her nerves.

***

Nothing was said when he later climbed into bed beside her that night, they lay with their backs turned on one another. After a few restless minutes, she heard the gentle rise and fall of his chest, realising he had fallen asleep whilst she still lay there, her mind racing. Eventually, she fell into a fitful sleep and by the time she had awoken; his side of the bed was empty. He'd already left the house without wishing her well or even saying goodbye. A lone tear coursed her cheek.

Getting herself ready for the day ahead with a heavy heart, she made herself a light breakfast of oatmeal and made her way to the theatre.

Jess blinked when Kathleen arrived. "I feared I'd never see you again," she said, as she was in the middle of clearing the mess left behind on the seats in the auditorium. "What happened to your sister-in-law afterwards?"

Kathleen managed a smile. "She had the baby, a healthy baby boy; she's going to name him, Joshua."

"Well that's good then, ain't it?"

Kathleen nodded. "Yes."

"Then what's the matter?" Jess touched Kathleen's arm with the look of compassion in her eyes.

"Dafydd found the note about my departure yesterday, and realised I was about to leave him. He was so upset. We spoke about it yesterday and I've told him of my intention to catch the train today instead and how I would like him to accompany me, but he's just not interested, Jess…" she gazed at the floor for a moment.

"Aw Kathleen, that will be male pride, I'm sure. He needs time to get used to the idea," Jess said cheerfully. "I had your trunk brought back to the theatre when you left. I guess you'll not be needing it now?"

"Oh no, you're mistaken. I'm still going to London," she said firmly. "I will leave for the train this afternoon and explain to the stage manager. I'm sure even he will understand more than my own husband does. I've written a letter to my agent and will post it before I leave." She extracted a white envelope from her pocket.

"I'll see to that for you." Jess took it from Kathleen's hand.

"Thanks." Kathleen handed her a few coins for the postage, which Jess pocketed with the letter.

"It sounds as though you've made your mind up, well and truly, so I reckon we should have a farewell cup of tea."

Kathleen nodded gratefully, she'd need something to sustain her for the journey.

Later, they said their goodbyes and the trunk was despatched to the railway station ahead of her.

As she sat on the platform, she heard the hiss of the train as it waited for passengers to alight. There were three brown carriages in waiting to take people as far as Cardiff, if needs be. Several people milled past her with suitcases, one was a family of husband and wife, and two young children. The little boy, who she guessed was about six-years-old, held a small wooden train in his hand and the little girl of about three, clung on to a china doll with flowing blonde hair. She swallowed hard, that could have been her and Dafydd in a few years' time with their own children, but now that might never happen.

Glancing one last time along the platform as it cleared, except for a guard who was keeping look out with a small flag and whistle, with a heavy heart she boarded the train behind a porter, who loaded her trunk on board ahead of her.

She stood to gaze out of the window as the guard blew the whistle for them to depart and smoke billowed out of the train sending up puffs of steam, enveloping the carriage windows, making it difficult for her to see outside the mist. She sat down with tears in her eyes and wept bitterly.

As one dream ended another was about to begin, breaking her heart in the process.

She became aware of someone brushing past her and a deep resinous voice said, "Is this seat opposite you taken, Madam?"

Recognition slowly dawned. It was the voice of her husband. "Dafydd!" she jumped out of her seat and hugged him. "How are you here? I thought you'd left early for work this morning?"

"I did," he said smiling, then seated himself down as she did opposite him, as the train jerked as it started pulling away. "I went in to explain to the landlord of the Vulcan Inn, who gave me a nice little bonus! I came to the theatre to tell you the good news, but you'd already left, so I came racing here. Oh Kathleen, did you think I'd let you go without me?" He took hold of her gloved hand in quiet reassurance.

She wept again, but this time there were tears of joy in her eyes as she gazed out of the window and saw the green hills of Abercanaid that they were leaving behind, and she listened to the thundering train wheels that led them away a little nearer to her dream that lay ahead.

Chapter Fifteen

Upon arriving in Cardiff, Kathleen and Dafydd took a horse and carriage ride to the Angel Hotel in Castle Street, situated opposite the famous castle itself. Breathless with excitement, Kathleen snuggled into her husband as the horse and carriage bumped its way along the street for the short journey to the hotel. The carriage driver drew up outside the hotel causing Kathleen to hold her breath and then let it out again.

"Well, I've never in all my born days, stayed in a hotel such as this," she said, admiring the hotel's splendour. "It certainly looks grand, Dafydd. Have you ever stayed here before?"

He shook his head. "No, my sweet. I just wanted us to spend one night in a lovely hotel as when we get to London we're going to have to be careful with our money. I've had all my earnings from the inn paid to me, along with a bonus, so wanted to treat you for one night."

The carriage driver dismounted, retrieving their trunk from the back of the Hansom, and summoned a young porter to take it into the hotel. Dafydd thanked the driver and paid him for the journey and then tipped the porter.

"We'll rest here tonight and tomorrow take the ten o'clock train to London," he announced. "Where would you have stayed, if I had not accompanied you?"

"I probably would have looked for somewhere a little less grand, maybe an inn or something like that."

He sniffed loudly. "That would not have been a wise thing to do, Kathleen, in this place on your own."

"Aye, 'tis right enough. Though Jess says she thinks it's safer to walk the streets of Cardiff than 'China' at night."

"She's probably right, but I wouldn't want you staying anywhere strange on your own."

He alighted from the carriage and stood nearby to help her descend, taking her arm and ensuring she stepped down safely.

The driver tipped his hat and rode off back in the direction from whence he came.

Inside the foyer of the hotel was such exquisite splendour, she'd never seen before: chandeliers, marble pillars, men and women attired in luxurious dress, she could only dream of such things.

As if reading her mind, Dafydd whispered in his wife's ear. "One day you and I will dress like those nobs."

She laughed. "T'will be a long time till then, Dafydd."

"It might come sooner than you think," he declared confidently.

They made a reservation at the booking desk and chose one of the cheapest rooms without booking any meals for the evening or following morning. "We'll eat out," Dafydd said, "that way we can afford to stay here."

She had to admit she wholeheartedly agreed with him. After spending some time resting and feeling refreshed in their room, they decided to go for a stroll around the streets of Cardiff. They already knew the area as they had recently married there, but had not stayed in such a beautiful hotel then.

"Is this why you brought me here?" Kathleen asked. "As we spent the week of our wedding staying in that rowdy tavern?"

He nodded. "I want us to have at least one special night before we leave for London."

She smiled and they linked arms as they left the hotel.

***

London was not what she expected it to be at all. It was beginning to get dark by the time they arrived and a thick mist had descended. "I've not seen anything like this since I lived near the marshes back home…" Kathleen muttered.

"Apparently, London is notorious for thick fog, it's a mist mixed with chimney smoke." Dafydd coughed. "It's going to make it all the harder to find our way."

Two young lads dressed in breeches, jackets and flat caps made their way towards them.

"Carry your trunk to a cab for a shilling, Sir!" one of them shouted.

"Tisn't a bad idea," Kathleen commented.

Dafydd nodded and dug deep into his pockets and handed the young lad a shilling. The other lad beside him stood there holding his grimy hand out.

Dafydd drew in a breath. "But your friend said, only a shilling."

"A shilling a piece, Guv'nor. He carries one end and I carries the other."

"I'll end up broke at this rate." He dug into his trouser pocket again and handed over the shilling to the boy.

The boys made off walking at a brisk pace, with the trunk between them. Dafydd and Kathleen found it hard to keep pace. Then they hit the mist again and had no clue where they were.

"The lads, did you see where they went?" Dafydd asked a man in a bowler hat who had just approached them.

"No, I didn't. Sorry. Did you just get off the train by any chance?"

"We did, yes indeed," Kathleen added.

The man shook his head. "It's the oldest trick in the book, I'm afraid. They wait for people's arrival at the station, offer to carry their bags for a bob or two, then run off with the luggage. You have little chance of catching the urchins in this pea souper of a fog tonight."

Dafydd stood there open-mouthed at the situation.

"My gown, my beautiful green velvet gown!" Kathleen cried, as realisation dawned. "I needed it for my stage audition. Now what shall I do?" She looked around in panic, but there was no sign of the lads anywhere in the fog.

"I can't believe I was so foolish," Dafydd chastised himself.

"You're not from around these parts, are you?" The gentleman asked kindly.

"No Sir, we're from a town called Merthyr Tydfil in Wales!" Dafydd announced proudly.

"Oh yes, I know of that place, it has a booming iron industry," the man said.

"Yes." Dafydd nodded.

"I tell you what," the man advised. "I'll give you both a lift. I take it you're looking for a hotel?"

"We need one that is quite near to Chester Square, Belgravia," Kathleen explained.

"They'll cost you a pretty penny near that area," the gentleman said. "I know of a couple of taverns around there, where you could spend the night and get your sea legs in the morning."

"Yes, that would be marvellous," Kathleen enthused. "We might well end up going back home tomorrow if I am not needed and I don't like it here."

"I very much doubt that," Dafydd said, as they followed the gentleman to his Hansom cab, which stood outside a large building across the street, beneath the glowing gaslight of a street lamp. The gentleman was obviously used to the area and knew the best things to do to avoid a crime himself.

"Mr. Samuel Carruthers at your service," he said, as he gesticulated toward the vehicle with a flourish of his hand.

They followed him to his cab, where his driver leapt down when he saw their impending approach and opened the cab door for them.

"Welcome to London," Carruthers said proudly. "I hope you'll both enjoy your stay here…"

***

They spent the night at the Black Feathers Inn, and although rowdy, it was comfortable and warm. The Inn keeper and his wife were friendly sorts. She, all heaving bosom and comfort for the poor weary soul and he, the convivial host, who at times could send a glare across the bar room that could cut a grown man in two, if provoked.

"'Ere ducks, that was an awful ordeal you both 'ad having your luggage taken away by two rapscallions. Was there anything valuable in yer trunk?" The inn keeper's wife, known by the name of Rosa, asked.

Kathleen sighed heavily. "My best green velvet dress that I was to wear for my audition at the theatre, my new shoes, and some perfumes and costume jewellery, those sorts of things. Nothing I can't live without, but I would have felt more confident on stage if dressed the part."

126

Rosa took her to one side of the bar, from where both husbands and wives were enjoying a drink. "Don't you fret none, dearie. I have a wardrobe full of clothes upstairs, I could lend you a nice gown."

Kathleen eyed her up and down, very much doubting they would fit into the one and same gown. "Thank you," she said, anyhow.

Rosa burst out laughing. "I know exactly what yer thinking, that I've more up top than you." She placed both palms beneath her own breasts and jiggled them in an ungainly fashion that both embarrassed and bemused Kathleen. "But some of them dresses, I've had years. I was only a little slip of a thing then. You come with me, dear."

She led Kathleen up a flight of stairs and showed her into bedroom with a wide wooden door and low rafters. The room was decorated in the most colourful fashion, containing a fancy Chinese print screen to undress behind. Colourful paintings and fans adorned the walls. Rosa flung open wide a double-door wardrobe as Kathleen gasped, clasping both palms together almost as if in prayer. "I've never seen as many outfits as this before in someone's house, only in the theatre…and this bedroom has such fine décor, too."

"Well dear, the gowns are entirely at your disposal. To the left are the clothes I wear every day, to the right are those that no longer fit, feel free to try any on."

Kathleen immediately rifled through the railing and after a while, drew out a sapphire blue, satin gown, with low-cut bodice and bow beneath. "This is exquisite," she enthused. "Please may I try it on? 'Tis just the ticket."

Rosa nodded enthusiastically and helped her remove her white high neck cotton blouse and tweed long skirt, leaving her in her corset and pantaloons. She draped Kathleen's clothes over the Chinese print screen. Then, she slipped the dress over Kathleen's head, so it fell over her hips, skimming her outline beautifully, and nipping her in at the waist level. Kathleen inhaled the strong scent of rose water and guessed it was Rosa's favourite perfume, turning, she caught her breath as she spied her own reflection in the mirror.

"I don't know what to say, Rosa, this is far more beautiful than the dress I had planned to wear. I hate to say it, but I'm almost glad it was taken away from me now!"

Rosa beamed. "That's not all ducks, I have a beautiful fur stole to go with it and a nice pair of shoes you can borrow if they fit."

The stole complimented the ensemble perfectly, unfortunately, Rosa had bigger feet, so Kathleen decided to wear her own slightly scuffed shoes instead, hardly visible beneath the gown.

"I don't know how to thank you," Kathleen said gratefully.

"No need dear, it's thanks enough for me to see you in that dress. You have a delightful figure. I'd like you to keep it as a gift from me, so as you realise not all us London folk are like those thieves what stole your trunk. I'd like to have the fur stole returned though, as I like to wear it meself sometimes, if Arnold takes me out to the music hall or theatre."

Kathleen turned and kissed the woman on her soft, powdered cheek. "You don't know how happy this has made me. I am so grateful to you, maybe someday I can return the favour…"

***

At five minutes to two, the following day, Kathleen and Dafydd stood outside the home of Clement Johnson, Theatrical Agent. His house was in the middle of a tree-lined street of cream coloured, three-storey-houses, with black wrought iron railings. Some had brass plaques on the doors indicating they were some sort of business premises, others appeared merely residential. Clement Johnson had one of the plaques secured to his wall, but it also appeared to be his home by the smart green drapes in the window and chandelier she could see inside.

They climbed the short flight of steps. Dafydd knocked on the black door knocker which was in the shape of a lion's head. He gave three short raps and the door swung open. They were met by a lady in a long black dress, white pinafore and white cap. He explained the reason for their visit and she led them through to a room with a chaise lounge one end and a large imposing walnut desk with leather chair the other side. The maid requested that they sit.

In front of the desk were two small, matching arm chairs. The walls were adorned with paintings of London, Big Ben and London Bridge, Buckingham Palace, St Paul's Cathedral and the like. An oil lamp burnt brightly in the window and a small fire flickered in the hearth.

Someone coughed. Kathleen turned to see Clement Johnson there. Dafydd immediately stood and shook the man's hand.

"I take it you're Kathleen's husband, Mr. O'Hara…" Clement asked, good-naturedly.

"Oh no, that's my maiden name, I'm Mrs Jenkin," Kathleen explained. "This is my husband, Dafydd Jenkin."

"Easy mistake to make," Dafydd said lightly.

"Please sit, Mr. Jenkin." Mr. Johnson's face took on a serious expression.

Dafydd and Kathleen sat, one in either arm chair. Clement Johnson seated himself opposite the pair, behind his desk. "I hope you're feeling rested, Kathleen, as I'd like you to sing for the theatre manager later this afternoon."

She nodded. She was already dressed for the part in Rosa's beautiful gown and fur stole. "Here?" she asked blinking several times.

"Er no, we'll take a cab to the theatre. It will be at the Royal Standard Music Hall in Victoria Street. It's just a short ride from here."

Kathleen's stomach flipped over. It was as if a thousand butterflies had decided to take flight. Sensing her anxiety, Dafydd squeezed his wife's hand.

"And if she passes the audition?" Dafydd asked, "What then?"

Clement Johnson's face broke out into a huge smile. "Then the world shall be her oyster. It would be a great start in London for your wife, Mr. Jenkin. She could even end up singing in Drury Lane. Although I would suggest she keeps her maiden name for her act."

Dafydd stiffened as his face reddened slightly. Kathleen couldn't be certain what he was thinking as she silently prayed he should not be angry with that decision. As if sensing the awkwardness of the situation, Clement Johnson sat forward in his chair and looking at both of them said, "It makes sense for you, Kathleen, to remain an O'Hara for the sake of your act as you will be sold as a young Irish star. The surname Jenkin is Welsh, so not befitting, if you understand me."

Dafydd relaxed as if suddenly accepting the situation. "But she'd still legally be my wife, Mrs Jenkin, wouldn't she?"

Kathleen giggled.

"Of course," Mr. Johnson smiled. "To the music world she will be Kathleen O'Hara, Irish singing sensation with the voice of an angel. To the rest of the world she will be Mrs Kathleen Jenkin."

"I see," Dafydd said thoughtfully. "And legally, if she is signed up, what do we need to do?"

"You need do nothing, Mr. Jenkin. I shall get the paperwork drawn up if your wife's audition goes well. She'll be required to sign some legal papers, that's all."

Kathleen beamed. "Thank you, Mr. Johnson."

Her new agent rang a little bell on his desk, and the same woman who had shown them both in, took instruction to return with a tray of tea and other refreshments.

Later, when they had partaken of homemade scones and tea out of the fanciest china cups Kathleen had ever seen in her life, Clement summoned a carriage to take them to the theatre at Victoria Street.

***

When the carriage drew up outside the Royal Standard Music Hall, Kathleen took in a sharp breath of excitement.

The agent paid the cab driver and helped Kathleen out of the carriage as Dafydd clambered out behind. They walked over to the tall imposing theatre. Outside the four-storey-building was a large placard bearing the names of the acts of the day. Top of the bill were the singing sisters, Matilda and Meg. The placard boasted of them being the finest singing sisters in the whole of

London. Further down the bill, a comedian, Jack Sommerfield; Daisy and her performing Dog, Rascal; The Amazing Acrobats known as, The Adelphi Brothers; and finally in smaller print, Dolly Day Dream, a juggling act.

"Now listen to me Kathleen, a word before you meet with the stage manager, you're as good as any act I've ever seen here, maybe even better. So please remember that thought before you perform. Do you have anything in mind to sing?"

She nodded. "There's a song I recently learned called, 'Silver Sonata',"

Clement Johnson rubbed his chin. "I can't say I've ever heard of it myself, maybe you'd be better sticking to a more well-known song? Do you have any others lined up?"

Kathleen straightened her countenance. "I do indeed. But would like to try the new song, if you've no real objection to it."

"Very well, my dear, you know best, but keep one or two other songs in mind, in case the manager doesn't like the new song."

She nodded."To be sure, Mr. Johnson."

Dafydd held the door open for his wife and Mr. Johnson to enter the theatre and he walked in behind them.

Well this could be the start of something new, Kathleen thought. *On the other hand after this audition, it might all, very well, be over...*

Chapter Sixteen

Clement Johnson led Kathleen and Dafydd through a side door back stage, where artists and performers were preparing for their acts. A man with a cage of doves walked briskly past the trio.

"Is this a rehearsal for tonight's performance, Mr. Johnson?" Kathleen blinked.

"No, my dear. They're all here for auditions. You might have to wait some time until you're called." Naively, she had assumed she would be the only one. So all these people had their own hopes and dreams, and were probably just like herself, trying to hit the big time.

Clement knocked sharply on a dressing room door. The door was opened by a blonde lady with tightly curled hair. She wore the most outrageous red plume feather headdress Kathleen had ever seen.

"This is Madeline, Kathleen. She'll take care of you. I'll be sitting with the theatre manager in the audience throughout. Now don't forget what I told you." He winked at her and patted her arm.

Dafydd cleared his voice. "Where shall I go, Mr. Johnson?"

As if remembering for the first time Dafydd was accompanying his wife, Mr. Johnson said, "Just sit somewhere quietly at the back of the theatre and enjoy the acts. Some will be better than others of course." He smiled.

Both men left the dressing area and made for the auditorium.

***

"Would you like me to help you with your stage make-up?" The woman asked Kathleen.

"Yes please. I normally do my own but I'm shaking that much, I fear I shall make a mess of it."

The woman smiled. "Yes, I know what you mean, only I've been to that many auditions lately, I'm becoming a dab hand at it." She gave a hollow laugh.

"You've been trying a long time then, Madeline?"

132

"Just call me Maddy, please. Yes. I used to have a regular act at a theatre not too far away from here, but it burned down in a fire. She leaned in close. Between me and you darling, I think the stage manager got drunk and accidentally set fire to the place. It was a mixture of brandy and cigars what did it, I am convinced of that. Only it don't help me none as I've been trying my hardest to find work ever since." One of the performers stood and left the room as she was called to the stage. "'ere sit down darling…" Maddy said, gesticulating towards the now empty chair.

Kathleen did as told and allowed Maddy to apply the stage make-up of face powder, rouge and lipstick. "Please don't go too heavy with it," Kathleen requested.

"Don't worry, dear, I can see you're a natural looker, but under them lights you'll need to show yourself off to your best advantage."

Kathleen nodded, not at all too sure that she'd done the right thing allowing the woman to apply her make up for her, but when she'd applied a final dusting of face powder over the complete look, she had to admit she'd made a real good job of it, even better than she'd have done for herself.

"Thank you," Kathleen smiled.

"I ain't finished yet…"

Maddy picked up a hair brush and hairpins and brushed Kathleen's hair till it shone and arranged it as a chignon knot, with loose tendrils framing her face.

Admiring her new look in the mirror from all angles, Kathleen stood and kissed Maddy's cheek. "Thank you ever so much, now if I could just control my nerves, I'll be fine."

"I can get you some gin if you like?" Maddy headed towards the door.

"Oh no, please don't do that…" A memory of the episode where she had her tea spiked with whiskey by Maggie Shanklin, came flooding back. "I rarely touch the stuff, it disagrees with me."

"As you wish darling, but half them performers out there take a swig before they go on stage to calm their nerves. Me, I can take it or leave it."

Maddy's name was called by someone from the echoing corridor. "Wish me luck!" she said, as she made for departure.

"I do truly wish you all the luck in the world..." Kathleen said kindly. Then Maddy disappeared and she was left to wait alone in the dressing room, it seemed she might be the last one to audition that day.

Maddy did not return, so she guessed that the woman had been sent away and felt really sad for her.

Finally, there was a knock on the door and a young man's voice called, "Kathleen O'Hara, to the stage please!"

Heart beating wildly, she was ushered along a long narrow dimly-lit corridor, through the wings and onto the stage. The brightness of the light almost blinding her as it dazzled her with its glare. She was amazed to see how much bigger the stage was here compared to the Temperance Hall in Merthyr.

A male voice shouted out of the darkness. "Please get ready to sing, Miss O'Hara..."

She had already handed her sheet of music to the agent and soon the strains of 'Silver Sonata' were being played on the piano and for a moment, she feared she'd forget the words, but somehow her mouth opened and it was as if it were someone else singing, not herself:

"I followed the moonlight's silvery path to your door,
And when I got there the moonlight was no more..."

When she had finished singing the love ballad, there was silence. Complete and utter silence in the inky darkness beyond. A wave of vulnerability coursed through her veins as she stood, exposed, out in front with the footlights and spot lights as they highlighted her small frame.

It was so quiet she could hear her own heartbeat and heavy breaths, and then she heard it, a clap and then another and another as people joined in. Whoever was in the audience liked her rendition.

She still couldn't see them and imagined Dafydd sitting there watching her, urging her to do well.

A man's voice, whom she didn't recognise, shouted: "Very good Miss O'Hara, please could you sing another, more well-known song this time?"

She nodded, her mouth dry now and feeling as though her legs might well buckle beneath her if she stood there much longer. She chose the 'Rose of Tralee', feeling more at ease as the strains of the gentle piano music drifted towards her and she joined in at precisely the right moment.

When she had finished singing, the same voice shouted out. "Yes, I've heard enough, Miss O'Hara. You're hired. But for the music hall I'd like you to include a couple more racy songs in your repertoire."

Kathleen stood there nodding, although she had little idea what the man meant by the term 'racy'.

"Thank you, Sir."

"I'd like you to report here, 10 o'clock sharp in the morning, your agent will sort out the paper work."

She nodded, then left the stage to remove her make-up, exhilarated and overflowing with happiness. She almost finished removing the final stages of her face powder and was brushing her hair back in its normal shoulder-length style, when she heard a knock on the door. Glancing up, she shouted, "Come in!" from the deserted room that looked a mess in amongst all the discarded outfits, cosmetics and empty tea cups.

She stood as a man entered. "Miss O'Hara, I'm the stage manager, Wilson Brown. That was a fine performance and I'd be glad to have you on board here." He flashed her a smile, making his already handsome face, look even more debonair.

"Thank you, Mr. Brown. I'll be here as arranged in the morning."

He escorted her along the corridor and down a set of steps near the stage. The lights were now on in the auditorium, and the only two people who remained in the audience were, Dafydd and Mr. Johnson. Clement Johnson was smiling broadly, but Dafydd looked a little uncertain, almost as if forcing a smile on his face.

135

As they left the building and made their way to a Hansom cab walking behind Mr. Johnson, Kathleen whispered to her husband, "What's the matter, Dafydd? Didn't you like my performance?"

He stopped a moment and looked at her. "Yes, of course I did. I just didn't like what the theatre manager said about you requiring a racy repertoire. Why should a wife of mine need to sing saucy songs?"

"Oh, that's what he meant. I didn't understand. I thought he meant he wanted me to sing faster songs."

Dafydd began to laugh, breaking the awkwardness between them. "Oh Kathleen, please don't ever change, your gentle innocence sometimes astounds me!"

She smiled and followed him to the awaiting carriage.

***

Following an evening of celebration with Clement Johnson where they ate out at a restaurant following his recommendation, and the wine was free flowing, it was time the next morning for Kathleen to show up at the theatre with her agent in tow. The contract was already signed and sealed. Dafydd took the time to explore the city and said he would send a telegram back home to his sister in Abercanaid, to relay the good news and details of where they could be contacted at the Black Feathers Inn.

Walking into the music hall in broad daylight had a different affect to the previous afternoon. Now a team of cleaners were employed to tidy up the area, and it was a buzz of activity as sets were being painted, lights were checked, and other things the public were not normally privy to, were put into place.

The theatre manager did not appear to be around but the stage manager, Wilson Brown, made a sudden appearance and seemed delighted to see her once again. Mr. Johnson waited until Kathleen was fully settled in and then said, "I hope you have a good day, m'dear. I have to attend some auditions at another theatre soon, so I will speak to you later to see how things progressed here today. Don't forget what the manager said yesterday about your repertoire."

She smiled nervously and nodded and took a breath of composure. "Yes. I will."

Mr. Brown escorted her into his office for a cup of tea. It was a small but tidy room with a desk where papers were neatly filed. Two chairs were positioned, either side. Hardly any room for more than two people, he closed the door behind him.

"So, how are you feeling today, Miss O'Hara? Has it finally sunk in yet you are about to make a name for yourself on the stage?"

She shook her head. "No, not really. 'Tis all I've ever wanted and now it's happening to me, it doesn't feel real somehow."

He grinned broadly. "Please take a seat," he gesticulated to the old arm chair and she sat down, arranging her skirts beneath her. Today, she just wore her simple tweed skirt and blouse, with best brooch at the collar. She was nowhere near as glamorous looking as yesterday and she had carefully returned the fur stole to Rosa for fear she should lose it or else it be stolen.

Wilson Brown took a seat opposite her. "I always love it when someone new begins at the theatre, you know…"

She looked across at him shyly. "Oh, why is that?"

"Because to begin with, people are fired with enthusiasm and have a lust for treading the boards. Unfortunately for some, as time marches on, they become jaded and wearisome. Having enough of the stage, learning new routines, or else become sick to death of the old. It no longer becomes such a joy for them to contend with."

"Oh, I hope that never happens to me."

"Well, we shall have to see that it doesn't, my dear."

There was a knock at the door. An elderly lady appeared with a tray in her hands that held two cups of tea and a plate of currant cake, her salt and peppered hair swept into a bun. Kathleen thought, that in her day, she was probably quite a beauty of sorts.

"This is Gracie, our longest running member of the stage, she's worked here since I was a lad hanging around outside at the stage door. She used to shoo me away with her broom." He laughed.

Gracie smiled, her piercing sapphire blue eyes twinkling. "Pay no mind to him, Miss, he weren't all that bad at all, used to help me sometimes just so he could get in 'ere free to see some of the acts."

To Kathleen's surprise, Mr. Brown's face flushed red, then changing the subject, he said, "Thank you, Mrs Smith."

Gracie nodded and turned to leave the room, closing the door behind her.

Wilson Brown passed Kathleen her cup of tea and took his own. "There's a sugar bowl on the tray if you'd like some?"

She shook her head and held up a vertical palm. "No thanks. I've learned to go without it. When I lived in Ireland, times were hard with famines and such, we had to make do with what we had and now, to be honest, I prefer to go without it in my tea."

He smiled at her. "What an honest person you are Kathleen O'Hara. I like that. I expect you still eat cake though?" He offered her the plate and she took a slice, trying to ensure she did not make crumbs on the office floor.

"Yes, thank you."

"Now tell me. Have you any questions for me before we begin a rehearsal later today?"

She thought hard for a moment. "Yes, I do have one, actually, what did the theatre manager mean to imply when he said he wanted me to sing racier songs? That baffled me."

Wilson Brown began to laugh. "I know what it is, there's another singer who has started at a nearby theatre. Her name's Daisy Marsh. She's become quite a hit with the gentlemen and even the ladies too. Her songs are full of innuendo, making people laugh. She's selling the theatre out. My guess is he would like you to rival her and do the same thing."

"B…but I don't know those kind of songs…"

"Not to worry, I know of a song writer, the same one who composes for Daisy. He'll come up with one or two for you to begin with, they're like signature songs for performers."

Kathleen felt uncomfortable at the thought. "Well beside the songs, what else do I need to do that's different?"

Brown let out a long breath. "To be honest with you, I think you need to have a word with the wardrobe mistress. Daisy Marsh wears low cut dresses and lifts her skirts to show her ankles every so often. Please don't look so alarmed."

Kathleen's hand flew to her mouth. "I really don't think I should be working here at all, 'tis no more than a bordello by the sound of it!" She placed both tea and cake on the desk and stood, her chin protruding out in defiance.

Brown's face changed to one of panic. "Please sit down, Miss O'Hara..." he said softly.

"I am not Miss O'Hara, I am Mrs Jenkin, I can see 't'was a mistake my coming here at all."

"I think, you'll find you have to stay now you've signed your contract, Madam." Tears sprung to her eyes, this wasn't what she had planned at all—she was to be promoted as 'voice of an angel' not 'voice of a whore'.

Brown stood and gently took her by the elbow, gently guiding her back to her chair. "Please don't upset yourself so, Mrs Jenkin. You've got a lot to learn about the ways of the London music halls. It's all an act, people know that. If you sing something a little risqué, it's only to make people laugh. They'll realise you are not one of the ladies from a bordello." He smiled and seated himself behind his desk.

She looked at him through a haze of tears and nodded. "I'm sorry Mr. Brown. What must you think of me? It just wasn't like this when I performed on stage in Merthyr Tydfil."

He nodded and extracted a white handkerchief from his top pocket, which he handed to her to wipe away her tears. "Look, what I really like about you is that you have a naïve quality to you and we shall build on that. It will be my suggestion to the theatre manager that you sing the words but act all innocent, blinking and blushing, so you look like an angel but act like a mischievous little madam without realising it. The audience will be in on the joke, which is far different to what Daisy Marsh is doing, the audience know she is being deliberately bawdy and lascivious with intent."

Relief flooded through Kathleen's veins, she was beginning to warm to Wilson Brown, he was a very kind man indeed.

"All right, Mr. Brown," she said finally, sniffing and dabbing her eyes with his handkerchief, "I'll give it a go."

The stage manager smiled and appeared to let out a breath of relief, and retrieving his handkerchief from Kathleen's hand, patted his brow.

After being fitted out with a couple of dresses at the wardrobe department, she accompanied Mr. Brown to the auditorium where the song writer was waiting at the piano. He was a middle-aged man, who occasionally picked up his pipe and smoked as he composed as if it somehow aided the entire process. Following the introductions, the man, whose name was Rodney Squire, she was to learn, said, "Pleased to meet you, Miss. I think I have just the tune for you. I've written several new songs, just need a few words to go with them, that's all. Should take me no more than an hour or so to get them written. I like to see the act and then think of the words."

He began to play a really jaunty number, his fingers tinkling over the ivories. Kathleen tapped her toes, the tune was uplifting. When he'd finished, Kathleen said, "I really like that tune, you are very talented Mr. Squire."

Squire smiled and took a long puff on his pipe, blowing a cloud of smoke into the air. "Now I need to think of some lyrics. Any instructions?" he asked, glancing at Mr. Brown for confirmation.

"Yes, could you put in some lines with dual meanings? Like you do for Daisy Marsh? I'd like to promote Miss O'Hara as an innocent lady who's singing songs that make the audience laugh, as she doesn't realise what she's saying."

Squire grinned broadly. "I know just what you mean, they are termed *double entendre*. I think I can manage that."

"We'll return in an hour or so then. Miss O'Hara can try out the song and learn the lyrics, if suitable…"

Squire was already hard at work, scribbling something down on a piece of parchment. Only vaguely taking in what was being said.

"Come on Kathleen," Wilson Brown said, lightly patting her shoulder. "We'll call a cab, I'm taking you somewhere…"

***

They arrived on a busy street twenty minutes later, milling with people this way and that, it was not a part of London Kathleen recognised and it seemed so busy.

"Where are we, Mr. Brown?" she asked, as the horse and carriage pulled up outside a large building with a long queue of people outside.

"This is the theatre I was telling you about, it's the Athena Coliseum, where Daisy Marsh performs. Those people are all queuing to see her afternoon performance. She's that popular, she performs on stage twice a day and always to a packed house."

Kathleen drew in a breath. "I cannot believe that one lady would entice such a large gathering."

"You need to believe it, Kathleen, as one day, I intend it to happen to you." Wilson Brown touched her gloved hand lightly. Causing her to shiver with which emotion, she had no clue, whether it was excitement, nervousness, or something entirely different.

The cab driver opened the door and helped Kathleen out of the carriage, then Brown disembarked and stood by her side. She brushed down her skirt and adjusted her bonnet. "If I had only known, I would have dressed for the occasion."

"Believe me, my sweet Kathleen, you look just fine as you are. Most of these folk are not overly dressed as it's a daytime performance, and the seats are so much cheaper, at night though, it is an altogether different matter."

He took her by the arm and walked her to the front of the queue, which was all but disappearing around the corner and beyond. Seeing the look of alarm on her face, he said, "Don't worry, we have no need to queue, I know the theatre manager and he owes me a favour."

As they entered the foyer, Brown whispered something to a man dressed in a black evening style suit, white shirt and black bow tie and tails. The man smiled and waved them through,

141

where they ended up in a little box area on the balcony, all to themselves.

"Please remove your shawl, Kathleen," Wilson Brown advised as they sat.

She glanced at him nervously. "Why should I need to do that?"

He cleared his throat as if realising she thought he might be being improper with her and said, "It's for your own benefit. Soon it will get quite warm in here, it always does and you won't feel the benefit of it when you leave the theatre, later."

She smiled, reassured by his comment and settled back in her seat to watch the performance as the place began to fill with people, hustling and bustling hither and thither. There was a loud thrum around the auditorium as people appeared to wait with anticipation.

Kathleen shot a glance at the man beside her. He was extremely handsome and gentlemanly in his countenance, having a fine chiselled jaw, jet black hair and rich brown eyes. He did not have Dafydd's strong appearance that so often had got her husband into trouble, but was milder mannered, yet she could sense he would handle himself well in an argument.

The lights dimmed, the curtains drew open and everyone clapped as the lights hit the stage, as a man dressed as a clown in colourful garb and bright orange wig, stood on the stage and performed jokes and somersaults that had the audience, rip roaring with laughter. Following a riotous round of applause, a juggling act took to the stage, but she could not concentrate in the darkness sitting beside Mr. Brown. There was something developing between them and she sensed that it should not be happening at all. Yet, maybe the feeling was all on her part and not his.

Then finally after three more acts, the star of the show, Miss Daisy Marsh, appeared. She wore a red velvet dress, trimmed with black lace. Carrying a parasol, she pranced around the stage. Then burst into a bawdy song that had the men cat-calling and their wives and girlfriends laughing and glancing towards the men beside them. Kathleen's cheeks blazed hot at the lewdness of the act.

As Daisy carried on singing, she occasionally lifted her skirts to show her ankle boots off and frivolously dropped them again, leaving the men to sigh laudably with disappointment.

Some of the terms used in her songs, Kathleen had never heard before. Mr. Brown assured her they were well-known Cockney rhymes, which amused her.

When the show was over all, the audience were quickly on their feet to applaud Miss Daisy Marsh, 'Good Time Girl from Guilford'. Kathleen and Brown stood themselves and applauded loudly. It had taken her some time to get accustomed to the act, but she found herself, much to her own surprise, really embracing it.

They left the theatre to avoid the crowds via a side door that Brown knew. Kathleen being somewhat surprised that it was still daylight for it felt as it should be night time as they'd been in the darkness of the theatre.

"Did you enjoy that performance, Kathleen?" Brown eagerly asked.

She nodded. "I did indeed, far more than I thought I would. I think I understand now about the racy repertoire." She smiled.

"Good. I knew you would."

"What time is it, please?" she asked, blinking.

Brown extracted a gold timepiece on a chain from his top pocket and flipped it open. "It's almost four o'clock," he said, snapping it shut and returning it once more to his pocket.

"Oh, I had no idea it was so late..."

"Does it really matter?" He frowned.

"I thought I would be heading home by now."

"Your husband will understand, it's your first day at the theatre and I wish to return there, to see what the song writer has come up with for you."

They took a cab back and Squire, being fired with enthusiasm, rushed to meet them upon their arrival. "It's all written," he said. "I've called it, 'Little Things Mean a Lot'. I've also been working on another song."

Kathleen beamed, realising it was the first song that had ever been written especially for her.

Squire sat at the piano and began to play and sing at the same time:

Please don't leave me in the lurch
We need to get to the church
I thought it was rather funny
That you called me 'your honey'
Little things mean a lot,
You've left me in a spot.
Please don't leave me in the lurch
We need to get to the church
I thought we were playing house
But we played cat and mouse
Little things mean a lot,
You've left me with a pot!
Please don't leave me in the lurch
We need to get to the church...

As he sang his head nodded back and forth and his eye expressions made Kathleen laugh behind her hand. But she was not laughing because it was so bad, but because it was so good and greatly amused her.

"That's wonderful!" she exclaimed, when her giggles had subsided. "Might I try it?"

Squire nodded.

Kathleen sang as Squire played the piano, and then she looked at Brown, who said, "That was good, but I think you need to put in some gestures of your own..."

She sang it again and when it came to the line 'little things mean a lot' Kathleen crooked her little finger making both men laugh that she'd understood the innuendo. As it came to the line, 'you've left me with a pot!' she turned side on and stuck out her stomach, to make it appear she was pregnant.

"Bravo!" someone shouted from the back of the auditorium and she turned to see the theatre manager himself, Mr. Langsford, stood there. "That's more like it girl!"

He walked towards them.

"Thank you, Sir," Kathleen said, "but I'd still like to sing one or two songs from the old country."

"And you will, young lass. You can sing one or two like that one, to get 'em warmed up and finish with a nice ballad like, 'The Rose of Tralee' you sang yesterday.

He dipped into his pocket, extracting a cigar and lit it, blowing out a long plume of smoke. "I think you're going to like working here, Kathleen," he said smiling, and then he left as quickly as he arrived.

"Right, Miss Kathleen O'Hara, our newest singing sensation, I'm taking you out to dine!" Brown announced as Squire closed the piano lid and left for the day, leaving the two of them alone. Before she had time to protest, he had taken her arm and was leading her out of the theatre into the night air.

Chapter Seventeen

The clock at Bailey's Luncheon Rooms said a quarter past six. Kathleen flinched. "I really must get back to my husband," she protested, as she began to think Dafydd might be concerned about her.

"Please stay a while," Wilson Brown soothed. "It's your first day on the job, you've just signed a contract to work at the music hall and have a new song written especially for you. Surely he won't mind?"

Kathleen shook her head, and pushed her half eaten steak meal to one side and set down her knife and fork. Somehow, she thought he *would* mind.

She stood. "Thank you very much for the meal, Mr. Brown, but I really should be getting back to my husband." She began walking towards the restaurant door. Brown jumped out of his seat and followed after her, taking her by the elbow.

"Look, hang on for a moment…" he said breathlessly, with a concerned look on his face, "I will escort you back home, it's not safe for a young woman to be out on the street unaccompanied, just allow me to settle the bill first."

She let out a breath, realising what he was saying made perfect sense, waiting a few moments whilst he paid the waiter and retrieved his hat and coat from the cloak room.

He hailed a Hansom for them outside the establishment. It was a long while before he said, once they were settled inside, "You don't entirely trust me, do you, Kathleen?"

She tensed in her seat and drew in a long breath before letting it go again. "I don't quite understand your meaning, Sir?"

"I mean... my intentions towards you. You fear they are unworthy somehow that I might make advances towards you. Is that not the case?"

She shook her head. "'Tis not that, Mr. Brown. I fear my husband should not like it if I remain out after dark chaperoned by a man like you."

Brown laughed. "Is he a jealous man, this husband of yours? I saw him at the theatre yesterday and he looks the strong, silent sort to me. He has an intense look in his eyes."

"Well, I have not had need to put him to the test on that score but I had a hard time convincing him of how serious I was to get on the London stage."

He softened his tone of voice. "Oh I see. Maybe he's the sort of husband then who would fear his wife becoming more of a success than he. What does this fellow do for a living, might I ask?"

She hesitated. "He's about to begin work as a police constable in Merthyr Tydfil, but before that he worked down the coal mine."

She heard Brown take in a gasp of astonishment in the darkness of the cab as it rattled along the cobbled street. "You do surprise me—that's quite a change of profession. Why did he leave the pit?"

"He was involved in an accident before I met him. There was an explosion at the colliery, killing 34 men and boys. It was awful by all accounts. He injured his leg. He's had other jobs since, but nothing that he's really settled to. I think though, he will make a fine police constable."

"You sound very proud of your husband?"

"Oh I am, it's just…"

It was one of those moments where she wished she hadn't began to express her doubts, but now it was too late.

"Just what?"

"Just that I don't know how we can work this out, if I am to stay in London and he join the police constabulary back home."

"Could he not work as a police constable in London, instead? He could join the Runners…"

"Runners?"

"The Bow Street Runners, my dear. I am toying with you a little…" He chuckled.

"I am glad you find my plight so amusing!" she snapped.

"No, the Bow Street Runners were a group of policemen established in the 1700s in London. They no longer exist, but he could perhaps join the Metropolitan Police here in the city?"

Realising he spoke with honourable intention, she relaxed. "'Tis a good idea, but I do not know if he would like that to be truthful."

"It might be worth mentioning it to him. You can only ask," he said kindly.

The cab drew up outside 'The Black Feathers Inn' and Brown handed some coins to the driver. "I shall see you tomorrow at 11 o'clock sharp for rehearsal, Kathleen. We'll go over that song together and see if the wardrobe mistress has your costume ready."

She thanked Mr Brown, watching as he rode off to his own abode in the cab as it clattered along the street with its driver perched on top.

***

There was plenty of life at the Inn as she entered, and she spied Rosa handing out a couple of foaming tankards to two men. One wore a battered top hat, whose long coat looked as though it had seen better days, and the other, sported a bowler hat and bow tie. The latter gentleman had the red nose of a regular partaker of alcohol. Rosa set down the tankards as the men eagerly snapped them up and started gulping away at them as though they were nectar from the gods.

"Well Kathleen, 'tis good to see you. How did your first day go at the theatre?" Rosa smiled, hands on hips.

The men stopped drinking, and stared at Kathleen.

"It went very well," she beamed. "I've even got a new song, written especially for me!" She held up a sheet of music.

"That's good to hear, dearie. Would you like something to eat, you must be famished?"

Kathleen shook her head. "I've already eaten," she said, with more than a sharp pang of guilt. "Have you seen my husband?"

"No, not since this morning, duck. Come through to the back room with me and we'll have a nice cup of tea, Arthur can manage here alone."

Rosa's terms of endearment amused Kathleen. She'd never heard anyone referred to as a 'duck' before. They had some strange sayings in London. Mind you, the Welsh also had odd sayings too, she concluded. Kathleen followed Rosa gratefully into the cosy back room. They enjoyed a nice cup of tea and a piece of Rosa's sponge cake, which was just as well as she'd wasted most of her meal at the restaurant.

"I'm so glad you managed to get the job at the theatre, Kathleen. That means you'll be staying and we can be good friends."

Kathleen nodded. "I'd like that, but I am not so certain about Dafydd though, he's due to begin work soon as a police constable in Wales. The timing 'tisn't right for us both."

Rosa shook her head. "You must not think that way, Kathleen. If a thing is meant to be then it shall be, my old mother, God rest her soul, used to say. 'Where there's a will there's a way and things can be worked out'. You'll see."

Kathleen was not so sure. She thanked Rosa and made for her room, waiting for Dafydd to return. He did not come back until an hour or so later, by which time, she was beginning to feel very cross with him at his absence.

She heard the door creak open and her husband stumbled into the room with a big smile on his face. "Where have you been?" she accused.

"I'm sorry, my Irish rose…" he hiccupped. "I met a fellow in a bar this afternoon while you were at rehearsal and I forgot…hic…the time. I am here now and I am several shillings, the richer…" He slumped down on the bed and immediately fell asleep.

She sighed deeply, being unsure quite what to do, never having seen her husband in this state before, though she had heard stories of his drinking from her sister-in-law, but she thought all that was behind him.

She turned off the light and got in bed beside him. The smell of alcohol filling the room and the sound of his snoring keeping her awake. It had been an eventful first day that was for sure, she hoped there'd be no more surprises tomorrow.

The following morning, Kathleen took no pleasure from the fact that her husband had a severe headache and had lost some of his winnings. "How did you win the money anyhow, Dafydd?" She raised her brows.

He let out a long groan from the bed. "I met this man in a pub and he told me about some cock fighting that was going on in the back yard, I made a couple of well chosen bets and won, unfortunately, I do remember now that I spent a lot of my winnings buying drinks for people in the pub."

"So you've made some new friends now, have you? The sort of friends, who will encourage you to spend your hard-earned money on placing bets, and lose it again on the evils of drink!"

"Please, don't get angry with me, Kathleen. I'm sorry, it won't happen again."

"But how can I be so sure, when you are left to your own devices all day on the streets of London? I am beginning to think t'would be better if you returned to Merthyr." She had said how she felt without even thinking about it, and now she had said it, she was full of remorse to realise she had cut him to the quick with her words.

He sat slumped on the edge of the bed, his shirt badly creased from lying heavily on it during the night. He looked up at her. "What can I say? Except for how sorry I am."

"Well, I have to go to the theatre now and shall expect you here for me when I get home tonight. Please keep away from taverns and mischief making new friends."

He shrugged. "How can I keep away? We are staying in one, *cariad.*"

She smiled for a moment, realising the truth in what he said. "Why don't you get yourself washed, put on a clean shirt and make enquiries about joining the Metropolitan Police Force?"

He sat wide-eyed. "Kathleen, I have never even considered that. I would like to serve my own townsfolk." He shook his head.

"I've gone and given you something to think about, now, that's for sure. Think about it while I am at work today. I had my breakfast whilst you were busy sleeping off the drink earlier, Rosa says she will keep something for you if you don't leave it too late."

He nodded gratefully. Kathleen tied the ribbons of her bonnet, wrapped herself in her woollen shawl and left the inn. All the while fuming with herself for leaving a lovely meal at the restaurant to rush back for a husband who hadn't the good grace to get himself home at a decent time and in a fit state at that.

***

"That's it, just lift your skirts a little, Kathleen…" Wilson Brown said, his eyes glittering with amusement at the music hall rehearsal.

"It's bad enough that this dress is cut so low, but now you are asking me to lift my skirts?" She blinked in amazement. Squire, who was sitting at the piano in preparation for a rehearsal of his song, said nothing, just puffed away on his pipe as if oblivious to it all.

"Well, if you're not comfortable with doing that, leave it for now," Brown reassured.

She harrumphed loudly and turned towards Squire. "Please begin, Mr. Squire, I should like to do justice to your great song!"

Squire beamed, playing the intro at the piano and Kathleen began singing, trying out the gesticulations earlier learned. Maybe if she was feeling a little bolder in the future she would hoist her skirts a little, but not right now, she felt too vulnerable.

After an hour or so of rehearsal, Brown called time on it and told Kathleen to take a break. She headed off towards the wardrobe department, with the intention of asking Mrs Miller, wardrobe mistress, if she could sew in a little extra lace along the line of her bosom as she wasn't entirely happy with having her cleavage on full view to all and sundry. As she walked the long corridor, she almost collided with a taller woman, a little older, with hair piled up high upon her head; it was a harsh colour blonde and Kathleen assumed the woman might have used peroxide, or else it was a wig.

"'ere be careful!" the woman shouted.

"Sorry," Kathleen trembled and looked at the woman for reassurance.

"You're that new gal, ain't you?"

Kathleen nodded. "Yes, I only started yesterday."

"Well my name is Constance de L'amour. And let me tell you, that song I just heard you singing should 'ave been mine!"

"Oh, I'm sorry I had no idea. It was suggested that I sing it yesterday. Would you like it if I had a word with Mr. Brown or the theatre manager about it? I could ask them to give it to you instead."

The woman flushed from the neck up. "Most certainly not, you cheeky young upstart!" She turned on her heel and flounced back down the corridor from whence she had came, as if she had forgotten something of importance.

Kathleen stood there open-mouthed, she had no intention of making enemies. She had enough of that with opera singer, Bella Montovani, at the Temperance Hall; noting that those female artistes with big egos also had fanciful names.

She walked on down the corridor and found Mrs Miller in her room with a measuring tape strung around her neck, busy adjusting a dress on a tailor's dummy. When she noticed Kathleen's approach, she removed a couple of pins from her mouth and secured them to the lapel of her own dress for later use. She raised an enquiring brow. "And what can I do for you, Miss O'Hara?" Her eyes met with Kathleen's own.

"I was just wondering, Mrs Miller, if you could add some extra lace to the bodice of this dress, to cover my cleavage a little more?"

Mrs Miller looked heavenward and tutted. "I wouldn't mess around with it dear, it's what the audience want to see. I understand you're not used to wearing such revealing costumes, but you will get used to it given time."

The seamstress turned her back on Kathleen and began attending to the dress on the dummy. Kathleen cleared her throat. "Very well, then, I understand and thank you for listening to me. Just one thing…who is the lady with the very blonde hair piled on her head. She has a small beauty spot on her cheek?"

Mrs Miller turned back around to face Kathleen, realising that her handiwork was no longer being called into question, and smiled. "That's Constance Painter. She goes by the name of Constance de L'amour to the audience." Lowering her voice to barely a whisper, she added, "A bit of a Prima Donna in her time if you ask me, but she's hanging on in here by the skin of her teeth, I think. The audience is tiring of her. Now don't go letting on I told you so!" She wagged a stern finger.

Kathleen shook her head. "Oh no, not I. Thank you, Mrs Miller." She left the wardrobe department and made her way to the small room the staff used to make tea, Mr. Brown had earlier told her she might use it. Now she understood why Constance had been so prickly with her earlier. It was sheer jealousy.

The rest of the day wore on and there was more rehearsal, by the time the day was ended, she no longer cared how much of her cleavage was on show, or even if she lifted the hem of her dress an inch or two, it was work, pure and simple and not a reflection of her own morals.

***

When she returned to 'The Black Feathers' early evening, she was pleased to see Dafydd already waiting in their room spruced up with clean shirt, she was just about to say something, when he held up a piece of buff coloured parchment. "Kathleen, I'm going to have to return to Merthyr. Lily has sent me a telegram." He read it out: "PLEASE RETURN. DAFYDD. TROUBLE FOR ME. LILY."

"What on earth could be so bad that Lily wants you back in Merthyr Tydfil, Dafydd?"

"I've no idea, but I'd better get back home tomorrow to find out."

She patted him on the shoulder, wondering how she would cope without him and what was wrong in Abercanaid?

***

Several days later, Kathleen received a letter from Dafydd informing her of the reason Lily had contacted him and requested his return. Cooper Haines, the father of her child, had shown up in Abercanaid, just as Maggie Shanklin had forecast he would and she feared trouble. Evan being a mild mannered man might not be able to handle the situation physically if needs must, but Dafydd would, with his boxing background and strong physique. As if Dafydd didn't have enough on his plate, he was due to start work at Merthyr Police Station.

Things were going well for her in London and it posed quite a dilemma now what she should do about the situation. That evening, she chatted it over with Rosa in the living room.

"I think you should allow Dafydd to work at Merthyr just to see if he takes to it, Kathleen. If he doesn't, all's well and good, then he can rejoin you here and find work somewhere. We could offer him a few hours now and again here serving and collecting tankards, until he finds a decent job for himself."

Kathleen nodded. "That would be more than kind of you, Rosa." She blew on her cup of tea before taking a sip. "But what will happen if he really takes to working for the constabulary, then what? I love it on stage in London. The crowds are really warming to me."

Rosa nodded wisely. "Well, if that turns out to be the case, then one of you is going to have to make a sacrifice for the other."

Kathleen rested her teacup on the saucer, realising that Rosa was absolutely right.

Chapter Eighteen

Kathleen missed Dafydd in bed at night. Often she'd sprawl out and touch the cold, empty space beside her, her soul crying out for him, but other times, was so engrossed in her stage performances and the adulation she got from the audience, it was hard to weigh up who or what meant most to her.

Mr. Squire had written a new song for her entitled, 'Don't Call me a Lady!', which had the audience in stitches as she pranced around the stage with a parasol, tripping over, revealing her petticoats. She realised if her husband knew her act was becoming so risqué, he'd be most angry, but he wasn't anywhere near, so she quashed the thought. Now she was the one selling to houses packed to the rafters and Daisy Marsh from the other theatre, who had been the 'Good Time Girl from Guilford', was fading in people's memories. She, who had once been the Queen of the Music Hall, now only performed occasionally.

Reviews for Kathleen's shows were excellent. She kept the clippings, but decided against sending them to her husband, for fear he should stop her performing due to the slight lewdness of the act.

A letter arrived the following week from him:

My Dearest Kathleen,

I think about you day and night and hope your performances are going well. The house is not the same without you. I started work this week at the police station. My new uniform fits well, but it felt so strange walking around the streets of Merthyr wearing it.

The police inspector and his good wife have been very kind to me. She keeps ensuring that I eat well and has baked me a couple of pies and some Welsh cakes this week. By the next time we meet, I'll be as large as an ox.

Cooper Haines is still staying in Merthyr at a hotel in the town. Well, he has the finances for it, but so far there hasn't been any trouble as predicted, though Lily and Evan are wondering if it will be the calm before the storm and are cursing Maggie Shanklin. I notice though that Lucy Howells, appears smitten with the man. Lily thinks it's the American accent she's drawn to. To my surprise, he has conducted himself well, so far at least. He's enamoured with his son, Joshua. I noticed Evan is a little quiet when the man is around, but that's only to be expected under the circumstances.

A lot of things have changed lately, but one thing that hasn't and will never change, is my love for you, cariad.

I hope to hear from you soon about all the things you are doing.

Your beloved,
Always and Forever,
Dafydd.

Kathleen's eyes filled with tears as she read and re-read the letter. Then she folded it and tied it with a red ribbon and placed it under her pillow.

She intended to write a letter to him the following morning and post it on the way to the theatre. Mr. Brown had informed her he was to hold a special meeting the following day for all the artistes.

What he had to say, she had no clue, but he had sounded serious, which concerned her a little. The Theatre Manager, Mr Langsford, would be in attendance too. She'd tried to get out of Mrs Miller what it was all about, but the woman just smiled as if she knew some secret she was not about to tell, making her suspect that it was good news rather than bad.

***

The following day, all the artistes and behind the scenes staff, were assembled in the auditorium along with Wilson Brown and the Theatre Manager himself, who spoke. He stood on the stage and addressed the gathering.

"It has come to my attention that some of you here are not giving it your best shot…" Kathleen's heart slumped into her shoes. Was he thinking that she was no longer any good? "I said some and I mean some, not all. Most of you do work hard, granted."

156

A loud whisper went around the auditorium and she heard one artiste say to another, "I think he plans to dispose of some artistes, that's the rumour I've heard..." Several nodded.

"Ssssh!" Kathleen hissed at them. "Let's hear what the gentleman has to say for himself."

"There is something very important coming up..." Mr Langsford continued, "In a few weeks' time, you are to perform for royalty itself, Queen Victoria shall be making a visit here!"

A collective gasp filled the auditorium and a member of the dancing troupe suddenly fainted and was brought back to her feet and made to sit down.

"Now, I don't wish you to be alarmed by this, but I need the absolute finest artistes for this performance, so I shall hold several auditions here over the next few days. Only the best performers shall be included in the show and even moved to the top of the bill."

A man standing behind Kathleen groaned loudly.

"I'll just read out the date and times for your auditions over the next couple of days. Anyone who can't attend or needs theirs rearranged, please see Mr. Brown, later."

Kathleen was to discover that her audition was at 1.30 pm the following day. Wilson Brown informed her that she should pick out her most successful songs, the ones that got the audience joining in, and especially any they gave a standing ovation for. She decided to go for the new song, 'Don't Call Me a Lady!' and her favourite, 'Rose of Tralee'. It would be most exciting if she performed in front of royalty, but realised there were other artistes who were already higher up the bill than she was.

When she returned to the dressing room, Constance de L'amour was already there waiting for her. "What yer going to sing?" she asked.

"Probably one of my favourites and a new song!"

"Oh that old Irish one, you want them to cry do you, Missie?" Scornfully she began to rub her eyes and cry out, 'Boo Hoo!" to antagonise Kathleen.

A surge of anger flooded through Kathleen's entire body as she shook with rage, she hit out at Constance, sending her flying across the dressing room, so that she stumbled into a chair and hurt her back.

"Now look at what yer gorn and done!" She shouted from the floor, wincing as two of the dance troupe helped her to her feet. "You little Madam! I don't know who you thinks yer are, swanning in 'ere and taking over the theatre…"

The other performers stood around taking in the scene before them.

"Yes, and I don't know who you think you are! Constance de L'amour indeed. What an utterly silly name!" Kathleen shouted, placing both hands on her hips and throwing back her long auburn tresses.

Constance stared, then slapped Kathleen hard across the face. Before anyone had a chance to prise the pair apart, Kathleen had Constance by the hair and yanked, astonished to see the hair still in her hand and Constance completely bald beneath it, apart from the odd tuft of mouse brown hair. Constance brought her hands to her head in horror.

"Forgotten something?" Kathleen flung the hair piece into Constance's face.

A few of the women laughed and she heard one say, "She had it coming to her!"

Kathleen turned and saw Mr. Brown standing behind her, shaking his head. "Miss O'Hara, please accompany me to my office right now…"

An audible, collective intake of breath from the women resounded around the room and meekly, Kathleen followed Mr. Brown to his office as Constance scrambled to replace her wig. Now Kathleen feared she had gone too far and would be out of the show completely.

As she entered his office, Mr. Brown gestured for her to sit down and closed the door behind them, before seating himself. "By rights, I should stop you having that audition tomorrow after what I just witnessed in the changing room."

She shook her head. "It's not how it appears, Mr. Brown. Constance started it…"

"I really do not wish to hear any more of your playground squabbles. Deal with it, Miss O'Hara. If the theatre manager got to hear of this, he might well dispense with your services, contract or no contract."

"I am sorry, it shall not happen again."

He let out a breath. "Good. I've brought you in here to tell you that there is a good chance, that if you perform well tomorrow, you will end up the top of the bill for the royal performance."

She took in a breath and let it out again. "I can't believe it. I haven't been here that long, Mr. Brown."

He smiled, seemingly having forgiven her for her earlier outburst. "It is not a question of how long you have been here for, but of how good you are. And you, Miss O'Hara, are very good indeed. The public love you. Both men and women like you, they love your wicked but innocent sense of humour. They adore the comedy you insert into your act. They love your voice and most of all they love, *you*." His brown eyes shone with amusement.

She sat herself back in the chair, trying to ingest all that he had just said to her. They loved her, the public really wanted her to perform. A warm glow engulfed her, she was so happy, she could have leapt out of the chair and kissed Wilson Brown. But she was a married woman and that was not an appropriate thing to do. Just wait until she told Dafydd. She hoped he'd be happy for her.

Brown beamed. "Don't forget…you still have a rehearsal to get through tomorrow, so don't mess it up!"

"I won't." She stood and then winked at him like her character might have done on stage, causing him to blush. She left the room floating on a cloud of ecstasy and hope.

***

Auditions went well the following day and Kathleen was pleased she was being selected to perform in front of Queen Victoria herself. Several performers failed to make the grade, including Constance de L'amour, who'd scowled throughout Kathleen's audition as she sat in the theatre, unnerving Kathleen.

The following week a special dress rehearsal was to be held a few days before the royal performance.

New costumes were made, fresh sets painted and the theatre itself spruced up. Special scenery had been made for Kathleen's performance, to make it look like a country garden with a wooden gazebo and trellis fencing. The carpenters had worked really hard, it was a masterpiece in itself. Artists had painted green rolling hills and trees, and a bright blue sunny sky. Colourful blooms adorned the stage. It really was magnificent, she'd never had a set especially created for her before.

As the artistes sat around waiting to be called for their particular performances, they chatted amicably, each wishing the other all the best. It was quite noisy in the dressing room as people got dressed, painted their faces, laughed and joked and even practiced a few lines of their song or ran through a musical scale or two.

Kathleen had been asked to see Mr. Brown before she went on stage about a direction she had been given, as to whether she should enter right stage or left. As she made her way down the corridor her nostrils twitched as she inhaled an acrid smell that hit the back of her throat, causing her to gag. It was both pungent and suffocating. Her lungs filled with the foul air and she realised immediately it was smoke. A loud crackling sound and the noise of something falling, made the hairs on the back of her neck prickle.

Fire!

She ran back to the dressing room to warn the artistes and told them to leave at the back door as it appeared to becoming from the stage area. Some of the women screamed as they pushed past one another to get out of the theatre. All too often there were stories of theatres and similar buildings being razed to the ground and even deaths occurring from such fires.

Breathlessly, and with heart pounding, Kathleen managed to find Mr. Brown in his office. His eyes widened with horror as she burst in through the door without knocking and alerted him. He immediately jumped out of his chair and ran off towards the fire, with her in pursuit behind him. "Don't follow me. Get out of here now this very instant, Kathleen!" he shouted, but she knew she couldn't leave him; something made her want to stay. As they entered the stage area, it became evident it was the scenery that was on fire, as flames licked up the side of the red, plush theatre curtains, the heat powerful, intense and all consuming.

"Stand back, Kathleen!" Mr. Brown ordered. He managed to beat the flames out on the curtain and found an old woollen blanket just off stage which he threw over the wooden gazebo, smothering the fire and immediately putting out the flames.

"Whew, that was a close call!" He looked at Kathleen as they both stared at the smouldering mess before them, in sheer disbelief. "It's just as well you noticed when you did as the whole place might have gone up in flames. I'm afraid your set is totally ruined."

She shook her head. "That doesn't matter to me. What does, is that there is no loss to limb nor life." She turned and kicked something against her foot. Noticing for the first time, it was a small cardboard box on the floor nearby. Stooping, she picked it up and examined it.

"What is it?" Brown asked.

"It appears to be a box of matches." Though it was not a label she had ever seen before, this brand was called 'Beacon'. There were various brands of matches around and the one she was most familiar with was, 'Bryant & May'.

He took the small box from her outstretched hand and examined it carefully. "There are a lot of match boxes being made all over London, in the homes of women to earn money…" he said thoughtfully. "It seems fairly obvious to me that someone with intent against yourself, planned to ruin your set for your performance Kathleen, and not only that, didn't care if they burned the whole theatre down in the process. Whoever it was, had only minutes ago lit this fire."

The blood in Kathleen's veins turned ice-cold when she realised the probable truth of what Brown was saying.

"Constance…" she muttered.

He drew close to her side. "Maybe. That's a possibility, there is bad blood between the two of you. But we have to be careful not to make any assumptions at this point. I shall inform the police of this matter later. Meanwhile, I need to ask the staff if they noticed anyone out of place here this afternoon and then begin rehearsals, otherwise we shall fall behind schedule. Fortunately, there is only little damage done here. It could have been a damn sight worse. I shall speak to the carpenters, to see if they can knock something else up for the set in time for the performance. It's going to cost this theatre more money for the men's wages, but it has to be done." He stood for a while gazing in despair at the scene before him, then moved the now smothered remains of the gazebo and trellis work to one side, sighing deeply.

Kathleen cleared her throat, which was slightly sore, and hoped it wouldn't affect her performance. She badly needed to get a glass of water. "Shall I bring the performers back inside now, Mr. Brown?"

Wilson Brown turned to look at her, still with a concerned look upon his face. "Yes please, if you would, Kathleen."

As she paced the corridor, she could still taste the thick acrid taste of smoke in her mouth. Heading towards the side door, she thought about Constance. It made sense that it would be her who would do such a thing. She had a grudge against Kathleen for stealing the limelight and had moved down the bill at the theatre, and even now, had not made the grade at the auditions. She decided to keep quiet about this to the other performers, but maybe they would figure this out for themselves. They were hardly stupid and several had witnessed the earlier scene between Constance and Kathleen in the dressing room that had all but humiliated the woman.

When the staff members were later assembled in the auditorium, no one admitted seeing anyone out of place at the theatre, who shouldn't be there, making Kathleen wonder if it could have been one of them who had lit the fire. Yet, why would anyone scupper their own plans to perform in front of the Queen? It just didn't make any sense at all.

Despite the singed curtains, ruined set, and the faint whiff of burning, the show went on as planned, much to Kathleen's delight.

***

Constance failed to turn up at the theatre the following day. So when Kathleen had finished, she asked Mrs Miller where the woman lived.

"Why would you of all people wish to know that, Kathleen?" Mrs Miller raised a silver eyebrow with suspicion.

"I just need to pay her a visit 'tis all. Nothing wrong with that is there? Mr. Brown said the other day after our altercation that I should sort it out."

The woman let out a long laboured breath. "Very well then. She lives a few streets away from here, I'll write her address down for you. I haven't been that way for years, take care as you go, as it's not the best of areas."

Mrs Miller wrote the address on the back of an old card that was used to keep shirt collars in place between performances. "Take a cab," she advised. "It's dark out there, you don't know who's around."

Kathleen nodded, but she had no intention of taking a cab, she wanted to save her hard-earned pennies to treat herself to a new fur stole similar to the one that Rosa had loaned her. If she was going to be a star, she needed to look the part. "Thank you, Mrs Miller," she said, taking the piece of card from the woman's outstretched hand, and making her way out of the theatre.

It took her a while to get her bearings and find the general area. She stopped a lady and gentleman to ask further directions.

The man tipped his hat and frowned beneath the street light. "You don't want to be going to Devil's Acre unaccompanied, young lady…" he warned, but pointed out the area anyhow and left her to walk through the mist and cobbles. The first thing that hit her was the undeterminable stench of rot and human waste. She gagged slightly and asked a passerby if they knew the home of Constance Painter. The old woman, who was wrapped up in a shawl, nodded and pointed to a small hovel down the lane.

Kathleen stood outside the door, which was all but rotted away, the only remaining window pane, broken and stuffed with old rags.

She tentatively knocked the door and was shocked to see the hunched appearance of an elderly woman, who when she explained who she was, allowed her inside. Two young barefooted children, both boys, were fighting over an old wooden train and in what, Kathleen assumed was the scullery, she heard a voice. "Who is it, Ma?"

Constance walked towards her, open-mouthed, dressed in a filthy gown and pinafore, her almost bald head wrapped in a scarf, sending waves of pity coursing around Kathleen's body.

"Oh it's you, Miss High and Mighty, now is it? Well what do you want?"

"Is there any where we could talk in private?" Kathleen forced a smile.

Constance took her roughly by the elbow and led her into the small scullery which had a paltry, barely-lit, fire grate. There were some basic household instruments, the odd cracked plate and bowl, wooden spoons, and tin mugs, upon a rickety wooden table.

"Yeah, now what do yer want?" She stood with both hands on hips.

Kathleen straightened, remembering the real reason for her visit, she had been so shocked at the conditions here, she'd almost forgotten why she was here in the first place. "Were you at the theatre yesterday afternoon by any chance?"

"No, of course I weren't. I wasn't picked for the rehearsal. Why do you ask?"

"Someone tried to set fire to my set, almost burned down the theatre."

Constance paled. "And you think I had something to do with it?"

Glancing around the room, Kathleen was no longer so sure. "I don't know, but you're the only person that bears me ill will."

"Do you think after all I have on me plate, that I would stoop so low? I have enough 'ere looking after my elderly mother, a houseful of kids and a drunken boot of an husband to contend with!" She threw up her hands in despair.

"I'm sorry to have bothered you then," Kathleen said, and turned to leave and as she did so, she spotted a box of matches on the table which Constance quickly snatched away.

"Give me those," Kathleen demanded and wrestled them from the woman's red-raw, chafed hands.

"I was only putting them out of harm's way from the nippers. Me son Jack tries to play with 'em and it's too dangerous."

Kathleen took the box and studied it. 'Bryant & May'. She felt so foolish. "I'm sorry Constance," she mumbled.

"I make the boxes and pack the matches here, for the company, gives me a bit of extra income. They don't pay a lot, but I get some free boxes of matches. Now I'm not working much at the theatre, I need to earn more money. Me hair's been coming out in 'andfuls from all the stress, was why I been wearing a wig from the wardrobe department, Mrs Miller kindly loaned me it. My old man's been drinking the money away, too. I don't intend doing this forever as I 'ear some of the women from the match factory got phossy jaw cos of it."

A pang of guilt hit Kathleen full force, especially after remembering how she grabbed the woman's hair to discover it was a wig in that fight they'd had. She lightly touched the woman's shoulder. "I'm so sorry I was mean to you, Connie...What is that phossy jaw you speak of?"

Constance's eyes filled with tears. "It's working with the white stuff used to make the matches. I never can say that big word. They become disfigured, the whole side of their faces turning green and black, later lots of foul smelling pus comes from it. They often die. And when it happens, the company throws the women, young and old away, like spent matches themselves. One young girl I knows, she's only thirteen, disfigured now for life she is. And I'm sorry too, Kathleen. I was only narky 'cause I feared you'd take my place and I'd no longer earn any more money to feed and clothe my kids."

Kathleen drew in a deep breath and let it out again. "I understand, Connie. If you will allow me to, I will speak to Mr.

Brown first thing tomorrow about your plight and see if he can get you some other work at the theatre. Then you can stop making those matches. I don't want you getting that phossy jaw like those poor unfortunates."

Constance nodded gratefully. She was a woman at the end of her tether by the seem of it. Before leaving, Kathleen pressed a couple of shillings in the woman's rough palm, then quickly made her way from Devil's Acre to find a cab to get home. The fur stole would have to wait for some other time.

Chapter Nineteen

The following day at the music hall, Kathleen noticed a couple of policemen speaking with Mr. Brown in his office. When they'd gone, he called her in.

"Close the door behind you, Miss O'Hara," he said quietly.

She did as told and sat down facing him. "Have you any idea who started the fire?" She asked.

He shook his head. "The Sergeant asked if I knew anyone who had some sort of grudge against this theatre or anyone working here. I told them no, for now, but I need to speak to Constance Painter today."

Kathleen chewed her bottom lip, then let out a long breath. "There's no need…" she wrung both hands.

"Oh and why is that, Kathleen?" He narrowed his gaze.

"Because I've been to see her…"

Brown's face reddened. "And who gave you permission to do so?"

"I'm sorry. I went to see her after leaving the theatre last night and now I feel positively sorry for the woman. She lives in a stinking hovel in Devil's Acre. I truthfully believe it wasn't her who did it. She has a hard time of it with her husband drinking the money away, and her elderly mother and nippers to care for. She's even taken to making matchboxes for Bryant & May. I spotted one there on the table as I was leaving and made an accusation. But I honestly, and with all my heart, do not believe it was her—in fact—I was going to suggest as she is barely working here these days that the theatre employs her in some other capacity."

Brown stood and gazed out of the window, with his back turned towards her. She noticed how broad his shoulders were for the first time, highlighted against the window pane. He was wearing a tweed waistcoat, trousers and white shirt, the sleeves held up by a pair of brass coloured sleeve garters. He dug his hands in his trouser pockets as if deep in thought for a moment. Then removing his hands and turning to face her, said, "I'll speak with the theatre manager about the matter. But what puzzles me is one moment you dislike Constance and now you're trying to help her." He stood with both hands on the desk staring down at her in what she felt was an accusatory manner.

"Yes, I am well aware it might sound strange to you, but after visiting her home yesterday, and seeing her plight for myself at first hand, my heart went out to the woman."

Brown smiled and seated himself back down. "Very well, I'll put in a good word for her. Now about the fire here, yesterday... I think everyone needs to be on their guard, *you* especially, Kathleen, until the culprit is caught."

She sucked in a breath and let it out again. "Yes, I will be very careful, thank you, Mr. Brown."

***

It was hard to concentrate on rehearsals as she glanced around at the other theatre staff, it could be anyone of those. But why would anyone wish to harm her or the theatre come to that? By the time she got back to The Black Feathers, Rosa was waiting for her with a letter in her hand. "This came for you today, Kathleen, after you'd left for the theatre." Her stomach slumped when she realised the handwriting was not that of her husband's.

"Thank you. This isn't from Dafydd, though. I wonder who else could be writing to me at this time? Not many would know I was in London, let alone staying with you."

Rosa smiled nervously as if fearing after what Kathleen had said that it might be bad news. "I'll make us a nice cup of tea, duck. You go and sit in me parlour and read it to yourself."

Kathleen nodded gratefully and entered the parlour, which Rosa kept as her 'bit of best' with its fancy lace curtains, ornate oil lamps and elaborate paintings; it was in total contrast to the busy bar just yards away. She seated herself and slit open the envelope with her thumb and extracted the crumpled piece of yellowed parchment inside and read:

Dear Kathleen,

I got sumone to help us rite this letter to you. I bumped into your husband the uvver day in his uniform at first I fought he had come to arrest me for sumfink. But he was pleased to see me and

168

gave me your adress in Lundon. I wud be hever so pleased if we cud stay in tuch.

Am missing you at the fetre, but am glad you got me the job there, tis much better than the wash house. The kids ave grown so fast and needs new clothes. Missus Perks from the props room gave me sum old costumes for the nippers and wiv a needell and cotton I can make some nice fings for them.

I hope tis all going well fer you. Let me now what is apening in your life wen you ave time.

Your gud friend Jess.

Tears welled up in Kathleen's eyes to read a friendly word from home, even if there were several misspellings in the letter. At least she got the gist of what Jess was trying to say. She wiped away the tears with the back of her hand and sniffed as Rosa entered the room with a tray of tea in her best china cups. Rosa liked to act like the lady of the manor. "'ere darling, what's the matter, why you been crying?" She looked at Kathleen with great concern and set down the tray, then sat beside Kathleen patting her back.

Kathleen looked at her. "They're not bad tears, Rosa, they're good ones. One of my friends, well, my only real friend from Merthyr, has contacted me. I miss her so much."

"I see, duck. Well that's good then, ain't it? Now I'll pass you a nice cup of tea and you can have a slice of my sultana cake. It'll do you good, you works long hours at that music hall."

Kathleen nodded and accepted the cup of tea. "Yes, I have to work longer hours at the moment for a special performance coming up soon."

"Special performance? Who for?"

Kathleen hesitated for a moment. "It's for Queen Victoria herself. But you mustn't tell anyone. Myself and the other performers, we've been sworn to secrecy, you see. Could I please borrow your fur stole again? I was going to buy one for myself, but that will have to wait now until I save up more money."

Rosa's eyes lit up. "How marvellous. To think, my fur stole will get seen by Queen Victoria herself. Gawd bless her soul!"

"T'will be a grand evening, Rosa, I will try to get complimentary tickets for you and Arthur."

Rosa beamed. "That's so very kind of you, Kathleen. Will Dafydd be coming along?"

"I very much doubt it." The truth was she hadn't even told him, she had toyed with the idea of sending a telegram, but feared he would not be able to take the time from his duties anyhow and the expense of the train journey would be costly.

"You wait until I tell me Arthur, he'll be well nigh over the moon, he will."

Kathleen smiled at Rosa's enthusiasm, finished her tea and cake and left for her room for the evening. Another night in bed without Dafydd, she fell into a fitful sleep, awoken by a strong feeling of nausea, just managing to make the porcelain chamber pot beneath the bed before the entire contents of her stomach were expelled.

She wiped her mouth with the back of her hand. Then poured some water from the bedside jug into a bowl and washed her hands and face, feeling so much better. Maybe it was Rosa's sultana cake that had disagreed with her, reassuring herself that hopefully, she'd feel better tomorrow.

***

Kathleen felt so much better the following day as she made her way to the theatre as rehearsals were underway. A new stage set had been constructed by the carpenters and painted white, so the trellis and the gazebo were almost as good as the originals. A fresh lick of paint was applied to the country scenery behind, and so things were ready to go. In the event, not much damage had been done, even the heavy stage curtains had been hardly damaged. Mrs Miller had sewn on some new gold fringing to cover the singed parts, so all looked as good as new.

Whilst taking a break, Kathleen poured herself a cup of tea and took just one sip, when a wave of nausea engulfed her and she needed to go outside for fresh air. Constance had noticed and followed her outside.

"What's the matter?" she asked, her eyes wide with concern.

"I don't know. Last night I vomited and today, I felt sick to my stomach as soon as I picked up my cup of tea and took it to my lips."

"'ere you know what this is, don't you? Same thing 'appened to meself. When I was pregnant I couldn't bear to drink a cup of tea."

Pregnant? It wasn't something she had even considered. She wasn't even with Dafydd all that much, but there would have been opportunity for her to catch, maybe that night they stayed at the posh hotel in Cardiff, or even when he had stayed for the few days in London with her the previous month.

A shockwave coursed through her veins, this wasn't what she had planned at all. "I can't be pregnant right now, it's going to mess up my singing career, and especially right now when all is going so well."

Constance stepped forward and touched her forearm. "Babies have a way of making it into the world in their own time and making an entrance …You're just going to have to accept it, Kathleen."

Kathleen shook her head. "No, 'tisn't what I want. Do you know of anyone who could see to it for me?"

Constance frowned. "I do know of an elderly woman who has ways and means, but it's not without its risks. A young woman died, bled to death she did. I don't think it's a good idea. You've got a husband, haven't you? Go back home to him, is my advice."

Tears sprung to Kathleen's eyes. "I don't want to go back home though, I've waited all my life to have this opportunity."

"I know," Constance said softly. "Look, you're a good person Kathleen and I'm sure you'll do the right thing. Why don't you arrange to go back home for a couple of days to see your husband? Take some leave from the theatre, it will still be 'ere when you return."

Kathleen nodded, she knew it made sense. "If Mr. Brown will allow me the time, I might do that. Has he mentioned anything to you about finding more work for you at the theatre?"

"Aye, he said he might have something for me soon, thanks to you. One of the dressers is finishing to work elsewhere next month, so he's hoping to give me her job and I can do the odd bit on stage as well, fill in as an understudy if needed."

"That's great news…" she sniffed.

"So, I'm grateful for you having a word with Mr. Brown and such. Are you feeling any better now?"

Kathleen nodded. "A little."

"Well if you can't drink that cup of tea, have a glass of water to settle your stomach," Constance said kindly, as they both went back inside.

Thankfully, for the remainder of the day Kathleen was fine, but the nausea returned again at night, so the following day, she sent Dafydd a telegram telling him she was coming back to Merthyr for a few days. Mr. Brown had approved her leave of absence, providing she was back the following Monday morning sharp.

***

The train journey back home was arduous as she tried to fight off the nausea rising within. She found if she got up in the morning and ate something immediately first thing before setting foot on the floor, it helped. Rosa had given her some home baked biscuits in a tin, so she kept those on the bedside cabinet and took some to nibble on the train journey.

When she arrived back in Merthyr, the first thing she did was call to the theatre to see Jess. She crept in silently through the side door of the Temperance Hall and caught Jess in the auditorium with her bucket of water and mop, feet up on the seats taking a well-earned rest. She stood staring at her for a few moments and then Jess's eyes flicked open.

"Oh Kathleen, is it really you?" She rubbed her eyes. "I feel as though I am really dreaming."

Kathleen took a seat next to her friend. "It's so good to see you again. How is everything? I got your letter."

"I'm glad of that. I had to get Mrs Harris from the wash house to help me write it. She didn't know it was you I was writing to or else she might 'ave 'ad a bleeding fit!" She laughed uproariously. "Me, writing to the new girl who went missing, her first day on the job at the wash house!"

Kathleen smiled. "I'm glad you're well, I've missed you so much."

"I've missed you, too. Let me put the kettle on and we'll have a nice cup of tea. I miss our chats."

They chatted about the old times quite amicably, and as Kathleen stood and was about to leave, Jess turned to her and asked, "So, why did you really come to visit me, Kathleen?"

Kathleen cleared her throat. "Because I wanted to see you of course." She forced a smile.

"No, I meant coming to visit me before you saw your own husband, the police station isn't far from 'ere."

Kathleen seated herself back down. "Oh Jess. I'm so worried. I think I might be pregnant."

Jess blinked several times. "Well that's good news, ain't it?"

"I don't really know. I think Dafydd might want this, but it will mean I will have to give up my singing career in London and return to Merthyr. Just when I was doing so well and all. I've even been made top of the bill for a special performance in front of Queen Victoria…"

Jess swallowed. "Talk about going up in the world. No wonder you don't want to come back here. But if you do, I'm sure you'd be welcomed back home at the theatre 'ere. Maybe you could still sing 'ere now and again?"

Kathleen nodded. "Aye maybe." She stood and Jess followed suit and they hugged one another. "I better go and find Dafydd and tell him the good news I suppose…"

She lifted her large carpet bag and turning, took one last look at Jess. This was the world she might well have to return to and she didn't know if that's what she really wanted to do at all.

Chapter Twenty

Heart racing, Kathleen set off through the busy high street for the nearby police station. As she approached the building, she noticed a familiar face stood outside as if waiting for someone. Tall, proud looking and handsome in his black frock coat and helmet, she began to walk towards her husband. Her footsteps quickened with each heavy breath, and then she was running towards him with great pride.

"Kathleen!" Dafydd blinked with surprise as she approached.

"Weren't you expecting me? I sent a telegram a few days ago." She took in a breath and let it out again, realising in her possible condition, rushing wasn't such a good idea.

He searched her eyes. "Yes, but I thought you wouldn't be arriving until tomorrow, I've arranged to take the day off."

They were standing outside the police station, so there was no real opportunity to fully embrace as she became aware of his sense of morality and duty towards the public. "Oh that's a shame, what time do you finish your shift, Dafydd?"

He held her by the elbows at arm's length. "Not until this evening. Look, I have to go soon I'm waiting for my colleague, but I'll speak to you when I get home…" Noticing another police constable leaving the building, he nodded at him and ran down the street behind him, as if they had just been alerted to an incident some place.

Some home coming this is, Kathleen thought. *I've come all this way and my husband is more interested in running off somewhere.* She realised it was part of his job, but a pang of disappointment hit her in the gut nevertheless.

She wanted to get herself back home to Abercanaid in case the nausea started up again, thankfully, she had not overloaded her bag for the journey. It would take her around a half hour or so to get home by foot walking along the canal bank.

By the time she arrived back at Chapel Square she was exhausted from the walk, maybe it was something to do with her condition. Normally, she found the distance fairly easy to contend with.

Letting herself into the house, which was now darkened with the growing hour, she dropped her bag and lit the oil lamp on the window sill in the living room. There were still the embers of a fire in the grate, so she set about rekindling it by adding sticks, and eventually some coal to build it up.

Soon, there was a nice fire going. The house seemed so small now compared to buildings in London, even Rosa's parlour at the Black Swan was twice the size of this.

She made herself a cup of tea and nibbled one of the biscuits she'd brought with her to ward off any nausea, all the while sitting in front of the fire. Then when fully rested, she rose to see what was in the kitchen for her husband's supper. To her distaste, she noticed a skinned rabbit on the kitchen table and some unfamiliar looking cakes on the windowsill. She guessed the Police Inspector's wife had been busy looking after her husband again, and experienced a pang of regret at having to leave Dafydd to his own devices for so long, at what was an important time for him.

Gritting her teeth, she put on a pinafore and started dicing the rabbit and sliced some onion to make a pie for Dafydd. There was still plenty of flour for pastry in the larder. She guessed that maybe one of his friends from the village had caught the rabbit on a recent hunting expedition in the mountains.

By the time her husband came home, she'd changed into a fresh dress from her wardrobe she'd left behind, brushed her hair until it shone, and by that time the pie was all but ready to eat with potatoes and carrots.

As her husband finally burst in the front door, she ran into his arms. "Something smells good!" he said brightly. "I'm sorry I couldn't stop to talk to you earlier. I had to follow the Sergeant in quick time, there was some sort of fracas going on at the Vulcan Inn. It was quite comical really. There were tankards and fists flying everywhere, but when I walked in, it all stopped as the room went silent when all my old regulars saw me in my uniform. They were shaking my hand and patting me on the back. The Sergeant said that in all his born days he had never seen any regulars at a pub being so welcoming to a policeman before!"

Kathleen smiled. "Where's your uniform?" she asked.

"I change at the police station, *cariad*. It's not a good idea for me to wear it home as not everyone knows me and might turn against me. It's the uniform they see and not the man beneath it."

"I understand."

They stood staring at one another for a moment, then he took her in his arms for a long, lingering kiss that went on and on, making her feel for that moment at least, that she was safe and secure.

"How are things going in London?" he asked, his eyes shining brightly, whilst searching her own.

"Pretty good, thank you, but please sit yourself down I need to talk to you after we've eaten."

Dafydd removed his coat and cap and sat himself down at the table. "And you've lit the fire too. There's nice. I'm so used to coming home to an empty house with a cold grate, these days."

She nodded sympathetically, patted his shoulder and went to dish up his pie and vegetables. "Here you are." She sat down opposite him.

"You're not eating yourself?" he frowned.

"I will later. I've been feeling nauseous of late…"

He looked up from his dinner plate.

"Nauseous? Why is that? Is it something you're eating at The Black Feathers maybe?"

She shook her head vehemently. "Oh no, nothing like that…" she twisted her handkerchief on her lap. "I think I might be pregnant, Dafydd."

A flicker of recognition dawned in his eyes and he was on his feet and hugging her. "This is all I have dreamed of. Now at last we can be a proper family and you can come back home."

A wave of revulsion hit her. This wasn't what she wanted to hear. She'd imagined him saying that it made all the difference and he would come to London to be with her. But he wasn't noticing her disappointment, just hell bent on the fact she was having his baby and in his mind she had all but left the London stage.

He sat down and began eating his meal with great gusto. Even if she were not happy, he was. When he had finished relishing each mouthful, he dipped in a hunk of bread to soak up the gravy from the pie. "I meant to tell you…" he said chewing. "There's a special concert planned at the chapel soon, can you attend?"

She shrugged. "I'm not entirely sure. I have to return to the London stage for a little longer at least as I am bound to perform in front of Queen Victoria herself soon and I am top of the bill…" she declared proudly, then held her breath to see how he might respond.

"That's nice, but I am sure Her Royal Highness can spare you. Please don't go back to London, Kathleen. I beg of you…"

It hurt to think he didn't even see what an honour it was for her to be top of the bill at the theatre and in front of the Queen herself. She smiled weakly and nodded, realising her dream was all but now coming to an end.

***

Kathleen and Dafydd spent the following hour or so that evening, together. By the end of that time, her husband was ready for his bed, exhausted by the amount of time he'd worked that day. He was only allowed one day off every two weeks, but the Inspector had allowed him an extra leave day the following day as there were special circumstances, but the time would have to be made up later on, by adding a couple of hours to each subsequent shift. So, as a consequence, Kathleen realised what a sacrifice he was making for her. It was apparent that Dafydd now lived and breathed for his new job, which was good to see in one aspect—he had a passion for it that she had not seen for the pit. The pay was a lot better too.

She decided to banish all thoughts of any anguish she might be feeling towards him, for wanting her to remain at home and not return to London, to enjoy her stay.

The following day they went shopping in the hustle and bustle of Merthyr, where Kathleen managed to find a second-hand fur stole which she fell in love with at one of the market stalls in the town.

"Oh, it's absolutely beautiful, Dafydd!" she cooed, wrapping it around her shoulders and stroking the smooth fox fur.

"Then you shall have it my sweet," he said, proudly handing over a crown and a couple of florins to the market trader.

She imagined herself walking around the streets of London, proudly showing off her new stole, she would even use it as part of her act in front of the Queen. Dafydd, of course, did not realise her reasons for wanting it, but it had cost him a lot of his wages.

She turned and kissed him on the cheek. "Thank you, kind Sir. T'will be an honour to wear this." Her thoughts turned to Connie and her family, whom she had given her savings to, due to their meagre circumstances. It would have been a while before she'd have afforded a new fur stole for herself.

"That concert is tonight at the chapel…" Dafydd said, breaking into her thoughts. "Lily and Evan have arranged it. There will be refreshment afterwards at the chapel hall. You must wear it then, *cariad*," he advised.

She nodded. "Maybe, though I don't think it's the correct occasion for it," she said wistfully. It would be nice to see Lily, Evan and the children again before she left for London. There would be a lot to catch up on.

***

Later that evening she got changed into the best gown she had hanging up in the wardrobe which was her green flowered tea gown. It seemed more suitable to wear than an evening dress for such an occasion. She opted to wear a matching green cape and bonnet, much to her husband's disappointment. "I thought you'd have worn your new stole?" he said, narrowing his eyes.

She turned when fully attired, looking him squarely in his eyes. "I think the fur stole would be too showy for Abercaniad, Dafydd. I should most dislike it if Maggie Shanklin and her cronies were to chastise me and gossip about my 'London Girl' ways! I do not want people to think I have risen above my station in life…"

He let out a breath. "But in a way, you have, *cariad*. But soon you shall be back where you belong."

She shivered involuntary. The more he spoke of her belonging in Merthyr, the more she longed to get back to the bright lights of the London stage. As if sensing something amiss, Dafydd approached her from behind as she gazed into the mirror above the mantel piece, wondering if she was imagining her dress was a little too snugly fitting. He placed both hands on her shoulders, "Please do not worry, Kathleen. All will work out for the best..."

She smiled and turned to face him. "I'm so glad you said that..." she replied thinking he was considering their options.

But instead he said, "I know you must be concerned about seeing your agent and the theatre manager about your intention to leave, but they will understand most of all that a woman's place is in the home serving both her husband and family..."

Her heart plummeted as she forced a smile. It was as if she now had to wear a mask of sorts, to conceal the heart break she had hidden beneath.

Not sensing any of her anguish, he took her hand and laid a kiss upon it. "Come on then Mrs Jenkin, we do not wish to be late for the concert at the chapel..." he said, tipping his hat and then leading her towards the door.

***

When they arrived, it was just beginning to get dark. The lights were on in the chapel as several people stood gathered around in small groups outside the entrance. Dafydd removed his hat in front of a group of ladies, and left her momentarily to speak with a small cluster of men whom he had worked with at Gethin Pit, excusing himself from her side, he said, "You go inside and find my sister, Kathleen. She is expecting you."

Kathleen nodded, wondering how she would feel entering the chapel again after all this time. In the twilight, she failed to immediately see Maggie Shanklin in the shadows, just outside the entrance to the chapel hall.

"Mrs Shanklin?" Kathleen said amicably, for once, when recognition dawned.

Maggie sniffed and put her nose in the air. Then as Kathleen's back was turned, mumbled, "Thought you'd be too grand now for the likes of us…"

Kathleen spun on her heel to face the woman who now had a sly grin upon her face. "No, not at all, Mrs Shanklin. I do not think I'm too grand for the people of Merthyr, far from it. There will always be a place in my heart for them. But then again you're Irish like me, aren't you? So you're not from Merthyr either!"

Maggie visibly stiffened under the light diffused both from the street lamp outside and the light within the entrance to the chapel hall. For time being at least, Kathleen had managed to silence the woman.

Once inside, the chapel hall was warm and welcoming. She quickly spotted Lily talking to some children from the school with their parents. She had Mollie at her side holding on to her skirts and baby Joshua in her arms in a shawl wrapped Welsh fashion, so the infant was entirely cocooned and supported near her breast. She beamed when she saw Kathleen approaching. "Oh, please excuse me for a moment," she apologised to her small audience as she led Kathleen over to a corner and hugged her close. "How I have missed you, dear sister-in-law!"

Kathleen felt the genuine love from Lily and hugged her warmly. "I've missed you too," she said. Kathleen made a fuss over the children. "And how is little Miss Mollie?" she said, ruffling the child's mop of curly hair. Mollie turned her face in towards her mother's skirt as if to hide, amusing Kathleen.

"She's gone very shy since Joshua's birth," Lily explained. "I think it's due to us having to share our attention with him. Evan is here somewhere, I know he'd like to ask a favour of you?"

Kathleen nodded as Lily led her away to find her husband, as they walked off with children in tow, Kathleen noticed people looking at her and whispering behind their hands and she hoped it was not with malicious intent.

As they approached Evan, where he was arranging what appeared to be some music sheets in order for the evening, he looked up and walked towards Kathleen, hands outstretched.

"So, good to see you, my dear," he took her arms and pecked her on both cheeks. "And how is the London stage?"

She smiled. "'Tis really grand, Evan. I'm enjoying performing there and soon I shall even get to perform in front of Queen Victoria herself!"

Lily gasped with delight, genuinely pleased for her sister-in-law. "That's wonderful, Kathleen."

Evan nodded. "That's really good news. Dafydd must be so pleased for you?"

Kathleen shook her head. "I don't think he wants me to go back to London. It was a great sacrifice that he allowed me to go in the first place and now that my circumstances have all but changed..." she chewed her bottom lip.

"Changed? In which way?" Evan asked.

She looked at both of them. "I am with child..." she whispered.

Lily smiled and patted her hand. "Believe me, Kathleen, I know how unsettling it can feel at first, especially if it was unexpected."

"Yes," said Evan reassuringly. "It might be an act of our Heavenly Father, to bring you both closer together."

Kathleen nodded wordlessly. Now she had told them both she felt in a state of shock as the anxiety about her future coursed around her body. "I would very much appreciate you both keeping the news to yourself at the moment as it's early days..." They both nodded. "What is the favour you wished to ask, Evan?"

He raised a brow and exhaled loudly. "I don't know whether I should now due to your condition?"

"Do not be foolish, Evan," Lily scolded light heartedly, "Kathleen isn't ill. What my husband was about to ask you was if you would do us the honour of performing this evening? It would mean a lot to us."

Kathleen nodded vigorously. "Yes, of course. I have missed performing these past few days."

"What will you choose to sing?" Evan asked.

For a moment, her mind froze to think of something suitable, after all, she could hardly perform one of her naughty musical hall numbers. "I think I shall sing '*Ar Hyd Yr Nos*' in Welsh," she said proudly. It was one of the only musical numbers that she could sing entirely in Welsh, and she knew it would gladden Dafydd's heart.

As she looked up with tears in her eyes at the thought of performing the number for him, she saw her husband striding towards her, red-faced with a stern gaze.

He pulled her roughly to one side by the elbow and whispered in her ear under the watchful gaze of his sister and brother-in-law. "Is it right what I've just been told, that you've been performing lewd songs on stage at the music hall?"

Kathleen stood there frozen to the spot as she opened and closed her mouth, but nothing came out. People were beginning to stare at Dafydd's riotous behaviour, though they would not have heard what he'd said.

"I think," said Evan wisely, "we need to discuss this in my office." He led them both to a small room just offside the chapel hall in between the chapel and his house.

Once inside with the door closed, Kathleen broke down in tears.

Chapter Twenty One

Kathleen glanced at her husband behind a haze of tears, not knowing quite what to say next. Dafydd's hands were clenched into fists at his side, making his knuckles white as his teeth gritted with fury.

"Please sit down, both of you…" Evan advised.

Both sat opposite Evan's desk on two hard backed chairs. Kathleen realised this was where the minister often brought members of his congregation who needed to chat with him.

"Now is this true, Kathleen? What Dafydd is saying that you've been performing lewd songs at the music hall?" Evan said with a frown.

Kathleen shook her head slowly and sniffed. Evan passed her a clean handkerchief from his jacket pocket. "Here, please take this," he said kindly.

"I've had a couple of songs written for me, but they're not that bad, they're just a little bawdy, that's all. I sing them in a comical fashion and the songs go down well with the audience. I make them laugh—often the lyrics have a double meaning—so it all depends on how people interpret them. In other words…whether their minds are clean or not!"

Evan linked his fingers on his desk, as if deep in thought. Dafydd buried his head in his hands, in sheer disbelief at what he was hearing from his wife.

"And Dafydd, how did the person who told you this about Kathleen find out for themselves?"

Dafydd looked up at Evan, purposely avoiding eye contact with Kathleen, it was almost as though he wore a pair of horse blinkers to block her out. "It was Maggie's husband, Thomas Shanklin, and a couple of his friends. They went to London looking for work a few weeks ago and stayed at a boarding house whilst there. The boarding house was full of theatrical sorts and there were some newspapers with theatre and music hall reviews, so he told me. Apparently my wife has been making a right spectacle of herself on stage and the men love her…" he shot Kathleen a sideward glance.

"And their wives and girlfriends too," she added, nodding.

"That may be so, Kathleen," Dafydd said, turning towards her, "but you have humiliated me, your husband. How do you think I felt hearing that from Tom Shanklin of all people? No wonder people have been looking at me with pity this past couple of weeks. I thought it was because I've become a policeman, not because my wife has been showing her bloomers to all and sundry!"

Kathleen's chin jutted out in defiance. "I have not shown anyone my bloomers!" She said sharply, nor anything else come to that. Those men have their story wrong! 'Tisn't fair. I shall be having harsh words with Mr. Shanklin when I see him next!"

Dafydd shook his head. "It's only your word against his!"

"Well, maybe if you took more interest in what I am doing, you would have realised all along how well I am doing and how loved I am by the public. I even cut out a few newspaper reviews for myself; I was going to show these to Lily later."

She opened her small drawstring bag and took out three newspaper cuttings. One was an illustration of her dressed in a white lacy dress and bonnet, twirling a parasol. It was from the night she first sang, 'Please Don't Leave Me in the Lurch!' The first song that had been written for her. She passed the newspaper clipping to Dafydd, who reluctantly took it from her outstretched hand and spread it out on the desk before him. It read:

EMERGING STAR ARISES FROM ROYAL STANDARD MUSIC HALL

A new singing star has emerged from The Royal Standard Music Hall this week, Miss Kathleen O'Hara formerly from Southern Ireland, residing more recently at Merthyr Tydfil South Wales, went down a storm with the audience last night. Miss O'Hara has a rich melodic voice which people are dubbing: 'The Voice of an Angel'. She sings with such clarity and purity that her act is a total contrast to the woman herself, with her 'devil may care act', where she gets the audience to sing along and ponder anew what exactly she's referring to. A very refreshing singer, and one to watch out for in the future!

Dafydd sat forward in his chair and studied the rest of the reviews, which just got better and better, his eyes widening with amazement. He looked at her in awe.

"Now, do you see anything there which indicates I show my bloomers? 'Tis a travesty to be tarred that way, that's what it is to be sure!"

Evan took a look at the clippings for himself and nodded, while Dafydd sat there open-mouthed. "I had no idea you had made such an impression, Kathleen. I knew you were good, but not about how acclaimed you've become!" he said. Tears filled his eyes and he squeezed his wife's hand in quiet reassurance. "Of course you must go back and perform in front of the Queen. I'm going to request time off from work to accompany you. I will go without pay if necessary."

Evan smiled with the wisdom of someone who realised that by talking things through, thus avoiding any misunderstandings, all would be well. He said, briskly, "Well there's another show that needs to go on and that's tonight's concert!" He looked directly at her. "I would like it, if you could perform your song at the end of the concert. If that is all right with yourself?"

She nodded. "Yes of course, Evan. I should be delighted."

"And one other thing, I shall read some of these reviews to the congregation myself before you perform to quell any gossip. You are not doing anything wrong that I can see." Evan beamed.

She smiled, and this time, her tears were tears of joy.

***

Lucy Howells was seated in the front pew beside a large well-dressed gentleman with bushy side burns. "Who's that?" Kathleen asked, as she waited to sing.

Lily let out a long breath. "It's Cooper Haines...I introduced him to Lucy and they seem to get along just fine."

"So the trouble you were expecting didn't happen?"

"At first, he showed up in Abercanaid with all guns blazing, but after a while, I realised he just wanted to see that Joshua was well cared for, after all, he is his son. Evan and I have spoken to

185

Mr Haines at length and allowed him contact. But he said he will take a back seat on the condition he be allowed to contribute to his welfare."

"But will Joshua be eventually told who his father is?"

Lily shook her head. "No. We all agree this is the best way."

"And Mr Haines, will he stay in Wales?"

"I'm not entirely sure. He likes it here and now there is an added attraction. Who knows maybe one day, he'll take on Lucy and her children. It's all he ever wanted a wife and family...but his heart is in Utah and he does have a store to run."

They were interrupted as Evan stood at the front of the chapel to speak. Kathleen noticed Cooper beaming as he patted Lucy's hand. The first to perform was a local male voice choir, who sang several Welsh songs and hymns, followed up by a group of children whom Lily had been teaching at the school. Kathleen remembered them so well and was surprised how they had grown so much since she last helped there.

Evan himself then spoke about the importance of friendship and keeping in touch and introduced Mr Haines as a visitor to his home, though nothing about him being Joshua's father. Kathleen guessed it must have annoyed Maggie Shanklin that her plan to cause trouble had backfired on her. Cooper Haines stood and turning nodded to the congregation and re-seated himself beside Lucy.

A young woman came toward the podium and seated herself on a small wooden stool next to a large mahogany harp, the lyrical stringed instrument creating such a beautiful sound that drifted upwards to the chapel rafters.

Then finally, Evan introduced Kathleen. Initially, several people looked at one another and a murmur arose from the pews. It was as if they were in sheer disbelief that Kathleen would be allowed to perform after the gossip that had been going around the village. But then Evan said, "Kathleen, my dear sister-in-law, has been performing recently at The Royal Standard Music Hall in Victoria, London..."

There was silence for a moment, broken by a cough from the back of the chapel. Then Evan carried on. "I know that some of you have been listening to idle tittle-tattle that has been circulating around the village yet again, but let me tell you all this…Kathleen has been doing very well for herself. She is doing nothing wrong, both men and women love her act which makes them laugh and I shall read out some of the recent reviews for you." He read them out to mutters of approval and heads turned to look at her, nodding and smiling which made her blush.

"Not only are these excellent reviews, but she shall be taking top billing soon at the music hall to perform in front of none other than Her Majesty, Queen Victoria herself!" There was a gasp from the congregation, a baby cried for a few seconds and was hushed by its mother. Then a cheer came from the back of the chapel and there was a spontaneous outburst of applause as heads turned once more. Kathleen nodded graciously and then it was time for her to perform, '*Ar Hyd Yr Nos*' as Evan called her forward. It was arranged for the harpist to accompany her as she sang.

In all her born days, she had not felt as nervous as she did right now.

She stood on the stage under the watchful eyes of so many people that she knew so well. Behind Cooper Haines and Lucy Howells was Elsa and William Morgan from the shop, the Shanklins behind those and many others too.

In the music hall the audience was blackened out as the lights shone on her and she felt sometimes alone until she heard the odd shout or cheer, but here in the chapel, the audience was in full view. The harpist played a short introduction and then, Kathleen took a deep breath and opened her mouth, but no sound emerged. She looked at the harpist blankly, who played the intro again as people in the congregation looked around at one another. But still nothing emerged, no sound.

She caught sight of Maggie's face and focused on it. The woman was smirking. No doubt as her plan to humiliate Lily had backfired, she now sought to humiliate Kathleen instead. Composing herself, Kathleen took one more deep breath and then heard herself singing:

"Holl amrantau'r sêr ddywedant...

Ar hyd y nos..."

Kathleen risked a glance around at the congregation and knew in her heart she had won them over as they sat there spellbound, totally enchanted by her voice, all except for one person, who rudely stood and marched out of the chapel, head down. Mrs Shanklin had lost this round, but Kathleen didn't care. She had won over the people in the community, who no doubt would inform others of her fine performance and the fact she was doing so well on the London stage, and in the end, that was all that really mattered.

***

The next few days went by in a flash. All too soon, Kathleen found herself ready to board the train to go back to the London stage.

"Never mind, *cariad,*" Dafydd said softly. "Soon enough we will be reunited again. The Inspector has allowed me a few days leave so I can join you next month in London."

She felt safe and warm in her husband's embrace, and then, he was kissing her passionately as the train began blowing up clouds of steam on the platform. He kissed her one last time and she boarded the train. Leaning out of the window blowing him kisses, Dafydd's face became obliterated from view, as the train started to pull out of the station.

"I love you Mrs Jenkin!" She heard him call after her.

"I love you too!" she shouted and waved her white lace handkerchief for fear he wouldn't see her face again in amongst the steam, but then it cleared and she could see her husband's face slip further and further away in the distance until it became a small dot on the platform.

She seated herself in preparation for the long journey that lay ahead. She had sorted out a couple of things. One was a visit to Doctor Owen, who'd confirmed her pregnancy, of around three month's gestation. He'd written her a letter to take to the stage manager outlining this fact, requesting that she be allowed several short breaks during the day. The other thing she had sorted was the sending of a telegram to Mr. Johnson, her agent, requesting that he pick her up from the station in his carriage. He had replied that he could indeed sort that very thing out for her. From now on, she planned on making things a lot easier for herself.

She took a backward glance at the hills of Abercanaid, before setting her sights on the long journey that lay ahead.

***

There was no time for any rest once she returned to London. The first thing Rosa did was to ask her how the Merthyr trip had 'gorn' as she put it. Kathleen had advised her that Dafydd was happy about the pregnancy, and the fact she would be appearing in front of the Queen, and would join her shortly.

"Well, you know he is always welcome 'ere, ducks…" she said kindly.

Kathleen felt weary and needed her bed, but not before her landlady had dished up a nourishing bowl of hearty soup with chunks of mutton, vegetables and a couple of dumplings. "You'll need to put a bit o' meat on yer bones, to nourish the young 'un growing inside you," she winked.

Although Kathleen wasn't overly hungry, she did her best to eat as much as she could but found herself yawning, thanking Rosa and leaving the parlour to get to her bed. She was needed back at the music hall first thing in the morning.

"Night, Rosa," she said, kissing her landlady on her soft powdery cheek.

Rosa smiled and patted Kathleen's hand. "I hope you feel rested in the morning, ducks. I've changed the bed for you and spruced up the room."

"Thank you, Rosa." Wearily, she climbed the stairs, found her bed, and it wasn't long before she drifted into a deep sleep.

***

The following morning, she awoke to a shaft of sunlight shining into the bedroom window via a chink in the curtain. The sound of birds tweeting reminding her it was early spring.

She sat up and stretched and was amazed to discover it was the first time in ages that she hadn't felt nauseous.

She had plenty of time, so asked Rosa for some hot water which she mixed with the cold from the flowered jug on a table

189

in the corner into the matching bowl, and gave herself a good wash down.

She brushed her hair until it shone and tied it with a blue ribbon.

Dressing in her blue gingham dress and short blue jacket, she pinched her cheeks so they looked pink and healthy and donned her blue matching bonnet. She looked good and felt quite well as she set off for the theatre with a spring in her step.

When she arrived, there were a lot of people in the corridor and dressing room milling noisily around. She looked to see if she could find Constance. Spotting her applying a thick pan cake effect make up in the corner of the dressing room, she called her name. Connie turned in her chair when she spotted Kathleen, then stood, hugging her warmly. "Kathleen, how did the trip back home go?"

Kathleen nodded. "Very well, thank you. I don't understand what's going on here?"

Constance smiled. "Nothing to worry about, Mr. Brown just included a few new acts and wants a run through for a dress rehearsal today. That's how I'm here earning a few extra coppers, thanks to you. It all helps, until that vacancy comes up as a dresser, next month."

Somehow this threw Kathleen off guard. She hadn't been expecting to see so many people present and had hoped to gently slot herself back in to work at the theatre. "I must see Mr. Brown," she said, excusing herself from Constance and walked down the corridor to his office.

She rapped on the door. "Enter!" he shouted. Looking genuinely pleased to see her as she marched in and closed the door behind herself.

"Mr. Brown..." she began.

He stood and kissed both of her cheeks. "Please, Kathleen. I trust that you are now well rested after your visit to Merthyr?"

She nodded and took a seat and then handed over the letter from Doctor Owen. He took it from her outstretched hand, studying it carefully.

"My doctor requests that I get plenty of breaks here, Mr. Brown," she said firmly.

He nodded. "You're pregnant, Kathleen. I had no idea." He blinked several times.

"Yes. That's why I returned to Wales to inform my husband."

He nodded. "And he's happy about the pregnancy?"

She stiffened. "Why on earth shouldn't he be, Mr. Brown?" she asked, mystified.

His face reddened. "It's just that sometimes things happen in the music hall between folk who are separated from their loved ones for a length of time."

Furious, she clenched her teeth. "Well, that hasn't happened to me, I ain't that kind of girl, I can assure you!"

He stood. "No, I didn't mean to imply…" He studied the letter again. "This is absolutely fine for you to take regular breaks, but I do have you lined up to learn one more new number that you'll sing with a dancing troupe. Do you think you could manage that?"

She let out a long breath, all anger dissipating into thin air and shrugging nonchalantly, said, "I'm not sure. It is short notice and I don't understand why more acts are being slotted in last minute?"

He shook his head. "It's not of my doing to be honest. It's the theatre manager, he's looking to impress Her Majesty."

"As long as I have plenty of breaks, I will learn the new routine."

He nodded amicably. "Very well, we shall make that a priority for you, my dear."

She left Wilson Brown's office, and as she made to walk back down the corridor, when he summoned her back to his room.

"Just another thing, Kathleen," he said, as he lowered his voice, ushering her back inside. "The police called again this week and they are positive that stage set fire a couple of weeks ago, was deliberate. They've asked me to keep a watchful eye, so I'd appreciate it if you did the same, please?"

She nodded. "Of course."

"And please keep this to yourself, the less who realise there's an on-going investigation, the better."

"You have my solemn word. Has anything untoward happened since I've been away?"

He let out a long breath. "Thankfully, no. But that doesn't mean to say something won't happen again."

She shivered involuntary and returned to the changing room, there was a full day ahead of her to get through.

***

Rehearsals were hectic, but went quite well. Kathleen was given her new song to learn to sing with the dancing troupe, it was called, 'Fancy Free and Foolish!" She managed to run through it with Wilson Brown and song writer, Rodney Squire. It was a jaunty, upbeat number which was great fun to perform.

"That's excellent, Kathleen!" Wilson beamed. Then drawing his pocket watch from his waistcoat pocket, said, "Well, that's it for the day, would you like to accompany me for a spot of high tea?"

Normally she would refuse, particularly if her husband was around, but now, there was no one to answer to, so she accepted.

"I'll just put on my jacket and bonnet, Mr. Brown, and then I will be ready to leave…"

She returned to the now empty dressing room, as everyone had long since departed. The theatre could be quite eerie when it was just getting dark outside, the only light the gas mantles flickering on the walls. She donned her bonnet, tying it with a flourish, then picked up her jacket noticing it felt different somehow. It was rugged not smooth. Her hands flew to her mouth in horror when she realised someone had slashed it to pieces.

Who would do such a thing? Her screams brought Wilson Brown, who came running down the corridor, his footfalls gaining momentum. She was speechless on his arrival as he stood in the door well, gasping for breath. He walked towards her and then, hugged her warmly, realising her distress after spying the slashed garment.

"Someone wishes to harm you, Kathleen…" he said solemnly. "And I'm not going to allow that to happen. You can borrow a stole or a shawl from the props department; I'm taking you immediately for a cup of tea!"

She nodded blankly as she watched him leave. He returned within minutes clutching a glamorous white fur stole and placed it on her shoulders. "You've had a nasty shock for one day. Come on. Let's get out of here!" he said firmly.

He led her along the dim corridor and out through a side door, where a carriage was already in wait, in the bustling street outside. "The Carlton Hotel, please driver!" he advised as they boarded. They settled themselves into the leather seats. Kathleen let out a breath and studied Wilson's face, he really was the most handsome of men. He caught her eye with a lingering look, causing her stomach to flip over, as the coach rattled along the deserted street and out of the area, towards a more affluent area of the city.

Chapter Twenty Two

At the restaurant of the Carlton Hotel, it was warm and well lit, and the sound of chatter filled the room. Wilson Brown chose a seated area in the corner, so they should not be disturbed by people passing in and out of the area.

"This is lovely…" Kathleen enthused.

"Yes it is, I often came here with my parents as a child for special occasions. Are you all right now?"

She smiled. "I'll survive. Thank you. I still can't think who would wish me so much harm?" Her voice trembled as she spoke.

He shook his head. "Nor can I…but if I catch the culprit…"

Kathleen was very touched the way Wilson Brown sprung to her defence. "I've no idea how we go about discovering who that person is though, or why they should wish to scare me so. I might write to my husband and tell him about this."

Wilson took her hand from across the table. "Oh no! I wouldn't do that at this point, there's no reason to worry him as yet. After all, as I explained, the police are already on to it. I shall call to the police station to see a constable in the morning."

She nodded. "I suppose you're right. It would only concern Dafydd for my welfare." The truth was she realised, in her state of confinement, he would insist she returned home.

A waitress in a long black dress, frilled white pinafore and matching hat, showed up at their table. "What would you like to order, Mr. Brown?" she asked, as she batted her eyelids. Kathleen had noticed how the ladies at the theatre responded to the handsome stage manager, flocking around him in droves and hanging on to his every word.

"Could we have a plate of cucumber sandwiches thinly sliced, no crusts and a selection of small cakes, with a pot of China tea for two, please?" He held the waitress's gaze for a moment or two, and then, she nodded and smiled, moving away from the table.

"Do you always have this affect on the ladies?" Kathleen laughed, almost forgetting the earlier incident.

"No, not at all. I just like to treat ladies like ladies, if you know what I mean."

Kathleen nodded. "So who do you think might be causing the trouble at the theatre?" she asked earnestly.

He shrugged. "It must surely be someone with access to a large pair of scissors, going by those long slash marks on your jacket."

She bit her lip. "I hadn't thought of that, the only place I've seen those lately is the wardrobe department with Mrs Miller. Surely it can't be her? I know she can get a little agitated sometimes, but I will not believe it of her!"

Wilson Brown moved his head from side to side as if in contemplation, rubbing his chin. "It might be her, or her assistant Flora, or even..." he paused.

Kathleen raised a brow. "Even who?"

"Constance..."

"Constance! But she hasn't started work in the wardrobe department as yet."

"No I know, but Mrs Miller needed some extra help with all the costumes she needs to get ready, so I sent her there for a couple of hours this morning before she had rehearsal today."

"She never mentioned it to me. I can't believe it after I visited her home and gave her..."

Mr. Brown penetrated her gaze. "You gave her what, Kathleen?"

Shaking her head, she continued, "I gave her a couple of shillings to tide her over as I was so touched by her plight."

Wilson wagged a finger. "You'll learn my girl. She's probably drunk that away already on a bottle of Mother's Ruin."

"Mother's Ruin?"

"Gin! Did you not realise she has a drink problem?"

"No. I did not."

"She's turned up to the theatre several times smelling like the inside of 'The Market Tavern'. I haven't dismissed her as she does her job adequately, and I feel sorry for her like you do."

Kathleen digested what Mr. Brown had said in disbelief. It was incomprehensible that if the woman was already hard up and had a drunken wastrel husband, she would drink the money away herself. "Oh dear. I had no idea. I've never noticed any alcohol on her breath myself."

"She makes sure she hides it. One of the chorus girls told me she covers herself in heavy cologne."

"I see, Mr. Brown." But she didn't see at all. How could a mother with young children and an elderly relative to care for, squander what little money she had? And now, she felt annoyed with herself for handing over that couple of bob when she could have kept it for her own needs.

A few minutes later, the waitress arrived with a silver trolley, bearing two plate stands. One contained lots of thinly sliced cucumber sandwiches, no crusts, which she had never seen before. The other, a selection of tiny iced cakes, a pot of tea and two beautiful delicate, matching china teacups and saucers.

Throughout the tea, they chatted amicably and Kathleen was so glad that at least someone at the theatre had her best interests at heart.

She was surprised to find a couple of hours had passed, realising Rosa would probably be concerned about her, she asked Mr. Brown to take her home. When they drew up outside 'The Black Feathers', she removed the fur stole and handed it back to him. He immediately raised his vertical palm and said, "No, you keep it Kathleen, after all you've been through, the theatre owes you that much at least. I'll square it with Mrs Miller tomorrow."

Surprised at his generosity, she thanked him, and the driver dismounted from the top of the cab, opened the carriage door and taking her hand, helped her safely on to the pavement outside.

***

When she entered the inn, Rosa immediately ushered Kathleen into the parlour. Her eyes as round as saucers when she spied the white fur stole. "'ere that's beautiful Kathleen…how did you get hold of that?"

Kathleen told her what had happened. "Yes I agree, it is very beautiful, no idea what type of fur it is though…" It made the fur stole Dafydd had bought her second hand, look quite cheap in comparison.

Rosa's eyes shone. "It might be ermine, cost a fortune that would, but what do I know?"

"Maybe it belonged to one of the opera stars who sang there some time ago…"

"Perhaps. That Mr. Brown sounds like a right gentlemen, if you ask me!"

Kathleen agreed and felt a warm glow inside, which she couldn't quite identify, but it made her feel safe and protected.

***

The following morning at the music hall, Kathleen avoided Constance like the plague, until eventually, the woman caught up with her in the corridor and rudely pushed her.

"'ere Miss High and Mighty, why are you ignoring me this morning?"

Kathleen held her breath, what could she say? Deciding that honesty was the best policy, she exhaled loudly. "Look, if you really want to know, someone slashed my best jacket to pieces whilst I was practising my new song yesterday."

Constance narrowed her eyes with suspicion. "And you think it was me?" she poked Kathleen roughly with her index finger, nostrils flaring. "You think I was that jealous, don't you?"

"Well er…whoever it was had to have access to a sharp pair of scissors…"

Constance roughly grabbed hold of Kathleen's arm and marched her to the rest room, which thankfully, was empty.

"Look Kathleen," she said forcefully, "do you think I would risk my position 'ere after all you've done for me?" Tears now filled the woman's sapphire blue eyes.

"I'm sorry, Connie. 'Twas Mr. Brown saying it had to be yourself or Mrs Miller as there are scissors in the wardrobe department. He also put doubts in my mind about your drinking problem."

"Drinking problem!" Connie threw up her hands in despair. "That was a long time ago. I've not touched a drop this past couple of years!"

Kathleen did not for one moment doubt the sincerity in the woman's voice. "I'm sorry," she said softly. "Please forgive me. It just feels like someone is out to get me. I do believe you. I'll make us a cup of tea, shall I?"

Connie nodded.

Over a cuppa they discussed who it might be causing problems for Kathleen, but neither thought it could possibly be Mrs Miller, though Connie said she would keep an eye out for any untoward behaviour from the woman or anyone else for that matter.

Feeling much better, Kathleen returned to rehearsals, she needed to get that new song absolutely spot on as she was expected to sing and dance with the troupe.

Once rehearsals were over, she made her way to Mr. Brown's office with a view to thanking him for his kindness the previous evening. The door to his office was slightly ajar and she smiled when she could see he had his feet up on the desk, smoking a cigar. She knocked tentatively.

"Enter!" he called out.

He immediately removed his feet from the table, depositing his smoking cigar on an old saucer. Beaming, he rose and kissed her softly on the cheek. "How are you today, my dear?" He said, his voice thick with emotion.

"Very well thank you, Mr. Brown. I just wanted to show my gratitude for your kind support last night."

"Oh think nothing of it, Kathleen. Please sit yourself down."

She seated herself opposite him. "Thank you. I've spoken to Connie and I honestly don't think it was her…"

He frowned momentarily. "I wouldn't discuss such matters with her, now you've put her on her guard."

"Oh…but really…I know it wasn't her…"

He harrumphed loudly. Then shook his head, making her feel quite foolish, but she knew in her heart it wasn't Constance. "So, you've had no more trouble today?"

"No, none whatsoever."

"Well just in case, I insist on taking you home this evening." Before she had a chance to refuse, he said. "No, you can't take the risk of going home alone, I shall escort you to your door…"

Realising his cigar had extinguished itself, he drew it to his lips and extracted a box of matches from his inside pocket. Kathleen tensed, immediately recognising the red and black label:'Beacon Matches'. These were the same matches she'd found on stage the day the fire started on set when Wilson Brown had come to her aid.

"What's the matter?" He raised his brows.

"Those matches…they're the same make as the box I found on stage when that fire started." She stared hard at him.

He shrugged. "They're only matches Kathleen. You can get them anywhere."

"Very well, if that is so, where did you purchase them? They are not a well known brand that I am aware of," she accused, leaning over his desk.

Brown squirmed in his seat. "I really can't remember now, does it really matter?"

"Yes it does to me…" she stood as realisation dawned. Her heart picking up rhythm, the blood pulsing around her body as she fought to make sense of the situation. "It was you, Mr. Brown, *you* set the fire on that stage and acted the part of the hero to impress me. Then last night, you slashed my jacket and benevolently offered me that fur stole to wear, then took me to tea at a swank hotel. But why?" Her voice was tremulous and her mouth dry.

The colour drained from Brown's face, and by his loss for words, she knew she had hit the nail on its head.

"I…I…don't know what to say, Kathleen." He stood and made his way towards her as she backed up a step.

"Keep away from me!" she shouted, holding up her hands in front of her.

"Please don't fear me. I did want to impress you. I've loved you Kathleen from the first time I set eyes on you and I wanted you to notice me and forget about that Welsh husband of yours, who has put his career in the police constabulary before your performance on stage. He doesn't deserve you, but I do. I worship the very ground you walk upon."

Kathleen could not believe her ears. She dropped both hands by her side as he fell to his knees. "And that fur stole?" she asked, as things were becoming clear upon past reflection. "It was not from the wardrobe department was it?"

He shook his head and then looked up at her. "I bought it for you. As a gift…with my love…" He said, clinging to her skirts.

She pushed him away. "Love!" she spat, throwing up her arms in anger. "How can that possibly be love? When you scare me half to death and ruin my best jacket?"

He slowly stood, then shook his head. Eventually, he held up his hands as if some sort of defence. Letting out a breath, he said, "Look, you were never going to come to any harm, were you? I asked you the day of the fire to see me in my office, that's how I knew you'd smell the fire and call me in time. If you hadn't arrived, I would have put it out myself. And that fur stole is far more expensive than that jacket of yours…"

The man could not see how upset she was by his actions, far more upset than from the actual incidents themselves. Wilson Brown was someone she trusted and now that trust was destroyed forever. "What I really cannot forgive you for, is implying that it was Mrs Miller or Constance who might have had something against me. Not only that, but you risked the lives of the people at the theatre. Several theatres have burned down in the past, due to the props and the lime in the lights igniting. How foolhardy you were! And all to try to win the love of a woman who does not love you, but loves her own husband!"

Wilson Brown stood there open-mouthed, with tears in his eyes. "I'm truly sorry, Kathleen…"

She turned sharply and headed for the door, she could no longer bear to be in the same room as the man and look at his face for one more moment. Leaving his office, she slammed the door loudly behind her and marched off down the corridor. How could she remain at the theatre now with this turn of events?

***

The rest of the day went by in a blur as Kathleen tried her best to avoid Wilson Brown. This could not be happening to her, surely? How was she going to manage working at the theatre now? That thought concerned her greatly.

At the end of the day, she took a cab to Clement Johnson's home to have a word with him about the situation. Seeming surprised to see her, he sat her down in his office, summoning the maid to fetch her a glass of water to calm her down.

"Believe me, I do understand your distress, Kathleen," he said, when she had explained the situation to him. "But I would think it quite unwise for you to pull out of the show now…" he advised.

She let out an exasperated breath. "You mean due to the signed contract?"

He shook his head. "No, I have a good lawyer who could get you out of that if needs be, I meant for your career. You are just about to hit the big time. My advice is that you stay put for the royal show at least."

She gazed thoughtfully into the flickering flames in the fire place, the ticking of the mantel clock getting louder with each thought.

They were interrupted by the maid bringing the glass of water. The agent looked at Kathleen and continued, "You must do as you deem fit my dear, if all of this is distressing for you, especially as you now have a baby on the way."

She patted her stomach. "Yes, any stress is not good for this little one. I shall go away and have a good think about it." She watched as the maid handed her the glass, which she gratefully accepted.

The maid then excused herself from the room.

"There is one other option…" Clement began, thoughtfully rubbing his chin. "I am on good terms with the theatre manager himself, I could ask that he remove Mr. Brown from the theatre all together. Though I do not believe he is a bad man. I think he genuinely has feelings for you and went about it entirely the wrong way."

Kathleen nodded. "I agree. No, please don't do that, I should hate it if he were fired because of me. I doubt if he will do anything like that again. I think the better option is if I were to leave after the royal performance. It will be best all round. I can go back to Wales and attend to the needs of my husband and this little one growing inside me."

"Very well," Clement Johnson conceded. "But always be aware that I would only be too pleased to see you back on the London stage, my dear." He smiled warmly.

It gladdened her heart to hear him say so.

***

On the night of the royal performance, Kathleen stood back stage, trembling. Someone had just entered the changing room claiming to have seen Queen Victoria herself seated in the royal box. Imagine her, little Kathleen O'Hara, performing in front of royalty!

She was wearing a beautiful white lace dress for her performance of 'Please Don't Leave Me in the Lurch!"—her signature song. The dress nipped in at the waist. It was tied with bow from a light blue sash. On her head she wore a wide-brimmed, white lace hat, adorned with cornflowers to match the bow. Mrs Miller added the sash with a view to concealing the pregnancy, but Kathleen asked her to include some padding to emphasise it, as it would make the act all the more comical as she strutted across the stage in search of her groom. And she was absolutely correct, as it went down a storm in rehearsal.

"'ere are you all right, darling?" Kathleen turned to see Connie stood behind her, all garbed up in show girl frock, long black evening gloves and large black hat with feather plume.

Kathleen nodded. "'Tis only nerves is what it is Connie…"

Connie frowned, her eyes darkening for a moment. "You haven't been yourself lately though, is something wrong?"

Kathleen took Connie away to the corner of the dressing room, so they were away from prying eyes and listening ears. She told her friend what had happened with Wilson Brown. Connie's eyes rounded like two large saucers. "Cor love a duck! I ain't ever thought that of the Guv'nor!"

"Ssshhh! In case anyone overhears…" Kathleen advised. "Anyhow, 'tis my last night here and t'will be grand to get back home to Wales."

Connie frowned. "Well, I for one, am going to miss you. Please write to me Kathleen…yer won't forget us, will you?"

Kathleen shook her head, feeling her eyes fill with unshed tears, she swallowed and sniffed. It would not be a good time to break down before this very special performance.

"No, how could I ever forget you, Connie? I will write, I promise. Now go break a leg!" Kathleen shouted as Connie left for the stage, blowing her a kiss.

There was Connie's performance to get through first, after that the dancing troupe with Connie or 'Constance De L'amour' as she was otherwise known, then they would all remain on stage for Kathleen's 'Please Don't Leave Me in the Lurch!', followed by a couple of Kathleen's other numbers, finishing with 'The Rose of Tralee'.

In the background, she could hear the muffled sounds of cheers and applause and swallowed hard while she thought of her own songs. All too soon, someone knocked the door, thinking it was someone calling her on stage, she opened it to see a beautiful basket of white roses, just like the opera singer, Bella Montovani, had been given by her beau at the Temperance Hall. She bent down to lift the basket, but there was no card, or else it had dropped off.

Dafydd was out there somewhere in the audience, waiting expectantly for her to perform. She hoped they were from him and not Wilson Brown. She sat for a couple of minutes in the deserted dressing room, gazing at the beautiful, white blooms, green-stemmed and white-ribboned.

Star billing at long last!

Then the call came and she walked towards the stage…

***

Standing in front of the audience with the spot light on her, Kathleen feared she would faint from the shock of it all, but instead she found herself dancing, singing and losing herself in the songs. The audience loved her and shouted, cheered, laughed and clapped loudly. It made her proud to think Her Majesty was sat out there somewhere in the darkness, after the performance she would get the opportunity to meet with her. But most of all she was proud that Dafydd was out there, urging her to do well.

At the end of the show, after singing, 'The Rose of Tralee', she received a standing ovation as people threw flowers on to the stage. She took three curtain calls in all. Quite breathless as the curtain closed for the final time. A gripping pain seized her stomach and doubled her up. Everyone had left the stage except for Constance who had been hanging around in the wings to see her.

She immediately ran to Kathleen's side. "What's the matter?" she asked, her voice was full of concern.

"It's the baby, I think..." Kathleen gasped clutching her stomach as she lowered herself to the floor.

It was then she watched Connie's eyes widen with horror. "Oh Kathleen!"

"What's the matter?" Kathleen asked with alarm.

"You're bleeding. I think you're losing the baby...."

Kathleen looked down to see the front of her beautiful white dress sodden with blood. At that point she watched as the stage ceiling above appeared to swirl around and around and then everything went black with the applause still ringing in her ears.

Chapter Twenty Three

Kathleen blinked, then groaned. "Where am I?" A shaft of light filtered in through the window as slowly in the semi-darkness, she realised she was in bed in her room at the Black Feathers, with Dafydd and Rosa at her side. For a moment, she wondered if she had dreamt last night's performance at the musical hall and was only now awaking. But seeing both beside her with a look of concern on their faces, she knew it had not been a dream, but very real.

Dafydd was seated and took Kathleen's hand, but then broke down and wept. Rosa's eyes misted over, she turned away and appeared to wipe her eyes on the back of the sleeve of her dress before returning to face her friend once more, now a look of composure on her face. "It's better yer rest now, Kathleen...Yer've had a bad turn..."

Kathleen pulled herself up in the bed, her insides aching fiercely. "Please tell me...it's the baby isn't it? Please tell me I haven't lost the baby?"

Rosa clenched a fist to her mouth and turned away once more. The expression said it all. Kathleen buried her head in the pillow and wept bitterly.

***

Six months later

Lily breezed into the school room at Abercanaid where Kathleen was giving singing lessons to a group of young children.

She clapped her hands brusquely. "Children, please be seated for your milk and biscuits. Mrs Morgan shall serve you. I need to speak with Mrs Jenkin."

The children didn't need asking twice as they ran off to the table in the corner and surrounded Mrs Morgan like animals feeding in a zoo.

Lily took Kathleen to one side. She had been back helping at the school since returning to Merthyr with Dafydd, after her devastating miscarriage. She missed the London stage, but it was an awful reminder of what had happened to her there. In the event she had never got to meet with Queen Victoria. And was later to learn that it was Wilson Brown who had summoned a carriage to take both herself and Dafydd back to the inn. Dafydd had swept her up in his arms and looked really alarmed according to Rosa. Kathleen had been unconscious throughout, until she'd woken next day to see her husband and landlady beside her bed.

She'd recuperated for a few days until a doctor deemed her fit to leave for Merthyr. Clement Johnson called around to see her before she left, telling her not to worry about her contract. She was never to see Mr. Brown or Connie again. A deep depression had engulfed her the past few months where she cared not for the theatre, nor her performance, but being at the school helped to keep her mind occupied.

Blinking, she brought herself back to the present moment, aware Lily was about to ask her something.

Lily extracted an envelope from her dress pocket. "I've got a letter here for Delwyn and Rose in Great Salt Lake. Please could you go to the post office for me, Kathleen? I might be too busy later and would like to catch the next post."

Kathleen nodded. "Sure I will, Lily."

Her sister-in-law slipped a couple of coins in Kathleen's hand to cover the postage. Kathleen collected her shawl and bonnet. "I won't be too long!" she shouted to Lily.

As she crossed the road, she spied Maggie Shanklin entering the post office and took a deep breath. The best thing to do, she decided, was to ignore the woman. After all, what could she do? They were only words.

The post office was quite busy and a queue had formed. As soon as Kathleen closed the door behind herself, she saw Maggie's head turn and caught her beady-eyed stare. Then the woman whispered to the lady beside her.

Kathleen hadn't set eyes on Maggie since the night she had performed at the chapel before leaving for London. The hairs on the back of neck bristled as she feared contact with the old crone.

Slowly the queue moved forward and Kathleen breathed a sigh of relief to realise that soon Maggie would be out of her hair. When her own turn came, she explained to the post master that she wanted to send the letter to Utah. The post master seemed to understand as she realised, Lily would have been there many times before with letters for Delwyn and Rose. He took both coinage and letter from her hand and bade her good day.

Outside in the fresh air, she was proud of how she had conducted herself in close proximity to her arch enemy and was about to return to the school, mission completed, when a hand clamped down heavily on her shoulder. Turning sharply, she came face-to-face with Maggie, whose eyes were now like two shiny black lumps of coal. The anger inside evident.

Maggie breathed heavily. "You filthy little trollop!" She spat in Kathleen's face. "You humiliated me in front of my friends at chapel. You're nothing but a little whore of Babylon on that London stage prancing around in yer bloomers!"

Kathleen took a handkerchief from her dress pocket and wiped her face as it grew hot with anxiety. "No, I am not!" She said forcefully, "And I do not show my bloomers, thank you very much!" She turned to walk away and cross the road, but Maggie grabbed her by the arm.

"I've got your card marked, you little floozy. Everyone in Abercanaid knows you're a little jumped up madam who has got too big for her boots!"

Kathleen stared Maggie in the eye, then without realising she was about to do it, slapped her hard across the cheek. "You jealous old crone. The green eyed monster has got the better of you, Mrs Shanklin."

Maggie touched her own cheek, it must have stung like hell itself, Kathleen guessed. Then the crone grabbed at Kathleen's hair tugging it forcefully. Kathleen pulled away and shouted, "It's too late for you, you're a middle-aged old boot who now worries about your husband whistling at women like me on the stage. And no wonder and all, after living with an evil ugly shrew like you!"

Kathleen bolted across the road, turning to glance over her shoulder to see Maggie running after her in a rage with her fist in the air. From seemingly nowhere, there was the heavy sound of clattering horse's hooves and Kathleen's eyes widened with horror as a horse and carriage veered out of control towards them. She managed to reach the pavement, but it hit Maggie full force before she had a chance to realise what was happening. Her face became contorted with shock as both horse and carriage rode over her with a sickening thump.

Engulfed with nausea, Kathleen's hands flew to her face in an attempt to block out the scene before her. She heard the carriage ride on ahead for some time before the driver was able to bring it to a halt and heard his heavy footsteps run back to the scene. Kathleen peeked through her splayed fingers to see the battered and bloodied body of Maggie Shanklin lying haphazardly on the road, her eyes opened wide with horror and mouth agape.

The post office door swung open and the crowd that had gathered inside came running out, one of the women shouting out Maggie's name. The driver of the horse and carriage knelt over Maggie's body. "I think she's dead!" he said, looking at Kathleen.

Kathleen heard a high pitched scream coming from somewhere, it was then she realised it was coming from her own self as tears streamed down her face.

Her legs began to buckle beneath her and a strong pair of hands caught her.

"Come back inside the school room!" She turned to see Evan stood there, realising he must have witnessed her altercation with Maggie. "Fetch Doctor Owen, quickly!" Evan instructed the crowd. The post master, who had been standing there with a blank expression, ran towards the doctor's house as the coach driver stayed with Maggie and someone brought a blanket to cover her with.

Lily came running out of the school and helped Evan escort Kathleen back inside. "It's my fault she's dead!" was all she was able to say.

"Make her a sweet cup of tea, not too hot," Evan instructed his wife as he led her past the watchful eyes of the children and towards his office.

Kathleen slumped down in a chair and he closed the door behind them.

"Now what happened out there?" he asked.

She put her head in her hands and wept pitifully.

**

Kathleen looked up through a veil of misted tears. "I don't know, Evan. I just went to post a letter for Lily…"

"I see," he said solemnly, seating himself opposite her, behind his desk. "And then what?"

"Well Mrs Shanklin was already in the post office, I did my best to avoid her, though I could see she was whispering about me. Then just when I thought I had got away with it…"

Evan narrowed his gaze. "Got away with what?"

Kathleen sniffed then straightened her countenance. "Well getting out of the post office without conflict…"

"I see," he replied, his features softening.

"But when I got outside she grabbed me by the arm and made some horrible accusations. She was most hateful in fact."

"So it was she who accosted you and not the other way around?"

Kathleen nodded. "Yes. She also pulled me by the hair and made to follow me into the road, but not after I slapped her face first…"

She began sobbing when she remembered how she had done that as a pang of guilt overtook her.

"I saw you crossing the road, Kathleen, but not your altercation with one another. The police could be called into this, so it might be best if we can find a witness."

This was far worse than she ever thought possible. "The police? But what will Dafydd think of me? You do believe me, don't you Evan?"

He was just about to answer, when Lily entered with a cup of tea, setting it down on Evan's desk for Kathleen. "Now you drink all of that Kathleen. I've put some sugar in it, it will do you good."

"Thank you, Lily."

Her sister-in-law left the room to return to the classroom.

"So Evan, do you believe me?"

"Yes, of course I do. I've known you long enough not to doubt you and to realise the nature of your character, though it matters not what I think, but if others find out, they might well blame you."

"I don't think anyone else saw us, except maybe for the carriage driver when Maggie followed after me."

"Good, let's hope it stays that way, now drink your tea and you best get yourself home, you've had a nasty shock. What time is Dafydd due home from work?"

"Not until 10 o'clock this evening." A thought just occurred to her. "I suppose he might well find out before I see him about this accident?"

Evan stroked his chin. "That's entirely possible. Look drink your tea and I'll walk you home before it gets dark…"

By the time Kathleen left with Evan, the carriage driver and the crowd had departed. Evan told her that Maggie's body had been taken to her own home in the vehicle, ironically, responsible for her demise. He said that he intended calling to see Tom Shanklin and the rest of the family later that evening and that he'd contact Mr. Frobisher, the undertaker, himself.

Chapter Twenty Four

A tall man, wearing a black top hat, tails, and black cravat, stood outside the chapel as Kathleen approached with Dafydd, both attired in their mourning dress.

"Who's that gentleman?" She whispered to her husband behind her hand.

He cleared his throat. "William Frobisher, the undertaker. He dealt with my mother's funeral."

"Oh." She fell into step with her husband, shivering as a funeral hearse being pulled by two black horses with matching plumes, drew up outside the chapel. The horses whinnied, their breaths hitting the cold air and sending out puffs of steam. They had blinkers over their eyes and behind the cortege, walked a young boy in a top hat. He carried a long pole with a black plume on the end, dressed in the same fashion as the undertaker himself.

Had it only been a few days ago when another horse drawn carriage had passed that way and killed Maggie Shanklin? Now groups of people congregated outside the chapel for her funeral. In any normal circumstance, Maggie herself might have stood there, gossiping with her cronies about the latest demise in the village. This time she was also present, except now she was in the coffin inside the hearse.

"Come on, we'd better go inside," Dafydd advised, almost as if sensing his wife's thoughts. He gently led her past the whispering hordes and into the chapel itself, where Evan was stood with Lily, welcoming the mourners. From the corner of her eye, Kathleen could see Mrs and Mrs Morgan settled in a pew with their daughter Betty, and Evan and Lily's two, Mollie and Joshua.

Finally, everyone came inside the chapel as the organist played a sombre piece of music that she didn't recognise, as the coffin of Maggie Shanklin was carried by the pall bearers who set it down in front of the pulpit. Kathleen swallowed hard as the undertaker closed the chapel doors. Evan took to the podium as Thomas Shanklin and children looked on from the front pew.

Tom's head was bowed low and in his hand he twisted a white cotton handkerchief as his children clung to him in their moment of grief.

"We are gathered here today…" Evan began, "to celebrate the life of Margaret Mary Shanklin, who was born in Donegal, Ireland. Maggie, as she was best known by the people of this village, came over to Wales with her family, as her father and brothers sought work at the Cyfarthfa Iron Works. The family decided to stay put in Merthyr Tydfil, where work was plentiful. Maggie met Thomas Shanklin at this very chapel and a courtship began. They married within the year, making their home in this village. Maggie and Tom went on to have four children…" he stopped to draw a breath as if now about to carefully phrase his words. Evan was an honest man, who rarely shied away from the truth.

"I've had permission to say this from Tom himself…Maggie had a mixed reception in this village. To some she was revered and treated with the utmost respect, but to others she was less well thought of. I do not wish to go into that here and I had my own issues with Mrs Shanklin myself, as many of you know. But even though she was reprimanded on several occasions, she was still made welcome by myself and my wife, Lily." He glanced across to his wife as if in support, and she nodded and smiled.

"One thing that cannot be held in question, however, is that Mrs Shanklin was a good wife to Tom as he tells me and a good mother to their children, who are now almost grown up and about to make their way forward in this world."

At that point one of the eldest daughters, sobbed pitifully, sending a shiver skittering up Kathleen's spine. Evan thankfully, cut his address short, and they sang the first hymn, 'The Lord is my Shepherd.' Kathleen had originally been asked to sing something, but felt unable to do so, following the circumstances of Maggie's death, although she now accepted she was not to blame.

Towards the end of the service, Thomas Shanklin rose from the pew and handed Evan an envelope, then whispered something in his ear. Evan extracted a letter from the envelope and announced, "Tom has asked me to read this letter out to you that Maggie left behind in the event of her death. He has not read it himself."

Evan began to read. "If you are reading or hearing this, then I have already passed over to the other side. My dearest Tom, I love you so much and I always will. Mary, Declan, Timmy and Rose, you are my darlings and I will always watch over you. My dear friends who rallied around to support me at difficult times, I will always have you in my heart, you know who you are. As for the rest of you in Abercanaid..."

Evan's eyes widened as he gazed at the letter in his hand, he looked at Tom for confirmation to continue. Tom nodded.

"I don't know if I should continue to read this," Evan said doubtfully.

A man from the back shouted, "Go on, it's the last thing she'll ever get to say to us!"

A couple of people tittered. Which Kathleen found distasteful to say the least.

"Very well," Evan continued. "If anyone would like to leave, I suggest you do it now..."

Several women stood, obviously afraid Maggie might say something about them, and left the chapel, as Evan waited to continue.

He coughed to clear his throat and adjusted his collar. Kathleen noticed his face was now beaded with perspiration. For a moment, she thought he'd abandon the letter and make an apology, but instead he extracted a handkerchief from his pocket, and mopping his brow, carried on reading. "As for the rest of you in Abercanaid...I can't say I shall miss you. You have caused me a tremendous amount of grief, particularly the one who thinks she is better than us all and a traitor to both womankind and her home country..."

Kathleen's face burned red hot as she became aware of all eyes on her.

"Look, I'll stop this if you like," Evan said, addressing Kathleen directly.

"No, please continue Evan, I have done nothing wrong!" Kathleen said forcefully, surprising herself with her clear, stoic tone.

He nodded. "She dresses like a harlot and sings like an angel. In fact she reminds me so much of myself at her age, I can't begin to tell you what it is. The same red hair and voice that people love. But my father made me cut my beautiful hair and it never grew the same again, and he forbade me to sing in front of others, even in church…"

It was all beginning to make sense now why Maggie appeared to despise her so much, she saw her lost youth in Kathleen.

"But you people of Abercanaid who have called me a busybody in the past, accusing me of poking my nose into your affairs, 'tis only because I try to help that gets me in trouble, my tongue is always truthful…"

Kathleen felt the hairs on the back of her neck, bristle.

Always trying to help, what about the time Maggie spiked her tea? That wasn't very helpful.

"You'll all miss me when I'm gone. I make no apologies to anyone for my past behaviour. I'm a good, God fearing woman, and I expect to go to the right place when I pass over, which is more than many of you religious hypocrites can say."

Evan held up the letter for people to see she had signed it. There was a long silence, a seemingly never ending one. Then a loud murmur travelled around the congregation, and much to Kathleen's surprise, people approached her afterward asking how she was. Maybe they pitied her after the things Maggie had said in the letter, and finally came to their own conclusions about the woman.

When the funeral was over and Maggie's coffin was loaded back into the hearse, everyone trooped through to the chapel hall where Lily and Mrs Morgan served tea and cake as Thomas Shanklin, his family and a few friends, attended the burial with Evan. Thankfully, the past could now be laid to rest, along with Maggie's body.

***

The following day, Kathleen was feeling a little off colour, so sent news to Lily via Dafydd that she would not be able to work at the school, by the afternoon, her nausea became so bad, that Dafydd worried if he should leave for his evening shift, but she insisted he go. She hoped no one might think that it was an upset from Maggie's funeral yesterday, but it wasn't, it was something else she had experienced not so long ago. She was pregnant again, she was sure of it. Last time it had been a shock to her system, but now she felt mentally prepared and planned on telling Dafydd as soon as she got it confirmed by Doctor Owen.

Later that evening, she knocked on the doctor's door.

"Well hello there, Kathleen. How are you this fine evening?" he greeted, when his housekeeper had led her into his consulting room.

"I've been feeling very nauseous this past couple of days, Doctor, and think I might be pregnant again," she said brightly.

He smiled, requesting she sit, and asked her a few relevant questions. She estimated she could be as much as two to three months pregnant.

"Could you please remove your outer garments, so I might examine you on the couch?" he asked.

She stepped behind a screen to remove her clothing and then lay on the bed for him to examine her. When he had finished prodding around, he looked at her gravely. "I'm afraid I don't think you're pregnant, my dear, I can't feel any sign of your womb hardening or transcending up the abdomen. Well not of that long a duration of pregnancy anyhow, it's possible you could be just a few weeks pregnant, I won't rule that out though." He shook his head. "But I am unable to conclusively say whether you are pregnant at this point in time."

She felt a strong wave of disappointment wash over her. "Oh? I was so sure too. I haven't seen my courses for the past three months or so, so I assumed along with the nausea that I was with child again."

"Try not to be too down-hearted, it's still early days since the miscarriage," he said brightly. "You're a strong, healthy woman.

Your body needs time to recover from the trauma. What does Dafydd say about this?"

She sat up on the couch. "Nothing, we haven't discussed it as such, Doctor Owen."

"I see." He looked at her sombrely over his glasses. "Well put your clothes back on and we'll have a little chat..."

She did as instructed, then Doctor Owen helped to allay her fears about future pregnancies, but a sense of foreboding had taken over her very being and she didn't like the feeling at all.

***

If Dafydd was concerned about Kathleen's wellbeing he wasn't saying so, and maybe was giving her some space after the miscarriage. Spring had turned into summer, and one afternoon when they were out for a stroll by the River Taff, he turned to her and said, "Kathleen, I think we should have another child. How do you feel about that?"

She turned to him and saw the longing in her husband's eyes and gently said, "I wish it were so, Dafydd, but so far nothing has happened at all. I didn't tell you at the time, but a few weeks ago I visited Doctor Owen as I thought I might be pregnant as my courses had stopped, but he examined me and could not confirm anything. Now my courses have returned once more..." she lowered her head, almost as though in shame.

"Do you know what I think it is, *cariad*?"

She shook her head and he took her hand in his. "I believe it's because you not only lost the child you were carrying but you gave up the stage too..."

Kathleen stared in disbelief at what her husband was saying. "You think so?" She blinked several times.

"I know so. The light has gone out of your life. I think you should get back to the Temperance Hall for now, the theatre manager would bite your hand off to get you to perform there, I'm sure."

She nodded with tears in her eyes. "Yes, you might be right, Dafydd. I feel so empty and unfulfilled inside now."

"That's only natural. There's an emptiness that needs to be filled inside you and if that is what you need to do, then so be it."

He squeezed her hand and then lifted her into the air, tears of joy sprung to her eyes, why hadn't she seen it before? She had been so wrapped up in the loss of the baby that she had lost sight of her pathway in life. Setting her down on solid ground once more, he said, "Just think about it, that's all."

Kathleen could hardly believe her ears that now her husband was telling her to go to the theatre and no longer holding back. Frowning for a moment, she turned to him and said, "There's something I haven't told you..." she bit her lip.

"What is it? I can assure you that whatever it is, it will not affect our relationship..."

She took a deep breath and let it out again. "It was Mr. Wilson Brown. He fell in love with me, but I did not realise."

Dafydd chuckled. "My dear Kathleen, is that all?"

She shook her head. "Please don't laugh at me. I didn't realise that it was *he* who set fire to the theatre curtains in order to rescue me and it was *he* who shredded my best jacket."

Dafydd's eyes darkened. "Why did you not tell me of this? I would have sorted the fellow out. I'd have laid him on his back."

"No believe me, that would not have been the answer."

He furrowed his brow. "How did you find out it was him?"

"He lit a cigar in his office one day. I noticed he used the same brand of matches as the person who had lit the fire had. They're called 'Beacon' and quite unusual for the London area."

Dafydd grinned broadly. "You are quite the little detective, Miss Kathleen O'Hara! I should make enquiries about you joining the Glamorgan Constabulary. But alas, there are no women there, only the cleaners and the Inspector's wife who looks after us all!"

"There's something else that bothers me and I've never got around to asking you?"

"What is that?"

"After my performance, I received a beautiful bouquet of white roses, there was no card attached. I never got to see them again, as of course I lost the baby, and later we returned to Wales. I've often suspected they were from him..."

Dafydd smiled, his eyes brimming with tears. "No, my precious. They were from me. I have never forgotten you mentioning how when Bella Montovani was top of the bill at the Temperance Hall, she had a beautiful basket of white roses on her dressing table and how you dreamed of the same thing one day."

Kathleen snuggled into her husband, feeling safe and secure as he stroked her hair. "I should have known. I just wanted to make sure they were from you and I had hoped they were."

"Well, now you know. Come on, let's get back home and we'll plan what you will say to the theatre manager tomorrow."

***

The following morning, Kathleen set off for the theatre. There was no sign of Jess when she arrived. She felt her stomach slump to her shoes when she saw another, older woman, cleaning up the auditorium.

"Excuse me, madam, but have you seen Jess anywhere?" she asked the woman.

The woman, whose face was heavily ingrained with wrinkles and only appeared to have a couple of teeth in her head, said, "She's in the dressing room. '*Fy Duw*! Haven't I seen you before some place?"

Kathleen smiled. "You might well have done." She guessed that the woman might have seen her on this very stage at some point.

She ran to the dressing room, arriving almost out of breath to see Jess hanging up a beautiful, white lace dress on a hanger.

"Jess!" she cried.

Jess turned and it took a couple of seconds for realisation to hit her, then she ran towards Kathleen and hugged her.

"Kathleen! How long have you been back home for? Is this just a visit or are you home for good?"

"For good. It's great to see you. I've missed you."

"Me too. When did you arrive, a couple of days ago?" Jess's eyes were shining brightly.

Kathleen shook her head. "More like a couple of months ago…"

218

Jess frowned. "And you took all this time to come to see me?"

"No, you don't understand the circumstances. I was on stage in front of Queen Victoria herself, and when the performance ended and the curtain closed, I collapsed."

"Collapsed? But what happened?"

"I had a miscarriage. It was awful Jess. I haven't been myself for this past couple of months. Then Dafydd suggested I came back here to work."

"Oh, you poor soul. I had no idea. I mean I knew you were doing well on the stage and all as the manager told us, and Clement Johnson called in here looking for new talent again another time. He told me all about you, but he never signed anyone up like he did you. I could tell he was bored by Bella Montovani." She giggled.

Kathleen joined in with the laughter. It was great to see her friend once more. Like the old days.

"Yes and guess what," Jess continued, "I've gone up in the world, now I'm a dresser!"

"That's great news. I'm so pleased for you." For the first time, Kathleen noticed that Jess seemed to have taken more care of her appearance, her hands no longer chapped and sore looking, her hair was wrapped on top of her head in a more elegant style and the dress she wore appeared to be an old costume from the theatre, which although had seen better days was still much smarter than her usual garb.

"If the manager takes you on here, I will get to help you dress, Kathleen!"

Kathleen beamed, realising they had both come so far. "Speaking of whom, where might I find him?"

"He's just nipped out to the market. He'll be back soon enough, stop and have a nice cup of tea?"

Kathleen did not need asking twice. It was like old times as they both sat in the rest room with a hot pot of tea, chatting and catching up on the latest news. Kathleen was to learn that Bella Montovani had left the theatre to marry her admirer, and a couple of new acts had since taken to the stage.

When Mr. Smith the theatre manager returned, he beamed broadly when he saw Kathleen waiting. "It's so good to see you, my dear," he said pecking her on the cheek. "How are things in London?"

She hesitated. "I'm no longer there, Mr. Smith. I came back to Merthyr for personal reasons and I would like to ask you if I could go back on the stage here?"

Mr. Smith frowned, causing her heart to skip a beat. "I don't know about that…maybe Merthyr will no longer be grand enough for you!" Then he laughed. "I'm only joking, my dear. You've come back at the right time. Bella has already left and there's no star billing now, with your previous record, the crowds will flock here!"

Relief flooded through her.

Mr. Smith was true to his word and within a fortnight, following adequate rehearsal, she was back on the stage once more, where she belonged.

Chapter Twenty Five

Kathleen's act went down a storm at the Temperance Hall. She had a couple of new songs written for her. Each time she performed, the shows sold out as people came from neighbouring towns, and even as far away as Swansea and Cardiff, as word spread like wild fire. Her name became well known in the newspapers and on the tip of people's tongues.

On the run up to Christmas that year it was rumoured that Joseph Parry, a locally born composer, had been in the audience, though Kathleen did not get to meet him, but felt honoured that he'd been there. Mr. Parry and his family had emigrated to Pennsylvania when he was a young boy, but later he'd returned to his homeland and penned the beautiful, yet haunting love song, Myfanwy. It was rumoured to be about a young woman he'd once fallen in love with.

As Christmas approached, Kathleen thought of buying gifts for everyone. She had done quite well for herself with her earnings and with her husband's police wage, it was going to be a good Christmas this year. In between rehearsals and that evening's performance, she went shopping in Merthyr High Street and bought a pearl brooch for Lily, fountain pen for Evan, a ball for Joshua, china doll for Mollie and for her dear husband, she purchased a beautiful pocket watch, which she had engraved from herself with love, along with the date. There was just one present left to purchase and that was a very special one indeed. It was for Jess. There was a milliner in the town that sold the most exquisite handmade bonnets. She chose a particularly pretty one with a rosebud pink silk bow and flower. She had it boxed up for Jess, her dearest friend.

The weather had become chilly and Kathleen had come to feel nauseated once again, she hardly dared hope that she might be pregnant. She would go and see Doctor Owen again, but she feared he would say the same thing.

Reluctantly, the following day when she was on a break from the theatre, she set off from Chapel Square to the doctor's house.

The surgery was busy when she arrived, as people sat there, some with hacking coughs and colds as the winter was particularly harsh. Eventually, she was summoned to see him by his surly-faced housekeeper.

"Ah Kathleen, what can I do for you today?" he asked expectantly.

"I hesitate to think I might be pregnant again..." She chewed her bottom lip.

"Please undress behind the screen and lie upon the couch."

The doctor rolled up his sleeves and emptied a jug of water into a bowl and washed his hands thoroughly with soap and water, drying them on a towel before examining her abdomen. From his facial expressions she could tell little, but this time the examination took longer.

"Please get yourself dressed," he ordered.

Once robed, they sat and chatted at his desk. "Yes, there is no doubt about it, I am happy to confirm your pregnancy, Mrs Jenkin. But how far gone do you think you are, my dear?"

"I thought about two months?" she said briskly.

He shook his head. "More like three I would say. Go and tell your husband the good news and come back to see me in a month or two, so I can see how you're progressing."

She smiled as she left the doctor's surgery, the other patients totally unaware of her good news. This time she hadn't put quite so much weight on, her dresses were a little snug but it was probably as she had lost a lot of weight after her miscarriage that she hadn't gained all that much.

She decided to wait until Christmas Eve before telling Dafydd the good news, although she was bursting with inward joy. It was the absolute best present she could ever give him, even better than the pocket watch.

On Christmas Eve itself, she had to work at the theatre where there was a special Christmas show which was sold out. The place was packed to the rafters. Before going on stage, Jess helped her into her costume which was a red satin dress, edged with black lace, which made Kathleen think of Parisian ladies for some reason. She had heard all about those high kicking ladies of

Paris who bared their bloomers at the infamous, Moulin Rouge, and then ended their act with the splits. She tittered to herself as she thought of how some of the people in the community would contend with this. An image of Maggie Shanklin appeared before her eyes, tutting and wagging a finger, which made her smile. In a silly kind of way she missed the old crone and decided to call on Tom and the children over the festive season, though what sort of reception she'd get, she had not a clue.

"You were far away then, Miss," Jess said.

"Oh Jess, I can never get used to you calling me Miss, you know." She rolled her eyes.

"Well you are a star now and always have been to me." Jess gazed in awe. Kathleen could see the adoration reflected in her eyes.

"Thank you for saying so, Jess." She hugged her friend warmly.

"There you are, all buttoned up!" Jess declared with a tear in her eye. She stood back and took a look at Kathleen. "You look beautiful. There's something different about you, you seem to be blossoming somehow…"

Kathleen smiled inwardly, she yearned to tell Jess her news but realised it was Dafydd who needed to be told and tonight, after this performance, would be the best time.

"I've left a Christmas present in the cupboard at the back of the dressing room for you!" Kathleen said brightly. "It's in a big box with a bow…"

"Oh thank you, so much. I'm sorry I couldn't afford one for you, Kathleen…" Jess looked down cast.

"Don't be silly, I just wanted you to share my good fortune, Jess, it's been a good year for me."

She blew Jess a kiss from her gloved hand and walked towards the stage, the applause ringing in her ears as the curtains parted and the spot lights shone on her.

*****

The performance went well and people threw flowers on to the stage in appreciation. Jess helped her off with her costume afterwards, and then Kathleen changed into her day dress. She couldn't walk around the town in a red dress, that would be positively scandalous, she'd get accosted for being a nymph of the pave, as the prostitutes in the town were often referred to. *It was strange how a colour made all the difference*, she thought. A red dress was acceptable for the stage as she was playing a part, but not acceptable as a decent married woman. She removed her heavy stage makeup and donned her cape and bonnet, then went to greet Dafydd at the end of the road, where he often met her after his shift at the police station. But he was nowhere to be seen and as it had become late, the taverns in the town were full of noisy revellers. She shivered at the thought of being alone. She waited a good twenty minutes then went over to the police station, but there was no sign of any officers of the law, only the Inspector's wife who greeted her and told her there had been a call for all available policemen to get over to China as some serious trouble had broken out.

Kathleen's heart began to thump loudly. Realising she was becoming distressed, the Inspector's wife draped a comforting arm around her shoulder. "He'll be all right, you'll see, dear. My husband has been in the profession for many a year and I've spent some sleepless nights, I can tell you…"

Kathleen sniffed loudly, trying to hold back her tears, the pregnancy was making her emotional. What if something happened to Dafydd and he never even got to know she was carrying his child? Now she wished she had told him a couple of days ago. "I'm being silly, I know…"

"That's understandable. You have not been a police wife for all that long. You will get accustomed to it, I can assure you. You sit down dear and I'll brew us a cup of tea. It can be hard sometimes being married to a policeman. When we marry an officer of the constabulary, we also marry the profession."

Kathleen nodded, she needed to be strong for Dafydd to support him, but most of all she needed to be strong for the new life she carried within.

She waited at the station with the Inspector's wife, the best part of an hour, and was about to suggest leaving, when the station door burst open. She glanced up to see a man in a dishevelled state being dragged in by two constables as they grappled to keep hold of him. The man's face was dirty and covered in blood and then, the moment he made eye contact with her, she knew who it was. Twm Sion Watkin, the bully from China. She feared he'd show recognition as she'd encountered him there herself and got away from him. Shivering apprehensively, she turned her head away. As they dragged him over to the counter, she heard one of the officers say, "Twm Sion Watkin, you are under the arrest for the murder of one of the whores from China, how do you plead? Guilty or not guilty?"

Kathleen sneaked a peek. Sioni said nothing, just growled and glared at Kathleen as if he somehow thought she was responsible for bringing him to justice.

"He'll probably hang for this offence," the Inspector's wife said soberly. "Everyone knows he killed that poor woman in that alleyway."

Kathleen knew only too well about that incident, as Dafydd had told her the prostitute he'd met that day at China, whilst she was working next door at the wash house, was dead. Though she wasn't about to tell the Inspector's wife that snippet of information, in case awkward questions were asked why they were there in the first place. The woman's murder had been headline news in the local newspaper. She just nodded, wordlessly.

Two other officers trooped into the station, one had a black eye, holding a truncheon in his hand, and the other seemed to be nursing a swollen fist. "He gave us a hard time I can tell you," the one with the black eye said, "but now we've finally got the blighter! Mind you, there was a large crowd of people protecting the scoundrel. They were throwing rocks and all kinds at us."

The officer with the swollen fist muttered something under his breath that sounded like a cuss word, then winced as if in severe pain.

"Right gentlemen," the Inspector's wife looked at them and clapped her hands with an air of authority, "when you have finished and locked this brutish oaf up safely where he belongs, behind bars, you shall find a big saucepan of cawl in the kitchen and some bread I've already sliced for you!"

A cheer went up amongst the officers and it made Kathleen feel warm-hearted to know that one of the men who was responsible for putting Twm Sion Watkin behind bars, was her own husband. But where was he?

At that moment a crowd of people waded in through the police station door, protesting at Sioni's arrest.

"Quick get them out!" The Inspector himself had now appeared and worked hard with his men to escort them roughly from the premises and bolt the door. When he had done so, Kathleen turned to him and asked, "But where's my husband, Constable Dafydd Jenkin?"

***

Before the Inspector had time to reply there was a loud banging on the door, which was now locked after the baying horde had got thrown out onto the street. The Inspector stepped forward and opened the door tentatively to find Dafydd stood there, his face swollen and slightly bloodied.

A loud cheer went up with the men as he was allowed entry through the door and the Inspector secured it once more behind him. The men gathered around and slapped him vigorously on the back.

"What on earth is going on?" Kathleen blinked several times.

"It's your man here," the Inspector replied. "He was the one responsible for locating and grappling with the bully, Twm Sion Watkin. We've been after him for months, but your husband led us to the brute and now he's safely behind bars. He put himself through some danger though in the process, but just as well he used to be a bare knuckle boxer, his strength put pay to that slippery eel as he fell like a large sack of spuds!"

Kathleen looked on proudly as the back slaps and congratulations continued for a while and there was a lot of hand shaking and complimentary comments.

The Inspector's wife took Kathleen to one side and whispered reassuringly, "Let him have his moment. They are far and few between..." she advised. "Take it from one who knows, your husband is a very brave man who seems to have a good understanding of people and a vast knowledge of China, where other constables fear to tread…"

Kathleen nodded. Of course, none of them here knew that Dafydd knew so much about the area as he had once upon a time taken to the drink and lived amongst the rogues and vagabonds himself, nor that he had paid to speak to a whore at Twm Sion Watkin's abode more recently. Neither did they know that Kathleen herself had been 'bought' by the bully as his 'new whore'. Both had outwitted the brute. But none of that mattered now and she decided to keep those nuggets of information to herself.

Seeing her for the first time, Dafydd grinned broadly and the crowd of constables parted, as he walked towards her. "I am so sorry, *cariad*. I was not there for you tonight. But this man has been evading us for months now. Come and I shall walk you home and we will get to our beds before midnight."

"No!" Kathleen said firmly. The room went quiet as people stared, fearing what she might say next, Dafydd's eyes widening. "You must stay a while, rest and eat with the others, then we shall see if we can get a carriage home to our beds. It is Christmas day tomorrow and neither of us have work, so it matters not whether we get to our beds on time, though I would very much like to rise at a reasonable hour to attend chapel. Evan has a special Christmas service at 11 o'clock planned…"

Realising that his wife wasn't about to scold him, but instead supportive of his role as a constable, he smiled and hugged her warmly. Then the other constables began chattering again as the Inspector's wife ushered them into the kitchen for sustenance by banging a wooden spoon on a large empty saucepan.

"Come on you, too, Kathleen…" she urged. Kathleen followed after them and took a seat around the table beside her husband, with the Inspector and his wife either side of the table.

When Dafydd had eaten his fill and she'd managed a small bowl of cawl herself, her husband took a tot of brandy with the others to celebrate the Christmas season, while she sipped a cup of tea with the Inspector's wife. Then Dafydd took Kathleen's hand in his as they went outside to hail a cab home, thankfully the angry horde outside, having now departed.

As the cab passed the Parish church, they heard the peal of Christmas bells as the clock chimed the hour of midnight. It was Christmas day itself.

"Merry Christmas, Mrs Jenkin," Dafydd said, placing a kiss on her cheek as the cab clattered along the road.

"Merry Christmas, Father Jenkin," Kathleen whispered.

"Father Jenkin?" Dafydd seemed unable to comprehend what she was saying to him.

"Yes, I found out a couple of days ago, that I am with child again. Doctor Owen has confirmed my pregnancy. All appears well and the pregnancy 'tis around three month's gestation…" she expressed with great joy and excitement.

"That's wonderful news, Kathleen…" he drew her into his arms and kissed her passionately as the bells continued to chime. "I think this will be the best Christmas yet…"

When they arrived at their destination, he helped his wife out of the cab and paid the driver, giving him a generous tip for Christmas. Then outside their house, in the cobbled street, he slipped his hand into his pocket and brought out a small black velvet box, tied neatly with a red ribbon, and handed it to her under the glow of the street lamp.

"What's this?"

"Kathleen…" Dafydd's voice took on a serious tone. "I had intended to give it you earlier on our walk home, but things didn't go to plan, please open it."

She gasped as she untied the ribbon and opened the box to see a beautiful gold ring displayed inside, sparkling and shining with several precious stones.

"It's an eternity ring, Kathleen. It's set with rubies and diamonds. I couldn't afford to get you an engagement ring before we wed, but now I am on good wages, I've been saving up to get you this. We've been married for just over a year and I want you to know my love for you will never die, it's eternal."

She smiled as the tears fell and he slipped the ring on her finger next to her wedding ring and her heart. It was then as she looked up towards the lamp, she saw the first snowflakes fall, like feathers from heaven.

"Oh, Dafydd you have made me so happy, and inside I have a very special present for you too…"

He unlocked the door. "Then come inside and please present me with it…" he said, taking her by the hand and leading her indoors. They were in their own home, just the two of them, cosy for Christmas and by this time next year, there would be another one to join them, a new baby, a creation of their love for one another.

Epilogue

Temperance Hall, Merthyr Tydfil, April 1878

Kathleen stood in the dressing room with Jess at her side. Jess's once dark, lustrous hair, now peppered with grey, but she'd lost none of her youthful spirit and since working at the theatre had come to look so much better, a picture of good health. Her small frame had filled out and she looked well-nourished.

Either side of Jess were Dafydd and Kathleen's two young children, ten-year-old Rebecca and five-year-old James.

Kathleen bent down and patted them on their heads. "Now you two can watch me singing from the wings, and your father will be in the audience along with a very special guest…"

"Who is that, Mam? Tell us please!" James jumped up and down with impatience.

"Oh very well, I shall tell you as long as you both promise to be well behaved for Jess?"

"We will, we promise!" Becky said brightly, as she took her younger brother's hand. "But who is it, please will you tell us?"

Kathleen smiled as she glanced around the dressing room and saw the huge basket of white roses from Dafydd on her dressing table, and beside those, a special letter from a very famous admirer of her work, who had asked her to perform his song just for him after hearing her perform at the same theatre years ago.

She hesitated a moment and said, "It's Doctor Joseph Parry…"

"Mr. Parry the composer?" Becky blinked.

"Yes, to be sure, none other than the famous composer from Merthyr himself!"

James tugged at her dress. "But why has a famous man asked you to sing, Mam?"

Kathleen laughed, realising that to her children she was just their mother, pure and simple, nothing special, not a famous theatre singer known far and wide. "Because," explained Kathleen, "he came here many years ago and liked my voice and this year, his opera 'Blodwen' was performed in Aberystwyth, and then went on to tour in different towns to much acclamation from everyone. He wrote a very special song a couple of years ago that he has asked me to sing for the people of Merthyr."

Becky nodded. "I see, Mam. I think I have heard that song and it's very pretty."

"It is indeed!" Jess agreed. "Now you pair stay with me and a couple of moments after your mother goes on stage, I will take you to the wings to listen to her perform. And if you do as you're told and keep quiet, afterwards you can both 'ave a glass of milk and one of my homemade biscuits!"

James whooped with joy and Becky's eyes lit up. Kathleen was so pleased that both her children loved Jess. At a time like this, the woman was a Godsend to her.

There was a knock at the door and someone shouted, "Two minutes until you're due on stage, Miss O'Hara…"

James frowned. "Why did that man call you Miss O'Hara? You're not, you're our mother, Mrs Jenkin."

Kathleen ruffled her son's hair and laughed. "It's my stage name, James. I am still Mrs Jenkin at home, but I was born an O'Hara. I'll explain more to you later."

Being mildly placated, James managed a smile and Rebecca turned to him and scolded him mildly. "Now be a good boy for us while Mam sings, won't you?"

He nodded. Which made Kathleen smile to realise her daughter had grown up into quite a little lady, who tried to mother her own brother sometimes. She bent down to kiss both children and blew Jess a kiss.

"Wish me luck!" She shouted over her shoulder.

"You shan't need it, but break a leg anyhow!" Jess called after her.

James frowned again as Jess had to explain she didn't really mean his mother should break a leg at all, it was an expression of good luck amongst show people.

Kathleen closed the door behind her, took a deep breath and headed towards the stage, her footfalls echoing down the corridor in time with her pounding heart. She swallowed as the curtains drew apart, all lights directed on her and the audience applauded like there was no tomorrow.

The strains of a familiar haunting, yet soulful song, filled the air. She began to sing the most beautiful love song she'd ever heard in her life, for Doctor Joseph Parry and the people of Merthyr, but most of all for her dear husband, Dafydd, who she loved so much. That song was, Myfanwy…